PENGUIN BOOKS

LITTLE RED RIDING HOOD
AND OTHER CLASSIC FRENCH
FAIRY TALES

JACK ZIPES is professor emeritus at the University of Minnesota. A specialist in folklore, fairy tales, and children's literature, he has translated such works as the fairy tales of the Brothers Grimm and Hermann Hesse, written more than twenty books of criticism, and edited a number of anthologies, including *Spells of Enchantment: The Wondrous Fairy Tales of Western Culture.* For Penguin Classics he has edited *The Wonderful World of Oz, Pinocchio,* and *Peter Pan.* He has been honored with the Distinguished Scholar Award by the International Association for the Fantastic in the Arts as well as fellowships by the Guggenheim Foundation and the National Endowment for the Humanities.

Little Red Riding Hood

AND OTHER CLASSIC FRENCH FAIRY TALES

Translated by JACK ZIPES

Selections from *Beauties, Beasts and Enchantments*

PENGUIN BOOKS

PENGUIN BOOKS

Published by the Penguin Group
Penguin Group (USA) Inc., 375 Hudson Street, New York, New York 10014, U.S.A.
Penguin Group (Canada), 90 Eglinton Avenue East, Suite 700, Toronto,
Ontario, Canada M4P 2Y3 (a division of Pearson Penguin Canada Inc.)
Penguin Books Ltd, 80 Strand, London WC2R 0RL, England
Penguin Ireland, 25 St Stephen's Green, Dublin 2, Ireland (a division of Penguin Books Ltd)
Penguin Group (Australia), 250 Camberwell Road, Camberwell,
Victoria 3124, Australia (a division of Pearson Australia Group Pty Ltd)
Penguin Books India Pvt Ltd, 11 Community Centre, Panchsheel Park, New Delhi – 110 017, India
Penguin Group (NZ), 67 Apollo Drive, Rosedale, North Shore 0632,
New Zealand (a division of Pearson New Zealand Ltd)
Penguin Books (South Africa) (Pty) Ltd, 24 Sturdee Avenue,
Rosebank, Johannesburg 2196, South Africa
Penguin Books Ltd, Registered Offices:
80 Strand, London WC2R 0RL, England

This edition published in Penguin Books 2011

1 3 5 7 9 10 8 6 4 2

The selections in this book are reprinted from *Beauties, Beasts and Enchantment: Classic French Fairy Tales*, translated and with an introduction by Jack Zipes (NAL Books, 1989).

CIP data available

ISBN 978-0-14-312023-0

Printed in the United States of America

Contents

Little Red Riding Hood

AND OTHER CLASSIC FRENCH FAIRY TALES

CHARLES PERRAULT

THE MASTER CAT,
OR
PUSS IN BOOTS

A MILLER bequeathed to his three sons all his worldly goods, which consisted just of his mill, his ass, and his cat. The division was made quickly, and neither notary nor attorney were called, for they would have soon consumed all of the meager patrimony. The eldest received the mill; the second son, the ass; the youngest got nothing but the cat.

Of course, the youngest was upset at inheriting such a poor portion. "My brothers may now earn an honest living as partners," he said, "but as for me, I'm bound to die of hunger once I have eaten my cat and made a muff of his skin."

The cat, who had heard this speech but pretended not to have been listening, said to him with a sober and serious air, "Don't trouble yourself, master. Just give me a pouch and a pair of boots to go into the bushes, and you'll see that you were not left with as bad a share as you think."

Although the cat's master did not place much stock in this assertion, he had seen the cat play such cunning tricks in catching rats and mice—hanging himself upside down by the heels or lying in the flour as if he were dead—that he did not abandon all hope.

As soon as the cat had what he had asked for, he boldly pulled on his boots. Then he hung the pouch around his neck, took the strings in his forepaws, and went to a warren where a great number of rabbits lived. He put some bran and lettuce into his pouch and, stretching himself out as if he were dead, he waited for a young rabbit little versed in the wiles of the world to look for something to eat in the pouch. He had hardly laid down when he saw his plan work. A young scatterbrain of a rabbit entered the pouch, and master cat instantly pulled the strings, bagged it, and killed it without mercy. Proud of his catch, he went to the king's palace and demanded an audience. He was ushered up to the royal apartment, and upon entering, he made a low bow to the king. "Sire," he said, "here's a rabbit from the warren of my lord, the Marquis de Carabas (such was the name he fancied to call his master). He has instructed me to present it to you on his behalf."

"Tell your master," replied the king, "that I thank him and that he's given me great pleasure."

After some time had passed, the cat hid in a wheatfield, keeping the mouth of the pouch open as he always did. When two partridges entered it, he pulled the strings and caught them both. Then he went straight to the king and presented them to him just as he had done with the rabbit. The king was equally pleased by the two partridges and gave the cat a small token for his efforts.

During the next two or three months the cat continued every now and then to carry presents of game from his master to the king.

One day, when he knew the king was going to take a drive on the banks of a river with his daughter, the most beautiful princess in the world, he said to his master, "If you follow my advice, your fortune will be made. Just go and bathe in the river where I tell you, and leave the rest to me."

The "Marquis de Carabas" did as his cat advised, little expecting that any good would come of it. While he was bathing, the king passed by, and the cat began to shout with all his might, "Help! Help! My lord, the Marquis de Carabas is drowning!"

At this cry the king stuck his head out of the coach window. Recognizing the cat who had often brought game to him, he ordered his guards to rush to the aid of the Marquis de Carabas. While they were pulling the poor marquis out of the river, the cat approached the royal coach and told the king that some robbers had come and carried off his master's clothes while he was bathing, even though he had shouted "Thieves!" as loud as he could. But in truth the rascal had hidden his master's clothes himself under a large rock. The king immediately ordered the officers of his wardrobe to fetch one of his finest suits for the Marquis de Carabas. The king embraced the marquis a thousand times, and since the fine clothes brought out his good looks (for he was handsome and well built), the king's daughter found him much to her liking. No sooner did the Marquis de Carabas cast two or three respectful and rather tender glances at her than she fell in love with him. The king invited him to get into the coach and to accompany them on their drive.

Delighted to see that his scheme was succeeding, the cat ran on ahead and soon came upon some peasants mowing a field.

"Listen, my good people," he said, "you who are mowing, if you don't tell the king that this field belongs to my lord, the Marquis de Carabas, you'll all be cut into tiny pieces like minced meat!"

Indeed, the king did not fail to ask the mowers whose field they were mowing.

"It belongs to our lord, the Marquis de Carabas," they said all together, for the cat's threat had frightened them.

"You can see, sire," rejoined the marquis, "it's a field that yields an abundant crop every year."

Master cat, who kept ahead of the party, came upon some reapers and said to them, "Listen, my good people, you who are reaping, if you don't say that all this wheat belongs to my lord, the Marquis de Carabas, you'll all be cut into tiny pieces like minced meat!"

A moment later the king passed by and wished to know who owned all the wheatfields that he saw there.

"Our lord, the Marquis de Carabas," responded the reapers, and the king again expressed his joy to the marquis.

Running ahead of the coach, the cat uttered the same threat to all whom he encountered, and the king was astonished at the great wealth of the Marquis de Carabas. At last master cat arrived at a beautiful castle owned by an ogre, the richest ever known, for all the lands through which the king had driven belonged to the lord of this castle. The cat took care to inquire who the ogre was and what his powers were. Then he requested to speak with him, saying that he could not pass so near his castle without paying his respects. The ogre received him as civilly as an ogre can and asked him to sit down.

"I've been told," said the cat, "that you possess the power of changing yourself into all sorts of animals. For instance, it has been said that you can transform yourself into a lion or an elephant."

"It's true," said the ogre brusquely. "And to prove it, watch me become a lion."

The cat was so frightened at seeing a lion standing before him that he immediately scampered up into the roof gutters, and not without difficulty, for his boots were not made to walk on tiles. Upon noticing that the ogre resumed his previous form a short time afterward, the cat descended and admitted that he had been terribly frightened.

"I've also been told," said the cat, "but I can't believe it, that you've got the power to assume the form of the smallest of animals. For instance, they say that you can change yourself into a rat or mouse. I confess that it seems utterly impossible to me."

"Impossible?" replied the ogre. "Just watch!"

Immediately he changed himself into a mouse, which began to run about the floor. No sooner did the cat catch sight of it than he pounced on it and devoured it.

In the meantime the king saw the ogre's beautiful castle from the road and desired to enter it. The cat heard the noise of the coach rolling over the drawbridge and ran to meet it.

"Your Majesty," he said to the king, "welcome to the castle of my lord, the Marquis de Carabas."

"What!" exclaimed the king. "Does this castle also belong to you, Marquis? Nothing could be finer than this courtyard and all these buildings surrounding it. If you please, let us look inside."

The marquis gave his hand to the young princess, and they followed the king, who led the way upstairs. When they entered a grand hall, they found a magnificent repast that the ogre had ordered to be prepared for some friends who were to have visited him that day. (But they did not presume to enter when they found the king was there.) The king was just as much delighted by the accomplishments of the Marquis de Carabas as his daughter, who doted on him, and now, realizing how wealthy he was, he said to him, after having drunk five or six cups of wine, "The choice is entirely yours, Marquis, whether or not you want to become my son-in-law."

After making several low bows, the marquis accepted the honor the king had offered him, and on that very same day, he married the princess. In turn, the cat became a great lord and never again ran after mice, except for his amusement.

MORAL

Although the advantage may be great
When one inherits a grand estate
From father handed down to son,
Young men will find that industry
Combined with ingenuity,
Will lead more to prosperity.

ANOTHER MORAL

If the miller's son had quick success
In winning such a fair princess,
By turning on the charm,
Then regard his manners, looks, and dress
That inspired her deepest tenderness,
For they can't do one any harm.

CINDERELLA,
OR
THE GLASS SLIPPER

ONCE upon a time there was a gentleman who took the haughtiest and proudest woman in the world for his second wife. She had two daughters with the same temperament and the exact same appearance. On the other hand, the husband had a daughter whose gentleness and goodness were without parallel. She got this from her mother, who had been the best person in the world.

No sooner was the wedding over than the stepmother's ill-humor revealed itself. She could not abide the young girl, whose good qualities made her own daughters appear all the more detestable. So she ordered her to do all the most demeaning tasks in the house. It was she who cleaned the plates and the stairs, who scrubbed the rooms of the mistress and her daughters. She slept on a wretched straw mattress in a garret at the top of the house while her stepsisters occupied rooms with parquet floors and the most fashionable beds and mirrors in which they could regard themselves from head to toe. The poor girl endured everything with patience and did not dare complain to her father, who would have only scolded her since he was totally under the control of his wife. Whenever she finished her work, she would sit down near the chimney corner among the cinders. Consequently she was commonly called Cindertail. The second daughter, however, was not as malicious as her elder sister, and she dubbed her Cinderella. Nevertheless, Cinderella looked a thousand times more beautiful in her shabby clothes than her stepsisters, no matter how magnificent their clothes were.

Now, the king's son happened to give a ball and to invite all the people of quality. Our two young ladies were included in the invitation, for they cut a grand figure in this country. Of course, they were very pleased and began planning which would be the best gowns and headdresses to wear. This meant more misery for Cinderella because she was the one who ironed her sisters' linen and set their ruffles. Nothing was talked about but the style in which they were to be dressed.

"I'll wear my red velvet dress," said the elder sister, "and my English point-lace trimmings."

"I only have my usual petticoat to wear," said the younger, "but to make up for that I'll put on my gold-flowered mantua and my necklace of diamonds."

They sent for a good hairdresser to make up their double-frilled caps and brought their patches from the best shopkeeper. They summoned Cinderella and asked her opinion, for she had excellent taste. Cinderella gave them the best advice in the world and even offered to dress their hair for them, a favor they were eager to accept. While she went about it, they said to her, "Cinderella, wouldn't you like to go to the ball?"

"Alas! Ladies, you're playing with me. That would not befit me at all."

"You're right. People would have a great laugh to see a Cindertail at a ball!"

Any other person but Cinderella would have messed up their hairdos, but she was good-natured and dressed them to perfection. They could eat nothing for nearly two days because they were so excited. More than a dozen laces were broken in making their waists as small as possible, and they were constantly standing in front of their mirrors. At last the happy evening arrived. They set off, and Cinderella followed them with her eyes as long as she could. When they were out of sight, she began to cry. Her godmother, who came upon her all in tears, asked what was troubling her.

"I should so like—I should so like—" She sobbed so much that she could not finish the sentence.

"You'd like to go to the ball. Is that it?"

"Ah, yes!" said Cinderella, sighing.

"Well, if you'll be a good girl, I shall enable you to go." She

led her from her chamber into the yard and said, "Go to the
garden and bring me a pumpkin."

Cinderella left immediately, gathered the finest pumpkin she
could find, and brought it to her godmother, unable to guess
how a pumpkin would enable her to go to the ball. Her godmother scooped it out, leaving nothing but the rind. Then she
struck it with her wand, and the pumpkin was immediately
transformed into a beautiful coach gilded all over. Next she
looked into the mousetrap, where she found six live mice. She
told Cinderella to lift the door of the trap a little, and as each
mouse ran out, she gave it a tap with her wand. Each mouse
sprouted into a fine horse, producing a fine team of six handsome, dappled, mouse-gray horses. Since her godmother had
some difficulty in choosing something for a coachman, Cinderella said, "I'll go and see if there's a rat in the rattrap. We
could make a coachman out of him."

"You're right," said her godmother. "Go and see."

Cinderella brought her the rattrap, which contained three
large rats. The fairy selected one with the most ample beard,
and after touching it, the rat was changed into a fat coachman,
who had the finest moustaches that had ever been seen. Then
she said, "Go into the garden, where you'll find six lizards
behind the watering pot. I want you to bring them to me."

Cinderella had no sooner brought them than her godmother
transformed them into six footmen, who immediately climbed
up behind the coach in their braided liveries and perched there
as though they had done nothing else all their lives. Then the
fairy said to Cinderella, "Well, now you have something to
take you to the ball. Are you satisfied?"

"Yes, but am I to go in these dirty clothes?"

Her godmother merely touched her with her wand, and her
garments were instantly changed into garments of gold and silver dotted with jewels. She then gave her a pair of glass slippers, the prettiest in the world. When she was thus attired, she
got into the coach, but her godmother warned her, "Above all,
do not stay past midnight. If you remain at the ball one
moment too long, your coach will again become a pumpkin;
your horses, mice; your footmen, lizards; and your clothes will

become cinder-covered rags." She promised her godmother she would not fail to leave the ball before midnight, and so she departed, overcome with joy.

Upon being informed that a grand princess had arrived whom nobody knew, the king's son went forth to greet her. He gave her his hand to help her out of the coach and led her into the hall where the company was assembled. All at once there was dead silence. The guests stopped dancing and the fiddlers ceased playing, so engrossed was everybody in regarding the beauty of the unknown lady. All that was heard was a low murmuring, "Oh, how lovely she is!" The king himself, old as he was, could not take his eyes off her and whispered to the queen that it was a long time since he had seen anyone so beautiful and so pleasant. All the ladies were busy examining her headdress and her clothes because they wanted to obtain some similar garments the very next day, if they could find the appropriate materials and tailors.

The king's son conducted her to the place of honor and then led her out to dance. She danced with so much grace that everyone's admiration increased. A very fine supper was served, but the prince could not eat anything because he was so wrapped up in watching her.

She sat beside her sisters and showed them a thousand civilities. She shared with them oranges and citrons that the prince had given her, and her sisters were quite surprised because they did not recognize her at all. While they were conversing, Cinderella heard the clock strike a quarter to twelve. She immediately made a low curtsy to the company and departed as quickly as she could.

As soon as she arrived home, she looked for her godmother, and after having thanked her, she said she wished very much to go to the ball again the next day because the king's son had invited her. While she was busy in telling her godmother all that had happened at the ball, the two sisters knocked at the door, and Cinderella opened it.

"How late you are!" she said to them, yawning, rubbing her eyes, and stretching as if she had only just awoken. However, she had not had the slightest inclination to sleep since she had left them.

"If you had been at the ball," said one of her sisters, "you would not have been bored. The most beautiful princess attended it—the most beautiful in the world. She paid us a thousand attentions, and also gave us oranges and citrons."

Cinderella was beside herself with delight. She asked them the name of the princess, but they replied that nobody knew her. Moreover, the king's son was stumped and would give anything in the world to know who she was. Cinderella smiled and said, "She was very beautiful, then? Heavens! How fortunate you are!—Couldn't I have a chance to see her? Alas! Jayotte, would you lend me the yellow gown you wear every day?"

"Indeed," said Jayotte, "I like that! Lend my gown to a dirty Cindertail like you! I'd have to be quite mad to do something like that!"

Cinderella fully expected this refusal and was delighted by it, for she would have been greatly embarrassed if her sister had lent her the gown.

The next evening the two sisters went to the ball, and so did Cinderella, dressed even more splendidly than before. The king's son never left her side and kept saying sweet things to her. The young lady enjoyed herself so much that she forgot her godmother's advice and was dumbfounded when the clock began to strike twelve, for she did not even think it was eleven. She rose and fled as lightly as a fawn. The prince followed her, but could not catch her. However, she dropped one of the glass slippers, which the prince carefully picked up. Without coach or footmen, Cinderella reached home out of breath and in shabby clothes. Nothing remained of her finery, except one of her little slippers, the companion to the one that she had dropped. The guards at the palace gate were asked if they had seen a princess depart. They answered that they had only seen a poorly dressed girl pass by, and she had more the appearance of a peasant than a lady.

When the two sisters returned from the ball, Cinderella asked them if they had enjoyed themselves as much as the first time and if the beautiful lady had been present. They said yes, but that she had fled as soon as the clock had struck twelve, and she had been in such haste that she had dropped one of her glass slippers, the prettiest in the world. The king's son had picked it up and had done nothing but gaze at it during the remainder of the evening. Undoubtedly, he was very much in love with the beautiful person who had worn the slipper.

They spoke the truth, for a few days later there was a flourish of trumpets. The king's son proclaimed that he would marry her whose foot would exactly fit the slipper. His men began by trying it on the princesses, then on the duchesses, and so on throughout the entire court. However, it was all in vain. Soon it was taken to the two sisters, who did their utmost to force one of their feet into the slipper, but they could not manage to do so.

Cinderella, who witnessed their efforts and recognized the slipper, said with a smile, "Let me see if it will fit me."

Her sisters began to laugh and ridicule her. The gentleman who had been entrusted to try the slipper looked attentively at Cinderella and found her to be very beautiful. So he said, "It is a proper request. I have been ordered to try the slipper on everyone without exception." He asked Cinderella to sit down, and upon placing the slipper under her little foot, he saw it go on easily and fit like wax.

The astonishment of the two sisters was great, but it was even greater when Cinderella took the other little slipper out of her pocket and put it on the other foot. At that moment the godmother arrived. With a tap of her wand Cinderella's clothes became even more magnificent than all the previous garments she had worn. The two sisters then recognized her as the beautiful person they had seen at the ball. They threw themselves at her feet, begging her pardon for the harsh treatment they had made her endure.

Cinderella raised and embraced them, saying that she forgave them with all her heart and begged them to love her well in the future. Adorned as she was, she was conducted to the young prince. He found her more beautiful than ever, and a few days later he married her. Cinderella, who was as kind as she was beautiful, gave her sisters apartments in the palace and had them married the very same day to two great noblemen of the court.

Moral

A woman's beauty is quite a treasure
We never cease to admire.
Yet graciousness exceeds all measure.
There's nothing of virtue higher.
The fairy, according to our story,
Contributed it to Cinderella's glory
And taught her what becomes a queen,
(Left in a moral to be gleaned.)

Beautiful ladies, it's kindness more than dress
That wins a man's heart with greater success.
So, if you want a life filled with bliss,
The truest gift is graciousness.

Another Moral

No doubt it is a benefit
To have strong courage and fine wit,
To be endowed with common sense
And other virtues to possess
That Heaven may dispense.
But these may prove quite useless—
As well as many others—
If you strive to gain success
And neglect godfathers or godmothers.

BLUE BEARD

ONCE upon a time there was a man who had fine town and country houses, gold and silver plates, embroidered furniture, and gilded coaches. Unfortunately, however, this man had a blue beard, which made him look so ugly and terrifying that there was not a woman or girl who did not run away from him.

Now, one of his neighbors was a lady of quality who had two exceedingly beautiful daughters. He proposed to marry one of them, leaving the choice up to the mother which of the two she would give him. Yet neither one would have him, and they kept sending him back and forth between them, not being able to make up their minds to marry a man who had a blue beard. What increased their distaste for him was that he had already had several wives, and nobody knew what had become of them.

In order to cultivate their acquaintance, Blue Beard took the sisters, their mother, three or four of their most intimate friends, and some young people who resided in the neighborhood, to one of his country estates, where they spent an entire week. Their days were filled with excursions, hunting and fishing, parties, balls, entertainments, and feasts. Nobody went to bed, for their nights were spent in merry games and gambols. In short, all went off so well that the younger daughter began to find that the beard of the master of the house was not as blue as it used to be and that he was a very worthy man.

The marriage took place immediately upon their return to town. At the end of a month Blue Beard told his wife that he was obliged to take a journey concerning a matter of great consequence, and it would occupy him at least six weeks. He asked her to amuse herself as best as she could during his

absence and to take her closest friends into the country with
her if she pleased, and to offer them fine meals.

"Here are the keys to my two great storerooms," he said to
her. "These are the keys to the chests in which the gold and silver plates for special occasions are kept. These are the keys to
the strongboxes in which I keep my money. These keys open
the caskets that contain my jewels. And this is the passkey to
all the apartments. As for this small key," he said, "it is for the
little room at the end of the long corridor on the ground floor.
Open everything and go everywhere except into that room,
which I forbid you to enter. My orders are to be strictly obeyed,
and if you dare open the door, my anger will exceed anything
you have ever experienced."

She promised to carry out all his instructions exactly as he had
ordered, and after he embraced her, he got into his coach and set
out on his journey. The neighbors and friends of the young bride
did not wait for her invitation, so eager were they to see all the
treasures contained in the country mansion. They had not ventured to enter it while her husband was at home because they had
been frightened of his blue beard. Now they began running
through all the rooms, closets, and wardrobes. Each apartment
outdid the other in beauty and richness. Then they ascended to
the storerooms, where they could not admire enough the elegance
of the many tapestries, beds, sofas, cabinets, stands, tables, and
mirrors in which they could see themselves from head to foot.
Some mirrors had frames of glass, and some of gold gilt, more
beautiful and magnificent than they had ever seen. They could
not stop extolling and envying the good fortune of the new bride.

In the meantime, she was not in the least entertained by all these
treasures because she was so impatient to open the little room on
the ground floor. Her curiosity increased to such a degree that,
without reflecting how rude it was to leave her company, she ran
down a back staircase so hastily that she nearly tripped and broke
her neck on two or three occasions. Once at the door she paused
for a moment, recalling her husband's prohibition. What misfortune might befall her if she disobeyed? But the temptation was so
strong that she could not withstand it. She took the small key, and
with a trembling hand she opened the door of the little room.

At first she could make out nothing, since the windows were shuttered. After a short time, though, she began to perceive that the floor was covered with clotted blood of the dead bodies of several women suspended from the walls. These were all the former wives of Blue Beard, who had cut their throats one after the other. She thought she would die from fright, and the key to the room fell from her hand. After recovering her senses a little, she picked up the key, locked the door again, and went up to her chamber to compose herself. Yet she could not relax because she was too upset. Then she noticed that the key to the room was stained with blood. She wiped it two or three times, but the blood would not come off. In vain she washed it, and even scrubbed it with sand and grit. But the blood remained, for the key was enchanted, and there was no way of cleaning it completely. When the blood was washed off one side, it came back on the other.

That very evening Blue Beard returned from his journey and announced that he had received letters on the road informing him that the business on which he had set forth had been settled to his advantage. His wife did all she could to persuade him that she was delighted by his speedy return. The next morning he asked her to return his keys. She gave them to him, but her hand trembled so much that he did not have any difficulty in guessing what had occurred.

"Why is it," he asked, "that the key to the little room is not with the others?"

"I must have left it upstairs on my table," she replied.

"Bring it to me right now," said Blue Beard.

After several excuses she was compelled to produce the key. Once Blue Beard examined it, he said to her, "Why is there blood on this key?"

"I don't know," answered the poor woman, paler than death.

"You don't know?" Blue Beard responded. "I know well enough. You wanted to enter the room! Well, madam, you will enter it and take your place among the ladies you saw there."

She flung herself at her husband's feet, weeping and begging his pardon. One glance at her showed that she truly repented of disobeying him. Her beauty and affliction might have melted a rock.

"You must die, madam," he said, "and immediately."

"If I must die," she replied, looking at him with eyes bathed in tears, "give me a little time to say my prayers."

"I shall give you a quarter of an hour," Blue Beard answered, "but not a minute more."

As soon as he had left her, she called for her sister and said, "Sister Anne"—for that was her name—"go up, I beg you, to the top of the tower and see if my brothers are coming. They promised me that they would come to see me today. If you see them, give them a signal to make haste."

Sister Anne mounted to the top of the tower, and the poor distressed creature called to her every now and then, "Anne! Sister Anne! Do you see anyone coming?"

And sister Anne answered her, "I see nothing but the sun making dust, and the grass growing green."

In the meantime Blue Beard held a cutlass in his hand and bellowed to his wife with all his might, "Come down quickly, or I'll come up there."

"Please, one minute more," replied his wife. Immediately she repeated in a low voice, "Anne! Sister Anne! Do you see anyone coming?"

And sister Anne replied, "I see nothing but the sun making dust, and the grass growing green."

"Come down quickly," roared Blue Beard, "or I shall come up there!"

"I'm coming," answered his wife, and then she called, "Anne! Sister Anne! Do you see anyone coming?"

"I see," said sister Anne, "a great cloud of dust moving this way."

"Is it my brothers?"

"Alas! No, sister, I see a flock of sheep."

"Do you refuse to come down?" shouted Blue Beard.

"One minute more," his wife replied, and then she cried, "Anne! Sister Anne! Do you see anything coming?"

"I see two horsemen coming this way," she responded, "but they're still at a great distance." A moment afterward she exclaimed. "Heaven be praised! They're my brothers! I'm signaling to them as best I can to hurry up."

Blue Beard began to roar so loudly that the whole house shook. So his poor wife descended to him and threw herself at his feet, all disheveled and in tears.

"It's no use," said Blue Beard. "You must die!"

He seized her by the hair with one hand and raised his cutlass with the other. He was about to cut off her head when the poor woman looked up at him. Fixing her dying gaze upon him, she implored him to allow her one short moment to collect herself.

"No, no," he said, lifting his arm, "commend yourself as best you can to Heaven."

At that moment there was such a loud knocking at the gate that Blue Beard stopped short. The gate was opened, and two horsemen burst through. With drawn swords they ran straight at Blue Beard, who recognized them as the brothers of his wife— one a dragoon, the other a musketeer. Immediately he fled, hoping to escape, but they pursued so quickly that they overtook him before he could reach the step of his door and passed their swords through his body, leaving him dead on the spot. The poor woman, who was nearly as dead as her husband, did not have the strength even to rise and embrace her brothers.

Since Blue Beard had no heirs, his widow inherited all his wealth. She employed part of it to arrange a marriage between her sister Anne and a young gentleman who had loved her a long time. Another part paid for commissions for her two brothers so they could become captains. The rest she used for her marriage to a worthy man who made her forget the miserable time she had spent with Blue Beard.

MORAL

Curiosity, in spite of its charm,
Too often causes a great deal of harm.
A thousand new cases arise each day.
With due respect, ladies, the thrill is slight,
For as soon as you're satisfied, it goes away,
And the price one pays is never right.

Another Moral

Provided one has common sense
And learns to study complex texts,
It's easy to trace the evidence
Of long ago in this tale's events.

No longer are husbands so terrible,
Or insist on having the impossible.
Though he may be jealous and dissatisfied,
He tries to do as he's obliged.
And whatever color his beard may be,
It's difficult to know who the master be.

LITTLE THUMBLING

ONCE upon a time there was a woodcutter and his wife who had seven children, all boys. The eldest was but ten years old and the youngest only seven. People were astonished that the woodcutter had had so many children in such a short time, but the fact is that his wife did not mince matters and seldom gave birth to less than two at a time. They were very poor, and having seven children was a great burden to them, since not one was able to earn his own living.

What distressed them even more was that the youngest son was very delicate and rarely spoke, which they considered a mark of stupidity instead of good sense. Moreover, he was very little. Indeed, at birth he was scarcely bigger than one's thumb, and this led everyone to call him Little Thumbling. This poor child became the family scapegoat and was blamed for everything that happened. Nevertheless, he was the shrewdest and most sensible of all the brothers, and if he spoke but little, he listened a great deal.

One year there was a disastrous harvest, and the famine was so severe that these poor people decided to get rid of their children. One evening, when they were all in bed and the woodcutter was sitting by the fire with his wife, he said with a heavy heart, "It's plain that we can no longer feed our children. I can't let them die of hunger before my eyes, and I've made up my mind to lose them tomorrow in the forest. We can do this without any trouble when they are making bundles of firewood. We only have to disappear without their seeing us."

"Ah!" the woodcutter's wife exclaimed. "Do you really have the heart to abandon your own children?"

Her husband tried in vain to convince her how their terrible poverty necessitated such a plan, but she would not consent to the deed. However poor, she was their mother. After reflecting on how miserable she would be to see them die of hunger, though, she finally agreed and went to bed weeping.

Little Thumbling had heard everything they said, for while he had been lying in his bed, he had realized that they were discussing their affairs. He had got up quietly, slipped under his father's stool, and listened without being seen. Going back to bed, he did not sleep a wink the rest of the night because he was thinking over what he should do. He rose early the next morning and went to the banks of a brook, where he filled his pockets with small white pebbles and then returned home. Little Thumbling revealed nothing of what he had heard to his brothers.

Later they set out all together. They entered a dense forest, where they were unable to see one another once they were ten paces apart. The woodcutter began to chop wood, and his children, to pick up sticks and make bundles. Seeing them occupied with their work, the father and mother gradually stole away and then fled in an instant by a small, winding path. When the children found themselves all alone, they began to cry with all their might. Little Thumbling let them scream since he was fully confident that he could get home again. He had dropped the white pebbles in his pockets all along the path.

"Don't be afraid, brothers," he said. "Our father and mother have abandoned us here, but I'll lead you safely home. Just follow me."

They followed him, and he led them back to the house by the same path that they had taken into the forest. At first they were afraid to enter the house. Instead, they placed themselves next to the door to listen to the conversation of their parents.

Now, after the woodcutter and his wife had arrived home, they found ten crowns that the lord of the manor had sent them. He had owed them this money for a long time, and they had given up all hope of ever receiving it. This put new life into these poor, starving people. The woodcutter sent his wife to the butcher's right away, for it had been many a day since they had eaten anything. She bought three times as much as was necessary for two persons, and when they sat down at the table again, she said, "Alas! Where are our poor children now? They would make a good meal out of our leftovers. But it was you, Guillaume, who wanted to lose them. I told you we'd repent it. What are they doing now in the forest? Alas! Heaven help me! The wolves have probably eaten them already! What a monster you must be to get rid of your children this way!"

When she repeated more than forty times that they would repent it and that she had told him so, the woodcutter lost his temper. He threatened to beat her if she did not hold her tongue. It was not that the woodcutter was not perhaps even more sorry than his wife, but that she browbeat him. He was like many other people who are disposed to women who can talk well but become irritated by women who are always right.

"Alas!" His wife was in tears. "Where are my children now, my poor children!"

She uttered these words so loudly that the children began to cry at the door, "Here we are! Here we are!"

She rushed to open the door, and embracing them, she exclaimed, "How happy I am to see you again, my dear children! You're very tired and hungry. And how dirty you are, Pierrot! Come here and let me wash you."

Pierrot was her eldest son, and she loved him most of all because he was somewhat redheaded, which was the color of her hair too. They sat down to supper and ate with an appetite that pleased their father and mother. They all talked at once and related how frightened they had been in the forest. The good souls were delighted to see their children around them once more, but their joy lasted just as long as the ten crowns. When the money was spent, they relapsed into their former misery and decided to lose the children again. And to do so they were determined to lead them much farther from home than they had the first time.

They discussed this in secret, but were overheard by Little Thumbling, who counted on getting out of the predicament the way he had before. Yet when he got up early to collect some pebbles, he found the house door double-locked. He could not think of what to do until the woodcutter's wife gave them each a piece of bread for their breakfast. Then it occurred to him that he might use the bread in place of the pebbles by throwing crumbs along the path as they went. So he stuck his piece in his pocket.

The father and mother led them into the thickest, darkest part of the forest, and as soon as they had done so, they took a side-path and left them there. Little Thumbling was not at all worried, for he thought he would easily find his way back by following the crumbs he had scattered along the path. But he was greatly surprised when he could not find a single crumb: the birds had eaten them all up. Now the poor children were in great trouble. The farther they wandered, the deeper they plunged into the forest. Night arrived, and a great wind arose, filling them with fear. They imagined that they heard wolves howling on every side of them. "They're coming to devour us!" They scarcely dared to turn their heads. Then it began raining so heavily that they were soon drenched to the skin. With each step they took, they slipped and tumbled into the mud. They got up all covered with mud and did not know what to do with their hands. Little Thumbling climbed up a tree to try to see something from the top. After looking all around, he saw a little light, like that of a candle, far-away on the other side of the forest. When he climbed down from the tree and reached the ground, he could no longer see the light. This was a great disappointment to him, but after having walked on with his brothers for some time in the direction of the light, he saw it again as they emerged from the forest. Then again, when they descended into the ravines, they kept losing sight of the beaming light and became frightened. Eventually, however, they reached the house where the light was burning and knocked at the door. A good woman came to open it and asked them what they wanted. Little Thumbling told her that they were poor children who had lost their way in the forest and begged her for a night's lodging out of charity. Seeing how lovely the children were, she began to weep and said, "Alas! My poor boys, don't you know where you've landed? This is the dwelling of an ogre who eats little children!"

"Oh, madam!" replied Little Thumbling, who trembled from head to toe just as all his brothers did. "What shall we do? It's certain that the wolves of the forest will devour us tonight if you refuse to take us under your roof. That being the case, we'd rather be eaten by your husband. If you're kind enough to plead for us, perhaps he'll take pity on us."

The ogre's wife, who believed she could manage to hide them from her husband till the next morning, allowed them to come in and led them to a spot where they could warm themselves by a good fire, for there was a whole sheep on the spit roasting for the ogre's supper. Just as they were beginning to get warm, they heard two or three loud knocks at the door. The ogre had come home. His wife immediately made the children hide under the bed and went to open the door. The ogre first asked if his supper were ready and if she had drawn the wine. With that he sat down to his meal. The mutton was almost raw, but he liked it all the better for that. He sniffed right and left, saying that he smelt fresh meat.

"It must be the calf that you smell. I've just skinned it," said his wife.

"I smell fresh meat, I tell you," replied the ogre, looking suspiciously at his wife. "There's something here I don't understand." Upon saying these words, he rose from the table and went straight to the bed. "Ah!" he exclaimed. "This is the way you deceive me, cursed woman! I don't know what's holding me back from eating you as well! It's a lucky thing that you're an old beast!"

He dragged the boys from under the bed one after the other. "Here's some game that comes just in time for me to entertain three ogre friends of mine who are coming to see me tomorrow." The poor children fell on their knees, begging for mercy, but they were facing the most cruel of all the ogres. Far from feeling pity for them, he was already devouring them with his eyes. He said to his wife, "They will be perfect as dainty bits once you make a good sauce for them." He fetched a large knife, and as he approached the poor children, he whetted it on a long stone that he held in his left hand. He had already grabbed one of the boys when his wife said to him, "Why do you want to do it at this hour of the night? Won't you have time enough tomorrow?"

"Hold your tongue," the ogre replied. "They'll be all the more tender."

"But you already have so much meat," his wife responded. "Here's a calf, two sheep, and half a pig."

"You're right," the ogre said. "Give them a good supper to fatten them up, and then put them to bed."

Overjoyed, the good woman brought them plenty for supper, but they could not eat because they were so paralyzed with fright. As for the ogre, he seated himself to drink again, delighted to think he had such a treat in store for his friends. So he emptied a dozen goblets, which was more than usual and affected his head somewhat, and he was obliged to go to bed.

Now, the ogre had seven daughters who were still quite young. These little ogresses had the most beautiful complexions due to eating raw flesh like their father. But they had very small, round gray eyes, hooked noses, and large mouths with long teeth, extremely sharp and wide apart. They were not very vicious as yet, but they showed great promise, for they had already begun to bite little children to suck their blood. They had been sent to bed early, and all seven were in a large bed, each having a golden crown on her head. In the same room there was another bed of the same size. It was in this bed that the ogre's wife put the seven little boys to sleep, after which she went to sleep with her husband.

Little Thumbling noticed that the ogre's daughters had golden crowns on their heads. Fearing that the ogre might regret not having killed him and his brothers that evening, he got up in the middle of the night. He took off his nightcap and those of his brothers, crept over very softly, and swapped them for the crowns of the ogre's seven daughters. These he put on his brothers and himself so that the ogre might mistake them for his daughters, and his daughters for the boys whose throats he longed to cut.

Everything turned out exactly as he had anticipated. The ogre awoke at midnight and regretted that he had postponed what he might have done that evening until the next morning. Therefore, he jumped out of bed and seized his large knife. "Let's go and see how our little rascals are doing. We won't make the same mistake twice." So he stole up to his daughters' bedroom on tiptoe and approached the bed in which the little boys were lying. They were all asleep except Thumbling, who was dreadfully frightened when the ogre placed his hand on his head to feel as he had in turn felt those of his brothers.

After feeling the golden crowns, the ogre said, "Upon my word, I almost made a mess of a job! It's clear I must have drunk too much last night." He then went to the bed where his daughters slept, and after feeling the nightcaps that belonged to the boys, he cried, "Aha! Here are our sly little dogs. Let's get to work!" With these words he cut the throats of his seven daughters without hesitating. Well satisfied with his work, he returned and stretched himself out in bed beside his wife. As soon as Little Thumbling heard the ogre snoring, he woke his brothers and told them to dress themselves quickly and follow him. They went down quietly into the garden and jumped over the wall. As they ran throughout the night, they could not stop trembling, for they did not know where they were going.

When the ogre awoke the next morning, he said to his wife, "Go upstairs and dress the little rascals you took in last night."

The ogress was astonished by her husband's kindness, never suspecting the sort of dressing he meant her to give them. Thus she merely imagined that he was ordering her to go and put on their clothes. When she went upstairs, she was greatly surprised to find her daughters murdered and swimming in their blood. All at once she fainted (for this is the first thing that most women do in similar circumstances). Fearing that his wife was taking too long in carrying out her task, the ogre went upstairs to help. He was no less surprised than his wife when he came upon the frightful spectacle.

"Ah! What have I done?" he exclaimed. "The wretches shall pay for it, and right now!" He threw a jugful of water in his wife's face, and after reviving her, he said, "Quick! Fetch my seven-league boots so I can go and catch them."

After setting out, he ran far and wide and at last came upon the track of the poor children, who were not more than a hundred yards from their father's house. They saw the ogre striding from hill to hill and stepping over rivers as easily as if they were the smallest brooks. Little Thumbling noticed a hollow cave nearby and hid his brothers in it, and while watching the movements of the ogre, he crept in after them. Now the ogre, feeling tired because his long journey had been to no avail, needed to rest, especially since seven-league boots make the wearer quite exhausted. By chance he sat down on the very rock in which the little boys had concealed themselves. Since the ogre was worn out, he soon fell asleep and began to snore so terribly that the poor children were just as frightened as they had been when he had grabbed the large knife to cut their throats.

Little Thumbling was not so much alarmed and told his brothers to run straight into the house while the ogre was sound asleep and not to worry about him. They took his advice and quickly ran home. Little Thumbling now approached the ogre and carefully pulled off his boots, which he immediately put on himself. The boots were very large and very long, but since they were fairy boots, they possessed the quality of increasing or diminishing in size according to the leg of the person who wore them. Thus they fit him just as if they had been made for him. He went straight to the ogre's house, where he found the wife weeping over her murdered daughters.

"Your husband is in great danger. He's been captured by a band of robbers, who have sworn to kill him if he doesn't give them all his gold and silver," Thumbling said to her. "He saw me just at the moment they had their daggers at his throat, and he begged me to come and ask you to give me all his valuables without holding anything back. Otherwise, they'll kill him without mercy. Since time was of the essence, he insisted I take his seven-league boots so that I might go faster and also so that you'd be sure I wasn't an imposter."

The good woman was very much alarmed by this news and immediately gave Thumbling all the money she could find, for the ogre was not a bad husband to her, even though he ate little children. So, loaded down with the ogre's entire wealth, Little Thumbling rushed back to his father's house, where he was received with great joy.

Many people differ in their account of this part of the story. They assert that Little Thumbling never committed the theft, and that he only considered himself justified in taking the ogre's seven-league boots because the ogre had used them expressly to run after little children. These people argue that they got their story from good authority and had even eaten and drunk in the woodcutter's house.

They maintain that after Little Thumbling had put on the ogre's boots, he went to the court. There, he knew, they were anxious to learn about the army and the outcome of a battle that was being fought two hundred leagues away. He went to the king and told him, "If you so desire, I will bring back news of the army before dusk." The king promised him a large sum of money if he did so, and Little Thumbling brought news that very evening.

Since this first journey gave him a certain reputation, he earned whatever he chose to ask. Not only did the king pay liberally for taking his orders to the army, but numerous ladies gave him any price he named for news of their lovers, and this became the best source of his income. Occasionally he met some wives who entrusted him with letters for their husbands, but they paid him so poorly that he did not even bother to put down what he got among his receipts.

After he had been a courier for some time and saved a great deal of money, he returned to his father. You cannot imagine how joyful his family was at seeing him again. He made them all comfortable by buying newly created positions for his father and brothers. In this way he made sure they were all established, and at the same time he made certain that he did perfectly well at the court himself.

MORAL

No longer may children be such a hardship,
If possessed of charm, good looks, and wit.
But if one's weak and falters in the fray,
He'll soon be mocked until he runs away.
Yet there are times when the child, the least expected,
May return with a fortune, his honor resurrected.

THE SLEEPING BEAUTY
IN THE WOODS

ONCE upon a time there was a king and a queen who were quite disturbed at not having any children. Indeed, they were so disturbed that no words can express their feelings. They visited all the baths in the world. They took vows, pilgrimages—everything was tried, and nothing succeeded. At last, however, the queen became pregnant and gave birth to a daughter. At the christening all the fairies who could be found in the realm (seven altogether) were asked to be godmothers so that each would give the child a gift. According to the custom of the fairies in those days, the gifts would endow the princess with all the perfections that could be imagined.

After the baptismal ceremonies the entire company returned to the king's palace, where a great banquet was held for the fairies. Places were laid for each, consisting of a magnificent plate with a massive gold case containing a spoon, fork, and knife of fine gold, studded with diamonds and rubies. But as they were all about to sit down at the table, an old fairy entered the palace. She had not been invited because she had not left the tower in which she resided for more than fifty years, and it was supposed that she had either died or had become enchanted.

The king ordered a place to be set for her, but he could not give her a massive gold case as as he had with the others because the seven had been made expressly for the seven fairies. The old fairy thought that she was being slighted and muttered some threats between her teeth. One of the young fairies who chanced to be nearby overheard her, and thinking that she might wish the little princess bad luck, hid herself behind the tapestry as soon as they rose from the table. "That way I'll have the last word and repair any evil the old woman might do."

Meanwhile, the fairies began to bestow their gifts upon the princess. The youngest fairy decreed, "She will be the most beautiful person in the world." The next fairy declared, "She will have the temperament of an angel." The third, "She will evince the most admirable grace in all she does." The fourth: "She will dance to perfection." The sixth: "She will play every instrument in the most exquisite manner possible."

Finally the turn of the old fairy arrived. Her head shook more with malice than with age as she declared, "The princess will pierce her hand with a spindle and die of the wound."

This terrible gift made the entire company tremble, and no one present could refrain from tears. At this moment the young fairy stepped from behind the tapestry and uttered in a loud voice, "Comfort yourselves, King and Queen, your daughter will not die. It's true that I don't have sufficient power to undo entirely what my elder has done. The princess will pierce her hand with a spindle. But instead of dying, she'll only fall into a deep sleep that will last one hundred years. At the end of that time, a king's son will come to wake her."

In the hope of avoiding the misfortune predicted by the old fairy, the king immediately issued a public edict forbidding all his subjects to spin with a spindle or to have spindles in their house under pain of death.

After fifteen or sixteen years had passed, the royal couple and their court traveled to one of their country residences, and one day the princess happened to be exploring it. She went from one chamber to another, and after arriving at the top of a tower, she entered a little garret, where an honest old woman was sitting by herself with her distaff and spindle. This good woman had never heard of the king's prohibition of spinning with a spindle.

"What are you doing there, my fair lady?" asked the princess.

"I'm spinning, my lovely child," answered the old woman, who did not know her.

"Oh, how pretty it is!" the princess responded. "How do you do it? Let me try and see if I can do it as well."

No sooner had she grasped the spindle than she pricked her hand with the point and fainted, for she had been hasty, a little thoughtless, and moreover, the sentence of the fairies had ordained it to be that way. Greatly embarrassed, the good old woman called for help. People came from all quarters. They threw water on the princess's face. They unlaced her stays. They slapped her hands. They rubbed her temples with Queen of Hungary's water. Nothing could revive her. Then the king, who had run upstairs at the noise, remembered the prediction of the fairies and wisely concluded that this must have happened as the fairies said it would. Therefore, he had the princess carried to the finest apartment in the palace and placed on a bed of gold and silver embroidery. One would have said she was an angel, so lovely did she appear, for her swoon had not deprived her of her rich complexion: her cheeks preserved their crimson color, and her lips were like coral. Her eyes were closed, but her gentle breathing could be heard, and that indicated she was not dead. The king commanded that she be left to sleep in peace until the hour arrived for her waking.

The good fairy who had saved her life by decreeing that she should sleep for one hundred years was in the Kingdom of Mataquin, twelve thousand leagues away. When the princess met with her accident, she was informed of it instantly by a little dwarf who had a pair of seven-league boots (that is, boots that enable the wearer to cover seven leagues at a single stride). The fairy set out immediately, and an hour afterward she was seen arriving in a chariot of fire drawn by dragons. The king advanced and offered his hand to help her out of the chariot. She approved of all that he had done. Yet since she had great foresight, she thought to herself that when the princess awoke, she would feel considerably embarrassed at finding herself all alone in that old castle. So this is what the fairy did:

With the exception of the king and queen, she touched everyone in the castle with her wand—governesses, maids of honor, ladies-in-waiting, gentlemen, officers, stewards, cooks, scullions, boys, guards, porters, pages, footmen. She also touched all the horses in the stables, their grooms, the great mastiffs in the courtyard, and little Pootsie, the princess's tiny dog lying on the bed beside her. As soon as she touched them, they all fell asleep, and they were not to wake again until the time arrived for their mistress to do so. Thus they would all be ready to wait upon her if she should want them. Even the spits that had been put down to the fire, laden with partridges and pheasants, went to sleep, and the fire as well.

All this was done in a moment, for the fairies never lose much time when they work. Then the king and queen kissed their dear daughter without waking her and left the castle. They issued a proclamation forbidding anyone to approach it. These orders were unnecessary, for within a quarter of an hour the park was surrounded by such a great quantity of trees, large and small, interlaced by brambles and thorns, that neither man nor beast could penetrate them. Nothing more could be seen than the tops of the castle turrets, and these only at a considerable distance. Nobody doubted but that was also some of the fairy's handi- work so that the princess might have nothing to fear from the curiosity of strangers during her slumber.

At the end of the hundred years, a different family from that of the sleeping princess had succeeded to the throne. One day the son of the king went hunting in that neighborhood and inquired about the towers that he saw above the trees of a large and dense wood. Every person responded to the prince according to the story he had heard. Some said that it was an old castle haunted by ghosts. Others, that all the witches of the region held their Sabbath there. The most prevalent opin- ion was that it was the abode of an ogre who carried away all the children he could catch and ate them there at his leisure, since he alone had the power of making a passage through the wood. While the prince tried to make up his mind what to believe, an old peasant spoke in his turn and said to him, "Prince, it is more than fifty years since I heard my father say that the most beautiful princess ever seen is in that castle. He told me that she was to sleep for a hundred years and was des- tined to be awakened by a chosen king's son."

Upon hearing these words, the young prince felt all on fire. There was no doubt in his mind that he was destined to accom- plish this wonderful adventure, and impelled by love and glory, he decided on the spot to see what would come of it. No sooner had he approached the wood than all those great trees and all those brambles and thorns opened on their own accord and allowed him to pass through. Then he began walking toward the castle, which he saw at the end of the long avenue that he had entered. To his surprise, the trees closed up as soon as he passed, and none of his attendants could follow him. Nevertheless, he continued to advance, for a young and amorous prince is always courageous. When he entered a large forecourt, everything he saw froze his blood with terror. A frightful silence reigned. Death seemed to be everywhere. Nothing could be seen but the bodies of men and animals stretched out and apparently lifeless. He soon discovered, however, by the shining noses and red faces of the porters that they were only asleep; their goblets, which still contained a few drops of wine, sufficently proved that they had dozed off while drinking. Passing through a large courtyard paved with marble, he ascended a staircase. As he entered the guardroom, he saw the guards drawn up in a line, their carbines shouldered, and snoring their loudest. He traversed several apartments filled with ladies and gentlemen all asleep; some standing, others seated. Finally he entered a chamber completely covered with gold and saw the most lovely sight he had ever looked upon—on a bed with curtains open on each side was a princess who seemed to be about fifteen or sixteen. Her radiant charms gave her such a luminous, supernatural appearance that he approached, trembling and admiring, and knelt down beside her. At that moment the enchantment ended. The princess awoke and bestowed on him a look more tender than a first glance might seem to warrant.

"Is it you, my prince?" she said. "You have been long awaited."

Charmed by these words, and still more by the tone in which they were uttered, the prince hardly knew how to express his joy and gratitude to her. He assured her he loved her better than he loved himself. His words were not very coherent, but they pleased her all the more because of that. The less eloquence, the more love, so they say. He was much more embarrassed than she was, and one ought not to be astonished at that, for the princess had had time enough to consider what she should say to him. There is reason to believe (though history makes no mention of it) that the good fairy had procured her the pleasure of very charming dreams during her long slumber. In short, they talked for four hours without expressing half of what they had to say to each other.

In the meantime the entire palace had been roused at the same time as the princess. They all remembered what their tasks were, and since they were not all in love, they were dying with hunger. The lady-in-waiting, as hungry as any of them, became impatient and announced loudly to the princess that dinner was ready. The prince assisted the princess to rise. She was fully dressed, and her gown was magnificent, but he took care not to tell her that she was attired like his grandmother, who also wore stand-up collars. Still, she looked no less lovely in it.

They passed into a salon of mirrors, in which stewards of the princess served them supper. The violins and oboes played antiquated but excellent pieces of music. And after supper, to lose no time, the chaplain married them in the castle chapel, and the maid of honor pulled the curtains of their bed closed.

They did not sleep a great deal, however. The princess did not have much need of sleep, and the prince left her at sunrise to return to the city, where his father had been greatly worried about him. The prince told him that he had lost his way in the forest while hunting, and that he had slept in the hut of a charcoal-burner, who had given him some black bread and cheese for his supper. His father, who was a trusting soul, believed him, but his mother was not so easily persuaded. Observing that he went hunting nearly every day and always had some story ready as an excuse when he had slept two or three nights away from home, she was convinced that he had some mistress. Indeed, he lived with the princess for more than two years and had two children by her. The first was a girl named Aurora, and the second, a son, called Day because he seemed even more beautiful than his sister.

In order to draw a confession from him, the queen often said to her son that he ought to settle down. However, he never dared to trust her with his secret. Although he loved her, he also feared her, for she was of the race of ogres, and the king had married her only because of her great wealth. It was even

whispered about the court that she had the inclinations of an
ogress: whenever she saw little children passing, she had the
greatest difficulty restraining herself from pouncing on them.
Hence, the prince refused to say anything about his adventure.

Two years later, however, the king died, and the prince
became his successor. Thereupon, he made a public declaration of his marriage and went in great state to fetch his queen
to the palace. With her two children on either side of her, she
made a magnificent entry into the capital.

Some time afterward the king went to war with his neighbor,
the Emperor Cantalabutte. He left the regency of the kingdom
to his mother, the queen, and placed his wife and children in
her care. Since he was likely to spend the entire summer in battle, the queen mother sent her daughter-in-law and the children
to a country house in the forest, as soon as he was gone, so that
she might gratify her horrible longing more easily. A few days
later, she followed them there, and one evening she said to her
steward, "I want to eat little Aurora for dinner tomorrow."

"Ah, madam!" exclaimed the steward.

"That is my will," said the queen (and she said it in the tone
of an ogress longing to eat fresh meat), "and I want her served
up with *sauce Robert*."

The poor man plainly saw that it was useless to trifle with
an ogress. So he took his knife and went up to little Aurora's
room. She was then about four years old, and when she
skipped over to him, threw her arms around his neck with a
laugh, and asked him for some sweets, he burst into tears. The
knife fell from his hands. Soon he went down into the kitchen
court, killed a little lamb, and served it with such a delicious
sauce that his mistress assured him she had never eaten anything so good. In the meantime he carried off little Aurora and
gave her to his wife to conceal in the lodging she occupied at
the far end of the kitchen court.

A week later, the wicked queen said to her steward, "I want
to eat little Day for supper."

Determined to deceive her as before, he did not reply. He
went in search of little Day and found him with a tiny foil in
his hand, fencing with a large monkey, though he was only

three years old. He carried him to his wife, who hid him where she had concealed his sister. Then he cooked a tender little goat in place of little Day, and the ogress thought it most delicious.

Thus far all was going well, but one evening this wicked queen said to the steward, "I want to eat the queen with the same sauce that I had with the children."

This time the poor steward despaired of being able to deceive her again. The young queen was now twenty years old, not counting the hundred years she had slept. Her skin was a little tough, though it was white and beautiful. Thus, where in the menagerie was he to find an animal that was just as tough as she was?

To save his own life he resolved he would cut the queen's throat and went up to her apartment intending to carry out this plan. He worked himself up into a fit and entered the young queen's chamber, dagger in hand. However, he did not want to take her by surprise and thus repeated respectfully the order he had received from the queen mother.

"Do your duty!" said she, stretching out her neck to him. "Carry out the order given to you. Then I shall behold my children, my poor children, that I loved so much."

She had thought they were dead ever since they had been carried off without explanation.

"No, no, madam!" replied the poor steward, touched to the quick. "You shall not die, and you shall see your children again, but it will be in my house, where I have hidden them. And I shall again deceive the queen mother by serving her a young hind in your stead."

He led her straight to his own quarters, and after leaving her to embrace her children and weep with them, he cooked a hind that the queen ate at supper with as much appetite as if it had been the young queen. She felt content with her cruelty and intended to tell the king on his return that some ferocious wolves had devoured his wife and two children.

One evening when she was prowling as usual around the courts and poultry yards of the castle to inhale the smell of fresh meat, she overheard little Day crying in a lower room because his mother wanted to slap him for having been naughty. She also heard little Aurora begging forgiveness for her brother. The ogress recognized the voices of the queen and her children and, furious at having been duped, she gave orders in a tone that made everyone tremble, "Bring a large copper vat into the middle of the court early tomorrow morning."

When it was done the next day, she had the vat filled with toads, vipers, adders, and serpents, intending to fling the queen, her children, the steward, his wife, and his maidservant into it.

"Bring them forth with their hands tied behind them," she commanded.

When they stood before her, the executioners began preparing to fling them into the copper vat when the king, who was not expected back so soon, entered the courtyard on horseback. He had ridden posthaste, and greatly astonished, he demanded to know the meaning of the horrible spectacle, but nobody dared to tell him. Then the ogress, enraged at the sight of the king's return, flung herself headfirst into the vat and was devoured by the horrible reptiles that she had commanded to be placed there. The king could not help but feel sorry, for she was his mother, but he speedily consoled himself in the company of his beautiful wife and children.

Moral

To wait so long,
To want a man refined and strong,
Is not at all uncommon.
But: rare it is a hundred years to wait.
Indeed there is no woman
Today so patient for a mate.

Our tale was meant to show
That when marriage is deferred,
It is no less blissful than those of which you've heard.
Nothing's lost after a century or so.
And yet, for lovers whose ardor
Cannot be controlled and marry out of passion,
I don't have the heart their act to deplore
Or to preach a moral lesson.

RIQUET WITH THE TUFT

ONCE upon a time there was a queen who gave birth to a son so ugly and misshapen that for a long time everyone doubted if he was in fact human. A fairy who was present at his birth assured everyone, however, that he could not fail to be pleasant because he would have a great deal of intelligence. She added that he would also have the ability to impart the same amount of intelligence to that person he came to love by virtue of this gift she was giving him. All this somewhat consoled the poor queen, who was very much distressed at having brought such a hideous little monkey into the world. Sure enough, as soon as the child was able to talk, he said a thousand pretty things. Futhermore, there was an indescribable air of thoughtfulness in all his actions that charmed everyone. I have forgotten to say that he was born with a little tuft of hair on his head, and this was the reason why he was called Riquet with the Tuft (Riquet being the family name).

At the end of seven or eight years, the queen of a neighboring kingdom gave birth to two daughters. The first of them was more beautiful than daylight, and the queen was so delighted that people feared her great joy might cause her some harm. The same fairy who had attended the birth of little Riquet with the Tuft was also present on this occasion, and to moderate the queen's joy, she declared that this little princess would be as stupid as she was beautiful. The queen was deeply mortified by this, but a few minutes later her chagrin became even greater still, for she gave birth to a second child who turned out to be extremely ugly.

"Don't be too upset, madam," the fairy said to her. "Your

daughter will be compensated in another way. She'll have so much intelligence that her lack of beauty will hardly be noticed."

"May heaven grant it," replied the queen. "But isn't there some way to give a little intelligence to my older daughter who is so beautiful?"

"I can't do anything for her, madam, in the way of wit," said the fairy, "but I can do a great deal in matters of beauty. Since there's nothing I would not do to please you, I shall endow her with the ability to render any person who pleases her with a beautiful or handsome appearance."

As these two princesses grew up, their qualities increased in the same proportion. Throughout the realm everyone talked about the beauty of the older daughter and the intelligence of the younger. It is also true that their defects greatly increased as they grew older. The young daughter became uglier, and the older more stupid every day. She either gave no answer when addressed, or she said something foolish. At the same time she was so awkward that she could not place four pieces of china on a mantel without breaking one of them, nor drink a glass of water without spilling half of it on her clothes. Despite the great advantage of beauty in a young person, the younger sister always outshone the elder whenever they were in society. At first everyone gathered around the more beautiful girl to admire her, but soon left her for the more intelligent sister to listen to the thousand pleasant things she said. In less than a quarter of an hour, not a soul would be standing near the elder sister while everyone would be surrounding the younger. Though very stupid, the elder sister noticed this and would have willingly given up all her beauty for half the intelligence of her sister.

The queen, discreet though she was, could not help reproaching the elder daughter whenever she did stupid things, and that made the poor princess ready to die of grief. One day, when she had withdrawn into the woods to bemoan her misfortune, she saw a little man coming toward her. He was extremely ugly and unpleasant, but was dressed in magnificent attire. It was young Riquet with the Tuft. He had fallen in love with her from seeing her portraits, which had been sent all around the world, and he had left his father's kingdom to have the pleasure of seeing and speaking to her. Delighted to meet her thus alone, he approached her with all the respect and politeness imaginable. After paying the usual compliments, he remarked that she was very melancholy.

"I cannot comprehend, madam," he said, "how a person so beautiful as you are can be so sad as you appear. Though I may boast of having seen an infinite number of lovely women, I can assure you that I've never beheld one whose beauty could begin to compare with yours."

"It's very kind of you to say so, sir," replied the princess, and there she stopped.

"Beauty is such a great advantage," continued Riquet, "that it ought to surpass all other things. If one possesses it, I don't see anything that could cause one much distress."

"I'd rather be as ugly as you and have intelligence," said the princess, "than be as beautiful and stupid as I am."

"There's no greater proof of intelligence, madam, than the belief that we do not have any. It's the nature of the gift that the more we have, the more we believe we are deficient in it."

"I don't know whether that's the case," the princess said, "but I know full well that I am very stupid, and that's the cause of the grief which is killing me."

"If that's all that's troubling you, madam, I can easily put an end to your distress."

"And how do you intend to manage that?" the princess asked.

"I have the power, madam, to give as much intelligence as anyone can possess to the person I love," Riquet with the Tuft replied. "And as you are that person, madam, it will depend entirely on whether or not you want to have so much intelligence, for you may have it, provided that you consent to marry me."

The princess was thunderstruck and did not say a word.

"I see that this proposal torments you, and I'm not surprised," said Riquet with the Tuft. "But I'll give you a full year to make up your mind."

The princess had so little intelligence, and at the same time had such a strong desire to possess a great deal, that she imagined the year would never come to an end. So she immediately accepted his offer. No sooner did she promise that she would

marry Riquet with the Tuft twelve months from that day than
she felt a complete change come over her. She found she possessed an incredible facility to say anything she wished and to
say it in a polished yet easy and natural manner. She com-
menced right away, maintaining an elegant conversation with
the prince. Indeed, she was so brilliant that he believed that he
had given her more wit than he had kept for himself.

When she returned to the palace, the whole court was at a
loss to account for such a sudden and extraordinary change.
Whereas she had formerly said any number of foolish things,
she now made sensible and exceedingly clever observations.
The entire court rejoiced beyond belief. Only the younger sister was not quite pleased, for she no longer held the advantage
of intelligence over her elder sister. Now she merely appeared
as an ugly woman by her side, and the king let himself be
guided by the elder daughter's advice. Sometimes he even held
the meetings of his council in her apartment.

The news of this change spread abroad, and all the young
princes of the neighboring kingdoms exerted themselves to the
utmost to gain her affection. Nearly all of them asked her
hand in marriage, but since she found none of them sufficiently
intelligent, she listened to all of them without promising herself to anyone in particular. At last a prince arrived who was
so witty and handsome that she could not help feeling attracted
to him. Her father noticed this and told her that she was at
perfect liberty to choose a husband for herself and that she
only had to make her decision known. Now, the more intelligence one possesses, the greater the difficulty one has in making up one's mind about such a weighty matter. So she thanked
her father and requested some time to think it over.

By chance she took a walk in the same woods where she had
met Riquet with the Tuft to ponder with greater freedom what
she should do. While she was walking, deep in thought, she
heard a dull rumble beneath her feet, as though many people
were running busily back and forth. Listening more attentively,
she heard voices say, "Bring me that cooking pot." "Give me
that kettle." "Put some wood on the fire." At that same moment
the ground opened, and she saw below what appeared to be a

large kitchen full of cooks, scullions, and all sorts of servants necessary for the preparation of a magnificent banquet. A group of approximately twenty to thirty cooks came forth, and they took places at a very long table set in a path of the woods. Each had a larding pin in hand and a cap on his head, and they set to work, keeping time to a melodious song. Astonished at this sight, the princess inquired who had hired them.

"Riquet with the Tuft, madam," the leader of the group replied. "His marriage is to take place tomorrow."

The princess was even more surprised than she was before, and suddenly she recalled that it was exactly a year ago that she had promised to marry Prince Riquet with the Tuft. How she was taken aback! The reason why she had not remembered her promise was that when she had made it, she had still been a fool, and after receiving her new mind, she had forgotten all her follies. Now, no sooner had she advanced another thirty steps on her walk than she encountered Riquet with the Tuft, who appeared gallant and magnificent, like a prince about to be married.

"As you can see, madam," he said, "I've kept my word to the minute, and I have no doubt but that you've come here to keep yours. By giving me your hand, you'll make me the happiest of men."

"I'll be frank with you," the princess replied. "I've yet to make up my mind on that matter, and I don't believe I'll ever be able to do so to your satisfaction."

"You astonish me, madam."

"I can believe it," the princess responded, "and assuredly, if I had to deal with a stupid person—a man without intelligence—I'd feel greatly embarrassed. 'A princess is bound by her word,' he'd say to me, 'and you must marry me as you promised to do so.' But since the man with whom I'm speaking is the most intelligent man in the world, I'm certain he'll listen to reason. As you know, when I was no better than a fool, I could not decide whether I should marry you. Now that I have the intelligence that you've given me and that renders me much more difficult to please than before, how can you expect me to make a decision today that I couldn't make then? If you seriously thought of marrying me, you made a big mistake in taking away my stupidity and enabling me to see clearer."

"If a man without intelligence would be justified in reproaching you for your breach of promise," Riquet with the Tuft replied, "why do you expect, madam, that I should not be allowed to do the same? This matter affects the entire happiness of my life. Is it reasonable that intelligent people should be placed at a greater disadvantage than those who have none? Can you presume this, you who have so much intelligence and have so earnestly desired to possess it? But let us come to the point, if you please. With the exception of my ugliness, is there anything about me that displeases you? Are you dissatisfied with my birth, my intelligence, my temperament, or my manners?"

"Not in the least," replied the princess. "I admire you for everything you've just mentioned."

"If so," Riquet with the Tuft responded, "I'll gain my happiness, for you have the power to make me the most pleasing of men."

"How can that be done?"

"It can if you love me sufficiently to wish that it should be. And to remove your doubts, you should know that the same fairy who endowed me at birth with the power to give intelligence to the person I chose also gave you the power to render handsome any man who pleases you."

"If that's so," the princess said, "I wish with all my heart that you may become the most charming and handsome prince in the world."

No sooner had the princess pronounced these words than Riquet with the Tuft appeared to her eyes as the most handsome, strapping, and charming man she had ever seen. There are some who assert that it was not the fairy's spell but love alone that caused this transformation. They say that the princess, having reflected on her lover's perseverance, prudence, and all the good qualities of his heart and mind, no longer saw the deformity of his body nor the ugliness of his features. His hunch appeared to her as nothing more than the effect of a man shrugging his shoulders. Likewise, his horrible limp appeared to be nothing more than a slight sway that charmed her. They also say that his eyes, which squinted, seemed to her only more brilliant for the proof they gave of the intensity of his love. Finally, his great red nose had something martial and heroic about it. However this may be, the princess promised to marry him on the spot, provided that he obtained the consent of the king, her father.

On learning of his daughter's high regard for Riquet with the Tuft, whom he also knew to be a very intelligent and wise prince, the king accepted him with pleasure as a son-in-law. The wedding took place the next morning, just as Riquet with the Tuft had planned it.

MORAL

That which you see written down here
Is not so fantastic because it's quite true:
We find what we love is wondrously fair,
In what we love we find intelligence, too.

ANOTHER MORAL

Nature very often places
Beauty in an object that amazes,
Such that art can ne'er achieve.
Yet even beauty can't move the heart
As much as that charm hard to chart,
A charm which only love can perceive.

LITTLE RED
RIDING HOOD

ONCE upon a time there was a little village girl, the prettiest in the world. Her mother doted on her, and her grandmother even more. This good woman made her a little red hood which suited her so well that wherever she went, she was called Little Red Riding Hood.

One day, after her mother had baked some biscuits, she said to Little Red Riding Hood, "Go see how your grandmother's feeling. I've heard that she's ill. You can take her some biscuits and this small pot of butter."

Little Red Riding Hood departed at once to visit her grandmother, who lived in another village. In passing through the forest she met old neighbor wolf, who had a great desire to eat her. But he did not dare because of some woodcutters who were in the forest. Instead he asked her where she was going. The poor child, who did not know that it is dangerous to stop and listen to a wolf, said to him, "I'm going to see my grandmother, and I'm bringing her some biscuits with a small pot of butter that my mother's sending her."

"Does she live far from here?" the wolf asked.

"Oh, yes!" Little Red Riding Hood said. "You've got to go by the mill, which you can see right over there, and hers is the first house in the village."

"Well, then," said the wolf, "I'll go and see her, too. You take that path there, and I'll take this path here, and we'll see who'll get there first."

The wolf began to run as fast as he could on the shorter path, and the little girl took the longer path. What's more, she enjoyed herself by gathering nuts, running after butterflies, and making bouquets of small flowers that she found along the way. It did not take the wolf long to arrive at the grandmother's house, and he knocked:

"Tick, tock."

"Who's there?"

"It's your granddaughter, Little Red Riding Hood," the wolf said, disguising his voice. "I've brought you some biscuits and a little pot of butter that my mother's sent for you."

The good grandmother, who was in her bed because she was not feeling well, cried out to him, "Pull the bobbin, and the latch will fall."

The wolf pulled the bobbin, and the door opened. He pounced on the good woman and devoured her quicker than a wink, for it had been more than three days since he had eaten last. After that he closed the door and lay down in the grandmother's bed to wait for Little Red Riding Hood, who after a while came knocking at the door.

"Tick, tock."

"Who's there?"

When she heard the gruff voice of the wolf, Little Red Riding Hood was scared at first, but she thought her grandmother had a cold and responded, "It's your granddaughter, Little Red Riding Hood. I've brought you some biscuits and a little pot of butter that my mother's sent for you."

The wolf softened his voice and cried out to her, "Pull the bobbin, and the latch will fall."

Little Red Riding Hood pulled the bobbin, and the door opened.

Upon seeing her enter, the wolf hid himself under the bedcovers and said to her, "Put the biscuits and the pot of butter on the bin and come lie down beside me."

Little Red Riding Hood undressed and got into the bed, where she was quite astonished to see how her grandmother appeared in her nightgown.

"What big arms you have, grandmother!" she said to her.

"The better to hug you with, my child."

"What big legs you have, grandmother!"

"The better to run with, my child."

"What big ears you have, grandmother!"
"The better to hear you with, my child."
"What big eyes you have, grandmother!"
"The better to see you with, my child."
"What big teeth you have, grandmother!"
"The better eat you with!"
And upon saying these words, the wicked wolf pounced on
Little Red Riding Hood and ate her up.

MORAL

One sees here that young children,
Especially pretty girls,
Who're bred as pure as pearls,
Should question words addressed by men.
Or they may serve one day as feast
For a wolf or other beast.
I say a wolf since not all are wild
Or are indeed the same in kind.
For some are winning and have sharp minds.
Some are loud, smooth, or mild.
Others appear plain kind or unriled.
They follow young ladies wherever they go,
Right into the halls of their very own homes.
Alas for those girls who've refused the truth:
The sweetest tongue has the sharpest tooth.

THE FAIRIES

ONCE upon a time there was a widow who had two daughters. The older one was often mistaken for her mother because she was so much like her in looks and character. Indeed, both mother and daughter were so disagreeable and haughty that it was impossible to live with them. The younger daughter, who looked exactly like her father and took after him in her kindness and politeness, was one of the most beautiful girls ever seen.

Since we naturally tend to be fond of those who resemble us, the mother doted on her elder daughter while she hated the younger. She made her eat in the kitchen and work from morning till night. Among the many things that this poor child was forced to do, she had to walk a mile twice a day to fetch water from a spring and tote it back in a large jug. One day, when she was at the spring, a poor woman came up to her and asked her for a drink.

"Why, of course, my good woman," she said, and the pretty maiden at once stooped and rinsed out the jug. Then she filled it with water from the clearest part of the spring and offered it to the woman, helping to keep the jug raised so that she might drink more easily.

After the woman had finished drinking, she said, "You are so beautiful, so good and kind, that I can't resist bestowing a gift on you"—for she was a fairy who had assumed the form of a poor peasant in order to discover just how kind this young girl was. "I shall give you a gift," continued the fairy, "that will cause every word you utter to become either a flower or precious stone."

When this beautiful girl arrived home, her mother scolded her for returning so late.

"I'm sorry for having taken so long," the poor girl said, and on saying these words, two roses, two pearls, and two large diamonds fell from her mouth.

"What do I see here!" said her mother, completely astonished. "I believe I saw pearls and diamonds dropping from your mouth. Where do they come from, my daughter?" (This was the first time she had ever called her "my daughter.")

As countless diamonds fell from her mouth, the poor child naively told her all that had happened.

"Upon my word," said the mother, "I must send my daughter. Come here, Fanchon! Do you see what's falling from your sister's mouth when she speaks? Wouldn't you like to have the same gift? You only have to fetch some water from the spring, and if a poor woman asks you for a drink, you're to give it to her nicely and politely."

"You'll never get me to walk to the spring!" the rude girl responded.

"I'm insisting," her mother replied, "and you'd better go this instant!"

She left, sulking as she went. With her she took the most beautiful silver bottle in the house. No sooner did she arrive at the spring than a magnificently dressed lady emerged from the forest and asked her for a drink. This was the same fairy who had appeared to her sister, but she now put on the airs and the garments of a princess to see just how rude this girl could be.

"Do you think I came here just to fetch you a drink?" the rude and arrogant girl said. "Do you think that I carried this silver bottle just to offer a drink to a fine lady? Get your own drink if you want one!"

"You're not at all polite," the fairy replied without anger. "Well, then, since you're not very obliging, I'll bestow a gift on you. Every word uttered from your mouth will become either a snake or a toad."

As soon as her mother caught sight of her, she cried out, "Well then, daughter!"

"Well then, my mother," her rude daughter responded, spitting two vipers and two toads from her mouth.

"Oh heavens!" her mother exclaimed. "What do I see? Your sister's to blame, and she'll pay for it!"

She dashed off to beat her, but the poor child fled and took refuge in a nearby forest. The king's son, who was returning from a hunt, encountered her there, and observing how beautiful she was, he asked her what she was doing there weeping all alone.

"Alas, sir! My mother has driven me from home."

Seeing five or six pearls and as many diamonds fall from her mouth, the king's son asked her to tell him where they came from. She told him the entire story, and the king's son fell in love with her. When he considered that such a gift was worth more than a dowry anyone else could bring, he took her to the palace of the king, his father, where he married her.

As for the sister, she made herself so hated that her own mother drove her out of the house. This wretched girl searched about in vain for someone who would offer her shelter, and finally she went off to a corner of the forest, where she died.

MORAL

> Diamonds and gold
> Can do wonders for one's soul.
> Yet kind words, I am told,
> Are worth more on the whole.

ANOTHER MORAL

> Virtue demands a great deal of effort,
> For one must indeed be very good-natured.
> Sooner or later it reaps its reward,
> Which comes indeed when it's least sought.

THE FOOLISH WISHES

ONCE upon a time there was a poor woodcutter whose life was so hard that he longed to rest in the infernal regions of the world beyond. This tormented soul maintained that in all his days on earth, heaven had never granted him a single wish.

One day he was grumbling to himself in the forest when Jupiter appeared with thunderbolt in hand. It is impossible to describe the fear of the good man, who threw himself on the ground and cried, "I don't want a thing. No wishes. No thunder. My lord, let me live in peace!"

"Have no fear," said Jupiter. "I've come because I've been moved by your complaints, and I want to show you how unfair you've been to me. So listen: I, who reign supreme over the entire world, promise to grant you the first three wishes you make, no matter what they are. Just see that they make you happy. And since your happiness depends on your wishes, think carefully before you make them." With these words Jupiter returned to the heavens.

The woodcutter, now cheerful, picked up his bundle of sticks and carried them home on his back. Never had his burden seemed so light. As he was running along, he said to himself, "I mustn't be hasty in this matter. It's important, and I must ask my wife's advice."

Upon entering his cottage, he called, "Hey, Fanchon! Let's make a large fire, my dear. We're going to be rich for the rest of our lives. All we have to do is to make some wishes."

He told her what had happened, and on hearing the story his wife promptly began forming a thousand vast schemes in her mind. Nevertheless, she realized the importance of doing everything prudently.

"Blaise, my dear," she said to her husband, "let's not spoil anything by our impatience. Let's both mull over in our minds what's best for us. I suggest that we sleep on it and put off our first wish until tomorrow."

"I agree with you," said the good man Blaise. "But now, get some of the good wine behind the stack of sticks."

On her return, he leisurely drank the wine by a large fire and enjoyed the sweetness of relaxation. Leaning back in his chair, he said, "Since we have such a good blaze, I wish we had some sausage. That would go well with it."

He had hardly finished speaking when his wife was astonished to see a very long sausage approaching her from the chimney corner like a serpent. First she screamed, but then realized that this incident had been caused by her husband's foolish wish. Overcome by vexation, she began to scold and berate the poor man.

"You can have an empire of gold, pearls, rubies, diamonds, or fine clothes," she said, "but all you seem to want is a sausage!"

"Ah well, I was wrong," he replied. "I made a bad choice. In fact, I made an enormously bad choice. I'll do better next time."

"Sure, you will," she snapped. "I'll be long gone before that happens. You've got to be an ass to make a wish like that!"

Her husband became enraged and thought how nice it would be to be a widower, and—between you and me—this was not a bad idea.

"Men," he said, "are born to suffer! A curse on this sausage and all other sausages. I wish to God that the sausage was hanging from your nose, you vile creature!"

The wish was heard in heaven, and moments after he had uttered those words, the sausage attached itself to the nose of the agitated woman. This unforseen miracle made her immensely angry. Fanchon was pretty and had a great deal of grace. And, to tell the truth, this ornament did not improve her looks. Even though it merely hung down over her face, it prevented her from speaking easily. Her husband now had such a wonderful advantage that he thought his wish was not all that bad.

"Despite this terrible disaster, I could still make myself king," he said to himself. "In truth, there's nothing that can compare

to the grandeur of sovereignty. But I must take the queen's feelings into account, for she'd suffer immensely if she had to take
her place on the throne with a nose more than a yard long. I
must see whether she wants to be a grand princess with that
horrible nose or whether she wants to keep living as a woodcutter's wife with a nose like everyone else's."

Fanchon knew that she who wielded a scepter had a lot of
power and that people must swear you have a well-formed
nose if you wear a crown. Yet after thinking about the matter
carefully, she realized that nothing could surpass the desire to
be pleasant-looking. Thus she decided to keep her own nose
rather than to become an ugly queen.

So the woodcutter did not change his lot. He did not become
a potentate, nor did his purse become filled with gold coins.
Happily he employed his last wish to have his wife restored to
her former state.

Moral

No doubt, men who are quite miserable,
Or blind, dumb, worried, and fickle
Aren't fit to make those wishes they should.
In fact, there are few among them who're able
To use such heaven's gifts for their own good.

DONKEY-SKIN

ONCE upon a time lived the most powerful king in the world. Gentle in peace, terrifying in war, he was incomparable in all ways. His neighbors feared him while his subjects were content. Throughout his realm the fine arts and civility flourished under his protection. His better half, his constant companion, was charming and beautiful. Such was her sweet and good nature that he was less happy as king and more happy as her husband. Out of their tender, pure wedlock a daughter was born, and she had so many virtues that she consoled them for their inability to have more children.

Everything was magnificent in their huge palace. They had an ample group of courtiers and servants all around them. In his stables the king had large and small horses of every kind, which were adorned with beautiful trappings, gold braids, and embroidery. But what surprised everyone on entering the stables was a master donkey in the place of honor. This discrepancy may be surprising, but if you knew the superb virtues of this donkey, you would probably agree that there was no honor too great for him. Nature had formed him in such a way that he never emitted an odor. Instead he generated heaps of beautiful gold coins that were gathered from the stable litter every morning at sunrise.

Now, heaven, which always mixes the good with the bad, just like rain may come in good weather, permitted a nasty illness to suddenly attack the queen. Help was sought everywhere, but neither the learned physicians nor the charlatans who appeared were able to arrest the fever, which increased day by day. When her last hour arrived, the queen said to her husband, "Before I die, you must promise me one thing, and that is, if you should desire to remarry when I am gone—"

"Ah!" said the king, "your concern is superfluous. I'd never think of doing such a thing. You can rest assured about that."

"I believe you," replied the queen, "if your ardent love is any proof. But to make me more certain, I want you to swear that you'll give your pledge to another woman only if she is more beautiful, more accomplished, and wiser than I."

Her confidence in her qualities and her cleverness were such that she knew he would regard his promise as an oath never to remarry. With his eyes bathed in tears, he swore to do everything the queen desired. Then she died in his arms.

Never did a king make such a commotion. Day and night he could be heard sobbing, and many believed that he could not keep mourning so bitterly for long. Indeed, some said he wept about his deceased wife like a man who wanted to end the matter in haste.

In truth, this was the case. At the end of several months he wanted to move on with his life and choose a new queen. But this was not easy to do. He had to keep his word, and his new wife had to have more charms and grace than his dead one, who had become immortalized. Neither the court, with its great quantity of beautiful women, nor the city, the country, or foreign kingdoms, where the rounds were made, could provide the king with such a woman.

The only one more beautiful was his daughter. In truth, she even possessed certain attractive qualities that her deceased mother had not had. The king himself noticed this, and he fell so ardently in love with her that he became mad. He convinced himself that this love was reason enough for him to marry her. He even found a casuist who argued logically that a case could be made for such a marriage. But the young princess was greatly troubled to hear him talk of such love and grieved night and day.

Thus the princess sought out her godmother, who lived at some distance from the castle in a grotto of coral and pearls. She was a remarkable fairy, far superior to any of her kind. There is no need to tell you what a fairy was like in those most happy of times, for I am certain that your mother has told you about them when you were very young.

Upon seeing the princess, the fairy said, "I know why you've come. I know your heart is filled with sadness. But there's no need to worry, for I am with you. If you follow my advice, there's nothing that can harm you. It's true that your father wants to marry you, and if you were to listen to his insane request, it would be a grave mistake. However, there's a way to refuse him without contradicting him. Tell him that before you'd be willing to abandon your heart to him, he must grant your wishes and give you a dress the color of the sky. In spite of all his power and wealth and the favorable signs of the stars, he'll never be able to fulfill your request."

So the princess departed right away, and trembling, went to her amorous father. He immediately summoned his tailors and ordered them to make a dress the color of the sky without delay. "Or else, be assured I will hang you all."

The sun was just dawning the next day when they brought the desired dress, the most beautiful blue of the firmament. There was not a color more like the sky, and it was encircled by large clouds of gold. Though the princess desired it, she was caught between joy and pain. She did not know how to respond or get out of her promise. Then her godmother said to her in a low voice, "Princess, ask for a more radiant dress. Ask for one the color of the moon. He'll never be able to give that to you."

No sooner did the princess make the request than the king said to his embroiderer, "I want a dress that will glisten greater than the star of night, and I want it without fail in four days."

The splendid dress was ready by the deadline set by the king. Up in the night sky the luster of the moon's illumination makes the stars appear pale, mere scullions in her court. Despite this, the glistening moon was less radiant than this dress of silver.

Admiring this marvelous dress, the princess was almost ready to give her consent to her father, but, urged on by her godmother, she said to the amorous king, "I can't be content until I have an even more radiant dress. I want one the color of the sun."

Since the king loved her with an ardor that could not be matched anywhere, he immediately summoned a rich jeweler and ordered him to make a superb garment of gold and diamonds. "And if you fail to satisfy us, you will be tortured to death."

Yet it was not necessary for the king to punish the jeweler, for the industrious man brought him the precious dress by the end of the week. It was so beautiful and radiant that the blond lover of Clytemnestra, when he drove his chariot of gold on the arch of heaven, would have been dazzled by its brilliant rays.

The princess was so confused by these gifts that she did not know what to say. At that moment her godmother took her by the hand and whispered in her ear, "There's no need to pursue this path anymore. There's a greater marvel than all the gifts you have received. I mean that donkey who constantly fills your father's purse with gold coins. Ask him for the donkey skin. Since this rare donkey is the major source of his money, he won't give it to you, unless I'm badly mistaken."

Now this fairy was very clever, and yet she did not realize that passionate love counts more than money or gold, provided that the prospects for its fulfillment are good. So the forfeit was gallantly granted the moment the princess requested it.

When the skin was brought to her, she was terribly frightened. As she began to complain bitterly about her fate, her godmother arrived. She explained, "If you do your best, there's no need to fear." The princess had to let the king think that she was ready to place herself at his disposal and marry him while preparing at the same time to disguise herself and flee alone to some distant country in order to avoid the impending, evil marriage.

"Here's a large chest," the fairy continued. "You can put your clothes, mirror, toilet articles, diamonds, and rubies in it. I'm going to give you my magic wand. Whenever you hold it in your hand, the chest will always follow your path beneath the ground. And whenever you want to open it, you merely have to touch the ground with my wand, and the chest will appear before you. We'll use the donkey's skin to make you unrecognizable. It's such a perfect disguise and so horrible that once you conceal yourself inside, nobody will ever believe that it adorns anyone so beautiful as you."

Thus disguised, the princess departed from the abode of the wise fairy the next morning as the dew began to drop. When the king started preparations for the marriage celebration, he learned to his horror that his bride-to-be had taken flight. All the houses, roads, and avenues were promptly searched, but in vain. No one could conceive of what had happened to her. Sadness and sorrow spread throughout the realm. There would be no marriage, no feast, no tarts, no sugar-almonds. The ladies at the court were quite disappointed not to be able to dine, but the priest was most saddened, for he had been expecting a heavy donation at the end of the ceremony as well as a hearty meal.

Meanwhile the princess continued her flight, dirtying her face with mud. When she extended her hands to people she met, begging for a place to work, they noticed how much she smelled and how disagreeable she looked, and did not want to have anything to do with such a dirty creature, even though they themselves were hardly less vulgar and mean. Farther and farther she traveled and farther still until she finally arrived at a farm where they needed a scullion to wash the dishclothes and clean out the pig troughs. She was put in a corner of the kitchen, where the servants, insolent and nasty creatures all, ridiculed, contradicted, and mocked her. They kept playing mean tricks on her and harassed her at every chance they had. Indeed, she was the butt of all their jokes.

On Sundays she had a little time to rest. After finishing her morning chores, she went into her room, closed the door, and washed herself. Then she opened the chest and carefully arranged her toilet articles in their little jars in front of her large mirror. Satisfied and happy, she tried on her moon dress, then the one that shone like the sun, and finally the beautiful blue dress that even the sky could not match in brilliance. Her only regret was that she did not have enough room to spread out the trains of the dresses on the floor. Still, she loved to see herself young, fresh as a rose, and a thousand times more elegant than she had ever been. Such sweet pleasure kept her going from one Sunday to the next.

I forgot to mention that there was a large aviary on this farm that belonged to a powerful and magnificent king. All sorts of strange fowls were kept there: chickens from Barbary, rails, guinea fowls, cormorants, musical birds, quacking ducks, and a thousand other kinds, which were the match of ten other courts put together. The king's son often stopped at this charming spot on his return from the hunt to rest and enjoy a cool drink. He was more handsome than Cephalus and had a regal and martial appearance that made the proudest battalions tremble. From a distance Donkey-Skin admired him with a tender look. Thanks to her courage, she realized that she still had the heart of a princess beneath her dirt and rags.

"What a grand manner he has!" she said, even though he paid no attention to her. "How gracious he is, and how happy must be the woman who has captured his heart! If he were to honor me with the plainest dress imaginable, I'd feel more decorated than in any of those I have."

One Sunday the young prince was wandering adventurously from courtyard to courtyard, and he passed through an obscure hallway, where Donkey-Skin had her humble room. He chanced to peek through the keyhole, and since it was a holiday, she had dressed herself up as richly as possible in her dress of gold and diamonds that shone like the sun. Succumbing to fascination, the prince kept peeking at her, scarcely breathing because he was filled with such pleasure. Her magnificent dress, her beautiful face, her lovely manner, her fine traits, and her young freshness moved him a thousand times over. But most of all, he was captivated by the air of grandeur mingled with modest reserve that bore witness to the beauty of her soul.

Three times he was on the verge of entering her room because of the ardor that overwhelmed him, but three times he refrained out of respect for the seemingly divine creature he was beholding.

Returning to the palace, he became pensive. Day and night he sighed, refusing to attend any of the balls even though it was Carnival. He began to hate hunting and attending the theater. He lost his appetite, and everything saddened his heart. At the root of his malady was a deadly melancholy.

He inquired about the remarkable nymph who lived in one

of the lower courtyards at the end of the dingy alley where it remained dark even in broad daylight.

"You mean Donkey-Skin," he was told. "But there's nothing nymphlike or beautiful about her. She's called Donkey-Skin because of the skin that she wears on her back. She's the ideal remedy for anyone in love. That beast is almost uglier than a wolf."

All this was said in vain, for he did not believe it. Love had left its mark and could not be effaced. However, his mother, whose only child he was, pleaded with him to tell her what was wrong, yet she pressured him in vain. He moaned, wept, and sighed. He said nothing, except that he wanted Donkey-Skin to make him a cake with her own hands. And so, his mother could only repeat what her son desired.

"Oh, heavens, madam!" the servants said to her. "This Donkey-Skin is a black drab, uglier and dirtier than the most wretched scullion."

"It doesn't matter," the queen said. "Fulfilling his request is the only thing that concerns us." His mother loved him so much that she would have served him anything on a golden platter.

Meanwhile, Donkey-Skin took some ground flour, salt, butter, and fresh eggs in order to make the dough especially fine. Then she locked herself alone in her room to make the cake. She washed her hands, arms, and face and put on a silver smock in honor of the task that she was about to undertake. It is said that in working a bit too hastily, a precious ring happened to fall from Donkey-Skin's finger into the batter. But some claim that she dropped the ring on purpose. As for me, quite frankly, I can believe it because when the prince had stopped at the door and looked through the keyhole, she must have seen him. Women are so alert that nothing escapes their notice. Indeed, I pledge my word on it that she was convinced her young lover would gratefully receive her ring.

There was never a cake kneaded so daintily as this one, and the prince found it so good that he immediately began ravishing it and almost swallowed the ring. However, when he saw

the remarkable emerald and the narrow band of gold, his heart
was ignited by an inexpressible joy. At once he put the ring
under his pillow. Yet that did not cure his malady. Upon seeing
him grow worse day by day, the doctors, wise with experience,
used their great science to come to the conclusion that he was
sick with love.

Whatever else one may say about marriage, it is a perfect
remedy for lovesickness. So it was decided that the prince
should marry. After he deliberated for some time, he finally
said, "I'll be glad to get married provided that I marry only the
person whose finger fits this ring."

This strange demand surprised the king and queen very
much, but he was so sick that they did not dare to say anything
that might upset him. Now a search began for the person
whose finger might fit the ring, no matter what class or lin-
eage. The only requirement was that the woman be ready to
come and show her finger to claim her due.

A rumor was spread throughout the realm that to claim the
prince, one had to have a very slender finger. Consequently,
every charlatan, eager to make a name for himself, pretended
that he possessed the secret of making a finger slender. Following such capricious advice, one woman scraped her finger like
a turnip. Another cut a little piece off. Still another used some
liquid to remove the skin from her finger and reduce its size.
All sorts of plans imaginable were concocted by women to
make their fingers fit the ring.

The selection was begun with the young princesses, mar-
quesses, and duchesses, but no matter how delicate their fingers were, they were too large for the ring. Then the countesses,
baronesses, and all the rest of the nobility took their turns and
presented their hands in vain. Next came well-proportioned
working girls who had pretty and slender fingers. Finally, it
was necessary to turn to the servants, kitchen help, minor servants, and poultry keepers, in short, to all the trash who with
their reddened or blackened hands hoped for a happy fate just
as much as those with delicate hands. Many girls presented
themselves with large and thick fingers, but trying the prince's

ring on their fingers was like trying to thread the eye of a needle with a rope.

Everyone thought that they had reached the end because the only one remaining was Donkey-Skin in the corner of the kitchen. And who could ever believe that the heavens had ordained that she might become queen?

"Why not?" said the prince. "Let her try."

Everyone began laughing and exclaimed aloud, "Do you mean to say that you want that dirty wretch to enter here?"

But when she drew a little hand as white as ivory and of royal blood from under the dirty skin, the destined ring fit perfectly around her finger. The members of the court were astonished. So delirious were they that they wanted to march her to the king right away, but she requested that she be given some time to change her clothes before she appeared before her lord and master. In truth, the people could hardly keep from laughing because of the clothes she was wearing.

Finally, she arrived at the palace and passed through all the halls in her blue dress whose radiance could not be matched. Her blonde hair glistened with diamonds. Her blue eyes, so large and sweet, whose gaze always pleased and never hurt, were filled with a proud majesty. Her waist was so slender that two hands could have encircled it. All the charms and ornaments of the ladies of the court dwindled in comparison. Despite the rejoicing and commotion of the gathering, the good king did not fail to notice the many charms of his future daughter-in-law, and the queen was also terribly delighted. The prince, her dear lover, could hardly bear the excitement of his rapture.

Preparations for the wedding were begun at once. The monarch invited all the kings of the surrounding countries, who left their lands to attend the grand event, all radiant in their different attire. Those from the East were mounted on huge elephants. The Moors arriving from distant shores were so black and ugly that they frightened the little children. People embarked from all the corners of the world and descended on the court in great numbers. But neither prince nor king seemed as splendid as the bride's father, who had purified the criminal and odious fires that had ignited his spirit in the past. The flame that was left in his soul had been transformed into devoted paternal love. When he saw her, he said, "May heaven be blessed for allowing me to see you again, my dear child."

Weeping with joy, he embraced her tenderly. Everyone wanted to share in his happiness, and the future husband was delighted to learn that he was to become the son-in-law of such a powerful king. At that moment the godmother arrived and told the entire story of how everything had happened and culminated in Donkey-Skin's glory.

Evidently, the moral of this tale implies it is better for a child to expose oneself to hardships than to neglect one's duty.

Indeed, virtue may sometimes seem ill-fated, but it is always crowned with success. Of course, strongest reason is a weak dike against mad love and ardent ecstasy, especially if a lover is not afraid to squander rich treasures.

Finally, we must take into account that clear water and brown bread are sufficient nourishment for all young women provided that they have good habits, and that there is not a damsel under the skies who does not imagine herself beautiful and somehow carrying off the honors in the famous beauty contest between Hera, Aphrodite, and Athena.

> The tale of Donkey-Skin is hard to believe,
> But as long as there are children on this earth,
> With mothers and grandmothers who continue to give birth,
> This tale will always be told and surely well received.

MARIE-JEANNE L'HÉRITIER

THE DISCREET PRINCESS,
OR THE ADVENTURES
OF FINETTE

DURING the time of the First Crusade, a king of a country in Europe decided to go to war against the infidels of Palestine. Before undertaking such a long journey, he put the affairs of his kingdom into such good order and placed the regency in the hands of such an able minister that he was entirely at ease. What worried this king most, though, was the care of his family. He had recently lost his wife, who had failed to give birth to a son before her death. On the other hand, he was the father of three princesses, all of marriageable age. My chronicle has not indicated what their true names were. I only know that people were quite simple during these happy times, and customarily gave eminent people surnames according to their good or bad characteristics. Thus they called the eldest princess "Nonchalante," the second "Babbler," and the third "Finette." All of these names suited the characters of the three sisters.

Never was anyone more indolent than Nonchalante. The earliest she ever woke up was one in the afternoon, and she was dragged to church in the same condition as when she got out of bed. Her clothes were all in disarray, her dress loose, sans belt, and often she wore mismatched slippers. They used to correct this mistake during the day, but could never prevail upon this princess to wear anything but slippers, for she found it extremely exhausting to put on shoes. Whenever Nonchalante finished eating, she would camp at her dressing table until evening. She employed the rest of her time until midnight by playing and snacking. Since undressing her took almost as long as getting her dressed, she never succeeded in going to bed until dawn.

Babbler led a different kind of life. Extremely active, this

princess spent little time caring about her looks, but she had
such a strong propensity for talking that from the moment she
woke to the time she fell asleep again, her mouth was never shut.
She knew everything about the bad households, the love liaisons,
and the intrigues not only at the court, but also among the most
petty of the bourgeoisie. She kept a record of all those wives who
stole from their families at home in order to make a more dazzling impression when they went out into society. She was
informed precisely about what a particular countess's lady-in-
waiting and a particular marquis's steward earned. In order to
be on top of all these insignificant affairs, she listened to her
nurse and seamstress with greater pleasure than she would to an
ambassador. Finally, she shocked everyone, from the king down
to his footmen, with her pretty stories. She did not care whom
she had for a listener provided she could prattle. Such a longing
to talk had another bad effect on this princess. Despite her high
rank, her familiarity emboldened young men around the court
to talk sweetly to her. She listened to their flowery speeches
merely so that she could have the pleasure of responding to them.
No matter what the consequences of her actions might be, she
had to hear others talk or gossip herself from morning till night.

Neither Babbler nor Nonchalante ever bothered to occupy
herself by thinking, reflecting, or reading. They never troubled
themselves about household chores or entertained themselves
by sewing or weaving. In short, these two sisters lived in eternal idleness and ignorance.

The youngest of the three sisters had a very different character. Her mind and hands were continually active, and she had
a surprising vivacity that was put to good use. She knew how
to sing and dance and play musical instruments to perfection.
She was remarkably nimble and successful in all those little
manual chores with which her sex generally amused themselves. Moreover, she put the king's household into perfect
order and prevented the pilferings of the petty officers through
her care and vigilance, for even in those days princes were
cheated by those who surrounded them.

Finette's talents did not stop there. She had great judgment
and such a wonderful presence of mind that she could immedi-

ately find ways to get out of any kind of predicament. By using her insights, this young princess had discovered a dangerous trap that a perfidious ambassador of the neighboring kingdom had set for her father in a treaty that he was about to sign. To punish the treachery of this ambassador and his master, the king changed the articles of the treaty, and by wording it in the terms that his daughter dictated to him, he in turn deceived the deceiver. Another time the princess discovered some cheating by a minister against the king, and through the advice she gave her father, he managed to foil this disloyal man. In fact, she gave so many signs of her intelligence that this is why they nicknamed her Finette, the cunning girl.

The king loved her far more than his other daughters and depended so much on her good sense that if he had not had any other child but her, he would have departed for the Crusade without feeling uneasy. However, his faith in Finette's good behavior was offset by his distrust of his other daughters. Therefore, to make sure that his family would be safeguarded in the way he believed he had done for his subjects, he adopted the following measures that I am now going to relate.

The king was on intimate terms with a fairy, and went to see her in order to express the uneasiness he felt concerning his daughters.

"It's not that the two eldest have ever done the least thing contrary to their duty," he said. "But they have so little sense, are so imprudent, and live so indolently that I fear that they will get caught up in some foolish intrigue during my absence or do something foolish merely to amuse themselves. As for Finette, I'm sure of her virtue. However, I'll treat her as I do her sisters to make everything equal. This is why, wise fairy, I'd like you to make my daughters three distaffs out of glass. And I'd like you to make each one so artfully that it will break as soon as its owner does anything against her honor."

Since this fairy was extremely skillful, she presented the king with three enchanted distaffs within seconds, taking great care to make them according to his conditions. But he was not content with this precaution. He put the princesses

into a high tower in a secluded spot. The king told his daughters that he was ordering them to live in that tower during his
absence and prohibited them from admitting any people what-
soever. He took all their officers and servants of both sexes from
them, and after giving them the enchanted distaffs, whose qualities he explained to them, he kissed the princesses, locked the
doors of the tower, took away the keys, and departed.

You may perhaps believe that these princesses were now in
danger of dying from hunger. Not at all. A pulley had been
attached to one of the windows of the tower, and a rope ran
through it, to which the princesses tied a basket that they let
down to the ground. Provisions were placed into this basket
on a daily basis, and after they pulled up the basket, they carefully coiled the rope in the room.

Nonchalante and Babbler led a life of despair in this desolate place. They became bored beyond expression, but they
were forced to have patience because they had been given such
a terrible picture of their distaffs that they feared that their
least slip might cause them to break.

As for Finette, she was not bored in the least. Her needlework,
spinning, and music furnished her with abundant amusement.
Besides this, the minister who was governing the state had the
king's permission to place letters into the basket, which kept the
princesses informed about what was happening in the kingdom
or outside it. Finette read all the news with great attention and
pleasure, but her two sisters did not deign to participate in the
least. They said they were too sorrowful to have the strength to
amuse themselves with such weighty matters. They needed cards
to entertain themselves during their father's absence.

Thus they spent their time by grumbling continually about
their destiny, and I believe they even said, "It is much better to
be born happy than to be born the daughter of a king." They
often went to the windows of the tower to see at least what was
happening in the countryside, and one day, when Finette was
absorbed in some pretty work in her room, her sisters saw a
poor woman clothed in rags and tatters at the foot of the tower.
She pathetically cried out to them about her misery and begged

them with clasped hands to let her come into the castle. "I'm an unfortunate stranger who knows how to do a thousand things, and I shall serve you with the utmost fidelity."

At first the princesses recalled their father's orders not to permit anyone to enter the tower, but Nonchalante was so weary of attending herself, and Babbler was so bored at having nobody to talk to but her sisters, that the desire of the one to be groomed and the other to gossip made them decide to admit this poor stranger.

"Do you think," Babbler said to her sister, "that the king's order was meant to include this unfortunate wretch? I believe we can admit her without anything happening."

"Sister, you may do whatever you please," Nonchalante responded.

Babbler had only waited for her sister to consent, and she immediately let down the basket. The poor woman got into it, and the princesses pulled her up with the help of the pulley.

When this woman drew nigh, her horrid dirty clothes almost turned their stomachs. They would have given her others, but she told them she would change her clothes the next day. At present, she could think of nothing but her work. As she said these words, Finette entered the room. She was stunned to see this unknown person with her sisters. They told her the reasons that had induced them to pull her up, and Finette, who saw that she could do nothing about it, concealed her disappointment at their imprudence.

In the meantime the princesses' new servant explored the tower a hundred times under the pretext of doing her work, but in reality to see what was located where in it. In truth, this ragged creature was none other than the elder son of a powerful king, a neighbor of the princesses' father. One of the most cunning men of his time, this young prince completely controlled his father. Actually, this did not require much ability, because the king had such a sweet and easy disposition that he had been named "The Gentle." As for this young prince, who always acted with artifice and guile, the people called him Rich-in-Craft, a name commonly shortened to Rich-Craft.

His younger brother had as many good qualities as Rich-Craft had bad ones. Despite their different characters, however, such a tight bond existed between these two princes that everyone was surprised by it. Besides the younger prince's good qualities, his handsome face and graceful figure were so remarkable that he was generally called Bel-a-voir.

It was Rich-Craft who had instigated the deceitful act of his father's ambassador who had tried to change the treaty, an act that had been foiled by Finette's quick mind. Ever since she had turned the tables on them, Rich-Craft, who had not shown a particularly great love for the princess's father before this, now developed an even stronger aversion for him. Thus, after he had learned about the precautions that the king had taken in regard to his daughters, he decided to have some pernicious fun by undermining the prudence of such a distrustful father. Accordingly, Rich-Craft obtained permission from his father to take a journey, and he found a way to enter the tower, as you have already seen.

In examining the castle, Rich-Craft observed that the princesses could easily make themselves heard by people passing by, and he concluded that he'd best stay in his ragged disguise for the rest of the day because if they realized who he was, they could easily call out and have him punished for his rash undertaking. That night, however, after the princesses had dined, he pulled off his rags and revealed himself as a cavalier in rich attire dotted with gold and jewels. The poor princesses were so frightened by this disclosure that they all ran from him as fast as they could. Finette and Babbler, who were very nimble, quickly reached their rooms, but Nonchalante, who was not accustomed to moving fast, was soon overtaken.

Rich-Craft threw himself at her feet. He declared who he was and told her that the reputation of her beauty and the sight of her portraits had induced him to leave his delightful court in order to pledge his eternal devotion and propose to her. Nonchalante was at such a loss for words that she could not answer the prince, who remained kneeling. Meanwhile he kept saying a thousand sweet things and made a thousand protestations, and he ardently implored her, "Take me this very moment for your husband." Due to her weak backbone, she did not have the strength to gainsay him and told him without thinking that she believed him to be sincere and accepted his proposal. No greater formalities than these concluded the marriage.

At that moment, however, her distaff broke into a thousand pieces.

Babbler and Finette were extraordinarily anxious. They had made it back to their separate rooms and locked themselves in. These rooms were at some distance from each other, and since neither princess knew anything about the other's fate, they did not sleep a wink all night long.

The next morning the wicked prince led Nonchalante into a ground apartment at the end of the garden, where she told him how greatly she was disturbed about her sisters. She dared not show herself to them, for fear they would find fault with her marriage. The prince told her he would make sure that they would approve and, after talking some more, he locked Nonchalante in her room. Then he searched carefully all over the castle to locate the other princesses. It took some time before he could discover in what rooms they had locked themselves, but eventually Babbler's longing to talk all the time caused her to grumble to herself.

Rich-Craft went to the door, looked through the keyhole, and spoke to her. He told her everything that he had previously told her sister. "I swear I entered the tower only to offer my hand and heart to you." This seducer was the consummate actor and played his role perfectly, for he had had a lot of practice. He praised her wit and beauty in exaggerated terms, and Babbler, who was convinced that she had great qualities, was foolish enough to believe everything he told her. She answered with a flood of words that showed how receptive she was. Certainly this princess had an extraordinary capacity for chatter to have acquitted herself as she did, for she was extremely faint after not having eaten a morsel all day. In fact, she had nothing fit to eat in her room because she was extremely lazy and had not thought of anything but endless talking. Whenever she needed anything, she usually depended on Finette, who was always prudent and kept an abundance of fine biscuits, pies, macaroons, and jams of her own making in her room. Weakened by her severe hunger pangs, Babbler was moved by the protestations that the prince made through the door. At last she opened it and was at the mercy of the artful seducer.

Given her hunger, they decided to adjourn to the pantry, where he found all sorts of refreshments, since the daily basket furnished the princesses with more than enough. Babbler was still at a loss to know what had happened to her sisters, but she got it into her head—and I am not sure what her reasons were—that they were both locked up in Finette's room and had all they needed. Rich-Craft used all the arguments he could to substantiate this belief and told her that they would go and find the princesses toward evening. Not entirely in agreement with him on this matter, she said they would go and find them as soon as they had finished eating.

In short, the prince and princess began eating with big appetites. When they were finished, Rich-Craft asked to see the most beautiful apartment in the castle. He gave his hand to the princess as she led him there, and when they entered, he began to exaggerate his love and the advantages she would have in marrying him. He told her, just as he had done with her sister Nonchalante, that she should accept his proposal immediately because if she were to see her sisters beforehand, they would certainly oppose it. "Since I'm one of the most powerful of the neighboring princes, they'll probably think I'm better suited for your elder sister, and she'll never consent to a match she might desire herself." After many words that signified nothing, Babbler acted just as extravagantly as her sister had done; she agreed to become Rich-Craft's wife.

She never thought about her glass distaff until it shattered into a hundred pieces.

Toward evening Babbler returned to her room with the prince, and the first thing she saw was the shards of her glass distaff littering the floor. She was very troubled by this sight, and the prince asked why she was so concerned. Since her passion for talking made her incapable of holding her tongue about any subject, she foolishly told Rich-Craft the secret of the distaff. The prince laughed evilly to himself because the princesses' father would now be wholly convinced of his daughters' bad conduct.

Meanwhile, Babbler no longer wished to search for her sisters, for she had reason to fear that they would not approve of her conduct. The prince himself proposed that he undertake this task and told her, "I know how to win their approval, never fear." After this assurance the princess, who had not slept at all that night, grew very drowsy, and when she fell asleep, Rich-Craft locked her in her room as he had previously done with Nonchalante.

Once this devious prince had locked up Babbler, he went into all the rooms of the castle, one after another. When he found them all open except one that was locked from the inside, he concluded that was where Finette had gone. Since he had created a routine of compliments, he used the same ones at Finette's door that he had used with her sisters. But this princess was not so easy to dupe, and listened to him for a good while without responding. At last realizing that he knew she was in that room, she told him if it were true that he had such a strong and sincere affection for her, he should go down into the garden and shut the door after him. Then she would talk to him as much as he wanted from the window of her room that overlooked the garden.

Rich-Craft would not agree to this, and since the princess persisted in refusing to open the door, this wicked prince lost his patience. Fetching a large wooden log, he broke the door in. However, he found Finette armed with a large hammer, which had been accidentally left in a wardrobe in her room. Her face was red with emotion, and her eyes sparkled with rage, making her appear even more enchanting and beautiful to Rich-Craft. He would have cast himself at her feet, but as she retreated, she said boldly, "Prince, if you approach me, I'll split your skull with this hammer."

"What's this I hear, beautiful princess!" Rich-Craft exclaimed in his hypocritical tone. "Does the love I have for you inspire you with such hatred?"

He then began to speak to her across the room, describing the passionate ardor that the reputation of her beauty and wonderful wit had aroused in him. "The only reason I put on such a disguise was to offer my hand and heart." He told her she ought to pardon the violent love that caused him to break open her door. Finally he tried to persuade her, as he had with her sisters, that it was in her interest to take him for a husband as soon as possible, and he assured her he did not know where her sisters had gone. This was because his thoughts had been wholly fixed on her, and he had not gone to the trouble of looking for them.

The discreet princess pretended to be appeased and told him, "I simply must find my sisters, and after that we will do what has to be done together." But Rich-Craft answered that he could not agree to search for her sisters until she had consented to marry him, for her sisters would certainly oppose their match due to their seniority. Finette, who had good reason to distrust this treacherous prince, became even more suspicious at this answer. She trembled to think of what disaster had befallen her sisters and was determined to avenge them. So this young princess told Rich-Craft that she would gladly consent to marry him, but since she was of the opinion that marriages made at night always turned out to be unhappy, she requested that he postpone the ceremony until the next morning. She added that she would certainly not mention a word of this to her sisters and asked him to give her only a little time to say her prayers. Afterward she would take him to a room where there was a very good bed, and then she would return to her own room until the morning.

Rich-Craft was not very courageous, and as he watched the large hammer, which she played with like a fan, he consented and retired to give her some time to pray. No sooner was he gone than Finette rushed to one of the rooms of the tower, and made a bed over the hole of a sink. This room was as clean as any other, but all the garbage and dirty water were thrown down the hole which was very large. Finette put two weak sticks across it and then made a clean bed on top of them. After that she quickly returned to her room. A few minutes later Rich-Craft made his appearance, and the princess led him into the room where she had made his bed and then retired.

Without undressing, the prince hastily threw himself onto the bed. His weight immediately broke the small sticks, and he began falling to the bottom of the drain, unable to stop himself. Along the way he received twenty blows on his head and was bruised all over. The prince's fall made a great noise in the pipe, and since it was not far from Finette's room, she knew that her trick had worked. It is impossible to describe the pleasant feeling and joy she had as she heard him muttering in the drain. He certainly deserved his punishment, and the princess had every reason to feel satisfied.

But her joy was not so consuming that she forgot her sisters, and her first concern was to go and look for them. It was quite easy to find Babbler. Rich-Craft had double-locked that princess in her room and had left the key in the door. So Finette entered eagerly, and the noise she made startled her sister, throwing her into a great state of confusion. Finette told how she had defeated the wicked prince who had come to insult them, and on hearing that news, Babbler was thunderstruck, for despite all her talk about how smart she was, she had been foolish enough to have ridiculously believed every word Rich-Craft had told her. The world is still full of such dopes like her. However, she managed to cover up the extent of her sorrow and left the room with Finette to look for Nonchalante.

They searched all the rooms of the castle, but in vain. At last Finette thought to herself that they should look in the garden apartment, where, indeed, they found Nonchalante half dead with despair and fatigue, for she had not had anything to eat all day. Her sisters gave her all the assistance she needed. Then they recounted their adventures to one another, and Nonchalante and Babbler were overcome with remorse. Afterward, all three went to bed.

In the meantime Rich-Craft spent a very uncomfortable night, and when day came, he was not much better. The prince found himself in an underground sewer, though he could not see how horrible it was because no light could penetrate there. Nevertheless, after he had struggled painfully for some time, he found the end of the drain, which ran into a river at a considerable distance from the tower. Once there, he was able to make himself heard by some fishermen, who dragged him out in such a state that he aroused their compassion.

Rich-Craft ordered the men to carry him to his father's kingdom to recover from his wounds in seclusion. The disgrace that he had experienced caused him to develop such an inveterate hatred for Finette that he thought less about getting well than he did about getting revenge.

Meanwhile, Finette was very sad. Honor was a thousand times dearer to her than life, and the shameful weakness of her sisters had thrown her into such despair that she had great difficulty overcoming it. At the same time; the constitution of her sisters took a turn for the worse as a result of their worthless marriages, and Finette's patience was put to the test.

Rich-Craft, long a cunning villain, had continued to hatch ideas since this incident so that he could perpetrate even greater villainy. Neither the drain nor the bruises disturbed him as much as the fact that he had encountered someone more clever than he was. He knew the effects that his two marriages had had, and to tempt the princesses, he had great boxes filled with the finest fruit placed beneath the windows of the castle. Nonchalante and Babbler, who often sat at the windows, could not help but see the fruit, and they immediately felt a passionate desire to eat some. They insisted that Finette go down in the basket to get some of the fruit for them. So great was the kindness of that princess and so willing was she to oblige her sisters that she did as they requested and brought back some fruit, which they devoured with great avidity.

The next day fruits of another kind appeared, and again the princesses wanted to have some. And again Finette complied with kindness. But Rich-Craft's officers, who were hiding and who had missed their target the first time, did not fail the second. They seized Finette and carried her off in plain view of her sisters, who tore out their hair in despair. Rich-Craft's guards were efficient and took Finette to a house in the country, where the prince was residing in order to regain his health. Since he was so infuriated with the princess, he said a hundred brutal things to her, which she answered with courage and greatness of soul worthy of the heroine she was. At last, after having kept her prisoner for some days, Rich-Craft had her brought to the top of an extremely high mountain, where he immediately followed. There he announced to her they were going to put her to death in such a manner that would sufficiently avenge all the injuries she had caused him. Then the wicked prince demonstrated his barbaric nature by showing her a barrel lined with knives, razors, and hooked nails all around the inside. "In order to punish you the way you deserve," he said, "we're going to put you into that barrel and roll you from the top of this mountain down into the valley."

Though Finette was no Roman, she was no more afraid of this punishment than Regulus was at the sight of a similar destiny. Instead of admiring her heroic character, however, Rich-Craft became more enraged than ever. Determined to put a quick end to her life, he stooped to look into the barrel, the instrument of his vengeance, to see whether it was properly furnished with all its murderous weapons.

Finette, who saw her persecutor absorbed in examining the barrel, swiftly pushed him into it and kicked the barrel down the mountain. As she ran away, the prince's officers, who had been appalled at how cruelly their master had planned to treat this charming princess, did not make the slightest attempt to stop her. Besides, they were so frightened by what had happened to Rich-Craft that they could think of nothing but how to stop the barrel, which was rolling pell-mell down the mountain. However, their efforts were for naught. He rolled down to the bottom, where they drew him out wounded in a thousand places.

Rich-Craft's accident made the gentle king and Prince Bel-a-voir extremely sad. As for the people of their country, they were not at all moved, since Rich-Craft was universally hated. They were astonished that the young prince, who had such noble and generous sentiments, could love his unworthy elder brother. But that was due to the loyalty and good nature of this prince, and Rich-Craft was always astute enough to exploit his compassionate feelings and make his brother beholden to him. Therefore, Bel-a-voir did not leave a thing undone to cure him as soon as possible. Yet despite all the care everyone took of Rich-Craft, nothing did him any good. On the contrary, his wounds grew worse every day, and it appeared that he would be suffering from them for a long time.

After escaping from this terrible danger, Finette returned safely to the castle, where she had left her sisters, but it was not long before she was faced with new troubles. Both of her sisters gave birth to sons, and Finette was mortified by such a predicament. However, her courage did not abate, and her desire to conceal her sisters' shame made her determined to expose herself to danger once more.

To accomplish her plan, she first took the precaution to disguise herself as a man. The children of her sisters she put into boxes in which she made little holes so they could breathe. Then she took these boxes and several others and rode on horseback to the capital of the gentle king.

When Finette entered the city, she learned of the generous manner in which Bel-a-voir was paying for any medicine that might help his brother. Indeed, such generosity had attracted all the charlatans in Europe. At that time there were a great many adventurers without jobs or talent who pretended to be remarkable men that had been endowed by heaven to cure all sorts of maladies. These men, whose entire science consisted of bold deceit, found great credence among the people because of the impression they created by their outward appearance and by the bizarre names they assumed. Such quacks never remain in the place where they were born, and the exoticism of coming from a distant place is often considered a proof of quality by the common people.

The ingenious princess, who knew all this, gave herself a very strange name for that kingdom. Then she let it be known that the Cavalier Sanatio had arrived with marvelous secrets that cured all sorts of wounds, no matter how dangerous and infected. Bel-a-voir immediately sent for this supposed cavalier, and Finette swept in with all the airs of one of the best physicians in the world and said five or six words in a cavalier way. That is, she was the perfect doctor.

The princess was surprised by the good looks and pleasant

manner of Bel-a-voir, and after conversing with him some time with regard to Rich-Craft's wounds, she told him she would fetch a bottle with an extraordinary elixir. "In the meantime I'll leave two boxes I've brought that contain some excellent ointments appropriate for the wounded prince." After the supposed physician left and did not return, everyone began to feel anxious. When at last they were going to send for him, they heard the bawling of young infants in Rich-Craft's room. This surprised everybody, for no one had seen any infants there. After listening attentively, however, they found that the cries came from the doctor's boxes. The noise was caused by Finette's little nephews. The princess had given them a great deal to eat before she came to the palace, but since they had now been there a long time, they were hungry and expressed their needs by singing a most doleful tune. Someone opened the boxes, and the people were greatly surprised to find two pretty babes in them. Rich-Craft realized immediately that Finette had played a new trick on him and threw himself into a rage. His wounds grew worse and worse because of this, and everyone realized that his death could not be prevented.

Seeing Bel-a-voir overcome with sorrow, Rich-Craft, treacherous to his last breath, thought to exploit his brother's affection. "You've always loved me, Prince," he said, "and you're now lamenting my imminent loss. I can have no greater proof of your love for me. It's true I'm dying, but if you've really ever cared for me, I hope you'll grant me what I'm going to ask of you."

Bel-a-voir, who was incapable of refusing anything to a brother in such a condition, gave him his most solemn oath to grant him whatever he desired.

As soon as he heard this, Rich-Craft embraced his brother and said to him, "Now I shall die contented because I'll be avenged. The favor I want you to do is to ask Finette to marry you after I die. You'll undoubtedly obtain this wicked princess for your wife, and the moment she's in your power, I want you to plunge your dagger into her heart."

Bel-a-voir trembled with horror at these words and repented the imprudence of his oath. But now was not the time to retract it. He did not want his despair to be noticed by his brother, who died soon after. The gentle king was tremendously affected by his death. His subjects, however, far from mourning Rich-Craft, were extremely glad that his death guaranteed the succession for Bel-a-voir, whom everyone considered worthy of the crown.

Once again Finette had returned safely to her sisters, and soon thereafter she heard of Rich-Craft's death. Some time later, news reached the three princesses that the king, their father, had returned home. He rushed to the tower, and his first wish was to see the distaffs. Nonchalante went and brought the distaff that belonged to Finette and showed it to the king. After making a very low curtsy, she returned it to the place whence she had taken it. Babbler did the same. In her turn, Finette brought out the same distaff, but the king now grew suspicious and demanded to see them all together. No one could show hers except Finette. The king was so enraged by his two elder daughters that he immediately sent them away to the fairy who had given him the distaffs, asking her to keep his daughters with her as long as they lived and to punish them the way they deserved.

To begin the punishment of these princesses, the fairy led them into a gallery of her enchanted castle where she had ordered the history of a vast number of illustrious women who had made themselves famous by leading busy, virtuous lives to be depicted in paintings. Due to the wonderful effects of fairy art, all these figures were in motion from morning until night. Trophies and emblems honoring these virtuous ladies were everywhere, and it was tremendously mortifying for the two sisters to compare the triumphs of these heroines with the despicable situation to which their imprudence had reduced them. To complete their grief, the fairy told them gravely that if they had occupied themselves like those they saw in the pictures, they would not have gone astray. She told them, "Idleness is the mother of all vice and the source of all your misery." Finally the fairy added that to prevent them from ever falling into the same bad habits again and to make up for the time they had lost, she was going to employ them in the most coarse and mean work. Without any regard for their lily-white complexions, she sent them to gather peas in the garden and to pull out the weeds. Nonchalante could not help but despair of leading such a disciplined life, and she soon died from sorrow and exhaustion. Babbler, who some time afterward found a way to escape from the fairy's castle by night, broke her skull against a tree and died in the arms of some peasants.

Finette's good nature caused her to grieve a great deal over the fate of her sisters, but in the midst of her sorrow, she was informed that Prince Bel-a-voir had requested her hand in marriage. What's more, her father had already consented without notifying her, for in those days the inclination of the partners was the last thing one considered in arranging marriages. Finette trembled at the news. She had good reason to fear that Rich-Craft's hatred might have infected the heart of a dear brother, and she was worried that this young prince only sought to victimize her for her brother's sake. So concerned was she about this that she went to consult the wise fairy, who appreciated her fine qualities in the same way she had despised Nonchalante's and Babbler's bad ones.

The fairy would reveal nothing to Finette and only remarked, "Princess, you're wise and prudent. Up to now you've taken the proper precautions with regard to your conduct, and that has enabled you to bear in mind that *distrust is the mother of security.* Remember the importance of this maxim, and you'll eventually be happy without needing the help of my art."

Since she was not able to learn anything more from the fairy, Finette returned to the palace extremely upset. Some days later she was married by an ambassador in the name of Prince Bel-a-voir and conducted to her spouse in a splendid equipage. After she crossed the border, she was escorted in the same magnificent manner upon entering the first two cities of King Gentle's realm, and in the third city she met Bel-a-voir, who had been ordered by his father to go and welcome her. Everybody had been surprised by the prince's sadness at the approach of a marriage that he had so zealously pursued. Indeed, the king had to reprimand him and send him to meet the princess against his inclinations.

When Bel-a-voir saw how charming she was, he compli-
mented her in such a confused manner that the courtiers, who
knew how witty and gallant he was, believed him so strongly
moved by love that he had lost his presence of mind. The entire
city shouted for joy, and there were concerts and fireworks
everywhere. After a magnificent supper, preparations were
made for conducting the royal couple to their apartment.

Finette, who kept thinking about the fairy's maxim, had a
plan. She won over one of the women, who had the key of the
closet of the apartment designated for her. She gave orders to
the woman to carry into that closet some straw, a bladder,
some sheep's blood, and the entrails of some of the animals
that had been prepared for supper. Then the princess used a
pretext to go in. Making a figure from the straw, she put into
it the entrails and bladder full of blood. Then she dressed it up
in a woman's night-clothes. After she had finished making this
pretty dummy, she rejoined her company, and some time later,
she and her husband were conducted to their apartment. When
they had allowed as much time at the dressing table as was
necessary, the ladies of honor took away the torches and
retired. Finette immediately placed the straw dummy in the
bed and hid herself in a corner of the room.

After heaving two or three deep sighs, the prince drew his
sword and ran it through the body of the supposed Finette. All
at once he saw the blood trickle out, and the straw body did
not move.

"What have I done?" Bel-a-voir exclaimed. "What! After so
many cruel struggles with myself—after having weighed
everything carefully whether I should keep my word at the
expense of a dreadful crime, I've taken the life of a charming
princess, whom I was born to love! Her charms captivated me
the moment I saw her, and yet I didn't have the strength to free
myself from an oath that a brother possessed by fury had
exacted from me. Ah, heavens! How could anyone think of
punishing a woman for having too much virtue? Well, Rich-
Craft, I've satisfied your unjust vengeance, but now I'll avenge
Finette by my own death. Yes, beautiful princess, this same
sword will—"

As he was saying these words, Finette heard the prince looking for his sword, which he had dropped in his great agitation. Since she did not want him to commit such a foolish act, she cried, "My prince, I'm not dead! Your good heart made me anticipate your repentance, and I saved you from committing a crime by playing a trick that was not meant to harm you."

She then told Bel-a-voir about the foresight she had had in regard to the straw figure. The prince was ecstatic to find Finette alive, and expressed his gratitude to her for her prudence and preventing him from committing a crime which he could not think about without horror. He could not understand how he could have been so weak and why he had not discovered the futility of that wicked oath sooner that had been exacted from him by his deceitful brother.

However, if Finette had not always been convinced that distrust is the mother of security, she would have been killed, and her death would have caused that of Bel-a-voir. Then afterward, people would have discussed the prince's strange emotions at their leisure.

Long live prudence and presence of mind! They saved this couple from the most dreadful of misfortunes and provided them with the most lovely destiny in the world. The prince and princess retained the greatest tenderness for each other and spent a long succession of beautiful days in such honor and happiness that would be difficult to describe.

CHARLOTTE-ROSE CAUMONT DE LA FORCE

THE GOOD WOMAN

ONCE upon a time there was a Good Woman who was kind, candid, and courageous. She had experienced all the vicissitudes that cause turbulence in one's life, for she had resided at the court and had endured all the storms that are commonplace there: treason, perfidy, infidelity, loss of wealth, loss of friends. Consequently, she became so disgusted with living where pretension and hypocrisy had established their empire and so tired of lovers who never were what they appeared to be that she decided to leave her own country and settle where she could forget the world and where the world would no longer hear about her.

When she believed herself far enough away, she built a cottage in an extremely pleasant spot. All she had to do then was to buy a flock of sheep, which furnished her with food and clothing. Not long thereafter she found herself perfectly happy. "So there does exist a way of life in which one can be content," she said, "and the choice I've made leaves nothing to be desired." She spent each day plying her distaff and tending her flock. Sometimes she would have liked a little company, but she was afraid of the trouble friends had always brought upon her.

She was gradually getting accustomed to the life she led when, one day, as she was gathering her little flock, the sheep began to flee from her, scattering all over the countryside. In fact, they fled so fast that there were soon hardly any sheep to be seen. "Am I a rapacious wolf?" she cried. "What's the meaning of this strange incident?" She called a favorite ewe, but it did not seem to know her voice. She raced after it, yelling, "I don't mind losing all the rest of the flock if only you would stay with me!" But the ungrateful creature continued its flight and disappeared with the rest.

The Good Woman was deeply distressed at the loss she had sustained. "Now I've got nothing left," she cried. "Maybe I won't even find my garden, or my little cottage will no longer be in its place." She returned slowly, for she was very tired from running after the sheep. After she exhausted a small stock of cheese, she lived off fruit and vegetables for some time. However, she began to see that the end was near.

"Fortune!" she cried. "You've sought in vain to persecute me even in this remote spot. Now you cannot prevent me from preparing myself for beholding the gates of death without alarm. After so much trouble, I shall descend with tranquility into those peaceful shadows."

She had nothing more to spin. She had nothing more to eat. Leaning on her distaff, she went into a little wood. In looking around for a place to die, she was astonished to see three little children come running toward her. They were all more beautiful than the brightest day imaginable. She was delighted to see such charming company, and they gave her a hundred caresses. As she sat on the ground in order to hug them more easily, one threw its arms around her neck, the other hugged her waist from behind, and the third called her "Mother." Long did she wait for someone to fetch them, believing that whoever had led them there would not neglect to come back for them. But the day passed without anyone appearing.

She decided to take them to her own home. "Heaven has sent me this little flock to replace the one I lost." There were two girls, who were only two or three years old, and a little boy of five. Each had a ribbon around its neck, to which was attached a small jewel. One was a golden cherry enameled with crimson and engraved with the word "LIRETTE." She thought, "This must be the little girl's name." The other had a medlar with "MIRTIS" written on it. And the little boy had an almond of green enamel around which was written "FINFIN." The Good Woman felt sure that these were their names.

The little girls had some jewels in their headdresses that were more than enough to put the Good Woman in comfortable circumstances. Soon thereafter she bought another flock of sheep and surrounded herself with everything necessary for maintaining her interesting family. She made their winter clothing from the bark of trees, and in the summer they had white cotton dresses that were bleached in a fine way. Even though they were quite young, they tended the flock, and this time the sheep were more docile and obedient to them than toward the large dogs that guarded them. These dogs were also gentle and attached to the children, who as they grew larger spent their days in most innocent ways. They loved the Good Woman, and all three were extremely fond of one another. They occupied themselves by tending their sheep, fishing with a line, spreading nets to catch birds, working in a little garden of their own, and using their delicate hands to cultivate flowers.

There was one rose tree that the young Lirette especially liked. She watered it often and took great care of it. She thought nothing so beautiful as a rose. One day she felt a desire to open a bud and find its heart. In doing so, she pricked her finger with a thorn. The pain was sharp, and she began to cry. The handsome Finfin, who seldom left her side, approached her, and when he saw how she was suffering, he also began to cry. He took her little finger, pressed it, and gently squeezed the blood from it.

The Good Woman, who saw their alarm at this accident, approached, and after learning what had happened, she asked, "Why were you so inquisitive? Why did you destroy the flower you loved so much?"

"I wanted its heart," Lirette replied.

"Such desires are always fatal," the Good Woman replied.

"But, Mother," Lirette pursued, "why does this beautiful flower that pleases me so much have so many thorns?"

"To show you that we must distrust the greater part of those things that please our eyes, and that the most pleasant objects hide snares that may be most deadly to us."

"What?" Lirette replied. "Shouldn't one love everything that's pleasant?"

"No, certainly not," the Good Woman said, "and you must take care not to do so."

"But I love my brother with all my heart," she replied. "He's so handsome and charming."

"You may love your brother," her mother replied, "but if he weren't your brother, you shouldn't love him."

Lirette shook her head, and thought that this rule was very hard. Meanwhile Finfin was still occupied with her finger; he squeezed the juice of the rose leaves on the wound and wrapped it up in them. The Good Woman asked him why he did that.

"Because I think that the remedy may be found in the same thing that has caused the evil."

The Good Woman smiled at this reason. "My dear child, not in this case."

"I thought it was in all cases," he said. "You see, sometimes when Lirette looks at me, she troubles me a great deal. I feel quite upset, and a moment later those same looks give me a pleasure I can't describe. When she scolds me sometimes, I'm very wretched, but if later she says one gentle word to me, I'm joyous again."

The Good Woman wondered what these children would think of next. Since she did not know their relation to one another, she dreaded that they would become too loving. "I'd give anything to learn if they are brother and sister." Her lack of knowledge about this point caused her much anxiety, but their extreme youth put her at ease.

Finfin already paid a great deal of attention to little Lirette, whom he loved much better than Mirtis. At one time he had given her some young partridges, the prettiest in the world, that he had caught. One that she reared became a fine bird with beautiful feathers. Lirette loved it inordinately and gave it to Finfin. It followed him everywhere, and he taught it a thousand amusing tricks. One day he took it with him when going to tend his flock. On returning home he could not find it and looked for it everywhere. He was greatly distressed by his loss, and Mirtis tried to console him without success. "Sister," he replied. "I'm despondent. Lirette will be angry, and nothing you can say will rid me of my grief."

"Well, brother," she said, "we'll get up very early tomorrow and go in search of another one. I can't bear to see you so miserable."

While she was saying this, Lirette arrived, and once she learned the cause of Finfin's grief, she said to him, "We'll find another partridge. It's just the condition in which I see you that gives me pain."

These words sufficed to restore serenity to Finfin's heart and countenance. "Why couldn't Mirtis restore my spirits with all her kindness," he asked himself, "while Lirette did it with a single word? Two is one too many—Lirette is enough for me."

On the other hand, Mirtis saw plainly that her brother made a distinction between her and Lirette. "There aren't enough of us here, being three," she said. "I ought to have another brother who would love me as much as Finfin does my sister."

Lirette had just turned twelve, Mirtis, thirteen, and Finfin, fifteen, when one evening after supper they were all seated in front of the cottage with the Good Woman, who would give them lessons in a hundred pleasant things. Young Finfin watched Lirette playing with the jewel on her neck and asked his dear mama what it was for. She replied that she had found one on each of them when they had fallen into her hands. Then Lirette said, "If mine would only do what I tell it to do, I'd be glad."

"And what would you like to have it do?" asked Finfin.

"You'll see," she said as she took the end of the ribbon. "Little cherry, I'd like to have a beautiful house of roses."

All at once they heard a slight noise behind them. Mirtis turned around first and uttered a loud cry. She had good reason to do so: one of the most charming cottages imaginable had replaced the Good Woman's cottage. It was not very high, but the roof was formed from roses that bloomed in winter as well as in summer. They entered it and found the most pleasant apartments magnificently furnished. In the middle of each room was a rose bush in full bloom and in a precious vase. As they entered the first room, they found the partridge that Finfin had lost. Onto his shoulder it flew and gave him a hundred caresses.

"Do I only have to wish?" Mirtis asked as she took the ribbon of her jewel in her hand. "Little medlar, give us a garden more beautiful than our own." No sooner had she finished speaking than a garden of extraordinary beauty appeared with everything that could be imagined in the most perfect condition.

The young children began immediately to run down the beautiful lanes among the flower beds and around the fountains.

"Wish for something, brother," Lirette said.

"But I don't have anything to wish for," he said, "except to be loved by you as much as you are loved by me."

"Oh," she replied, "my heart can satisfy you on this account. That doesn't depend on your almond."

"Well, then," Finfin said, "little almond, little almond, I wish that a great forest would rise near here in which the king's son would go hunting and then fall in love with Mirtis."

"What have I done to you?" the beautiful girl replied. "I don't want to leave the innocent life we lead."

"You're right, my child," said the Good Woman, "and I admire the wisdom of your sentiments. Besides, they say that this king is a cruel usurper who's put the rightful sovereign and his entire family to death. Perhaps the son is no better than his father."

The Good Woman, however, was quite unsettled by the unusual wishes of these wonderful children. That night she retired into the House of Roses, and in the morning she found a large forest close to the house. It formed a fine hunting ground for our young shepherds, and Finfin often hunted deer, harts, and roebucks there. He gave the lovely Lirette a fawn whiter than snow, and it followed her just as the partridge followed him. When they were separated for a short period of time, they wrote to each other and sent their notes by these messengers. It was the prettiest sight in the world.

The little family went on living peacefully like this, occupying themselves in different ways according to the seasons. They tended their flocks year round, but in the summer their work was most pleasant. They hunted a good deal in the winter with bows and arrows, and sometimes they went such a long distance that they returned to the House of Roses almost frozen and dragging their feet behind them.

The Good Woman would receive them by a large fire and would not know which one to begin warming first. "Lirette, my daughter Lirette," she would say, "place your feet here." And taking Mirtis in her arms, "Mirtis, my child," she would continue, "give me your beautiful hands to warm. And you, my son, Finfin, come nearer." Then placing all three of them on a sofa, she would take care of them in the most charming and gentle manner.

Thus did they spend their days in peace and happiness. The Good Woman was struck by the affection between Finfin and Lirette, for Mirtis was just as beautiful and charming as Lirette, yet Finfin certainly did not love her as fervently as the other. "If they are brother and sister, as I believe their beauty indicates," the Good Woman said, "what shall I do? They're so similar in everything that they must assuredly be of the same blood. If this is the case, then their affection for each other is dangerous. If not, I could make it legitimate by letting them marry. And since they both love me so much, their union would give me joy and peace in my old age."

In her uncertainty she ordered Lirette, who was rapidly approaching womanhood, never to be alone with Finfin. For better security she instructed Mirtis to always go with them. Lirette obeyed her without any objections, and Mirtis also did what she had commanded. Meanwhile the Good Woman had heard about a clever fairy in the vicinity and decided to look for her and find out something about the past of these children.

One day, when Lirette wasn't feeling well and Mirtis and Finfin were out hunting, the Good Woman thought it a convenient opportunity to go in search of Madame Tu-tu, for such was the name of the fairy. Leaving Lirette at the House of Roses, she had not gone far before she came upon Lirette's fawn, which was heading toward the forest. At the same time she saw Finfin's partridge coming from it. They came together right near her, and she was astonished to see a little ribbon around each one of their necks with a paper attached to it. She called the partridge, which flew to her, and took the paper. It contained these lines:

> Soar to Lirette, dear bird, take to the air.
> Cut off from her presence, I languish.
> Give her my love and make her hear
> My ardor and silent anguish,

For her heart is much too cold, I fear.
Oh I'd be content one day to see
That Lirette might change and come to care
The way I do with great sincerity.

"What words!" The Good Woman cried. "What phrases! A simple friendship doesn't express itself with so much warmth." Then she stopped the fawn, which came to lick her hand, and she unfastened the paper from its neck, opened it, and read these words:

The sun is setting—you're hunting yet.
You left while it was turning light.
Come back, dear Finfin, I think you forget,
Without you my day is like eternal night.

"They're acting just as people did when I was in society," the Good Woman remarked. "Who could have taught Lirette so much in this desolate spot? What can I do to cut the root of such a pernicious evil before it has a chance to grow?"

"Eh, madame, why are you so anxious?" the partridge asked. "Let them alone. Those who are guiding them know better than you."

The Good Woman was speechless, for she realized that the partridge must possess some kind of supernatural power. In her fright the notes fell from her hands, and the fawn and the partridge picked them up. The one ran and the other flew, and the partridge cried out so often "Tu-tu" that the Good Woman thought it must be that powerful fairy who had caused it to speak. She regained her senses a little after thinking about this incident, but she no longer felt equal to her undertaking and retraced her steps to the House of Roses.

Meanwhile, Finfin and Mirtis had hunted the entire day, and since they had become tired, they placed their game on the ground and sat down to rest under a tree, where they fell asleep. The king's son had also gone hunting in the forest that day. He became separated from his entourage and came to the spot where our young shepherd and shepherdess were resting.

He looked at them some time with wonder: Finfin had made a pillow out of his game bag, and Mirtis's head reclined on Finfin's chest. The prince thought Mirtis so beautiful that he quickly dismounted from his horse to examine her features more closely. He judged by the bags they were carrying and their simple apparel that they were only some shepherd's children. He sighed from grief, having already sighed from love, and this love was followed instantly by jealousy. The position in which they lay made him believe that such familiarity could result only from lovers' affection.

Uneasy, he could not stand their prolonged repose, so he touched the handsome Finfin with his spear. Finfin jumped up, and upon seeing a man before him, he passed his hand over Mirtis's face and woke her. In calling her "sister," he immediately gave the young prince the reassurance that he needed. Mirtis stood up quite astonished, for she had never seen any other man but Finfin. The young prince was the same age as she, and he was superbly attired. His face had a charming expression, and he began saying many sweet things to her. She listened to him with a pleasure that she had never before experienced, and she responded to him in a simple manner, full of grace. Finfin saw that it was getting late, and the fawn had not arrived with Lirette's letter. Therefore, he told his sister it was time to go.

"Come, brother," she said to the young prince, giving him her hand, "come with us to the House of Roses." Since she believed Finfin to be her brother, she thought any man who was as handsome as he must be her brother, too. The young prince did not need much urging to follow her. Finfin threw the game he had shot on the back of his fawn, and the handsome prince carried Mirtis's bow and game bag.

This was the way they arrived at the House of Roses. Lirette came out to greet them and gave the prince a warm welcome before turning toward Mirtis. "I'm delighted that you've had such a good catch."

They all went together to find the Good Woman, and the prince enlightened her about his high birth. She paid him the respect due such an illustrious guest and gave him a fine room in their home. He remained two or three days, long enough to complete his conquest of Mirtis, which was in keeping with the wish that Finfin had made with his little almond.

Meanwhile, the prince's entourage had been astonished to have lost track of him. They found his horse, and they looked for him everywhere. His father, the wicked king, was furious when they reported they could not find him. His mother, a charming woman who was the sister of the king whom her husband had cruelly murdered, was in a state of extreme grief at the loss of her son. In her distress she secretly sent a messenger in search of Madame Tu-tu, an old friend of hers whom she had not seen for some time because the king hated her and had insulted her outrageously by harming a person she had dearly loved.

Madame Tu-tu arrived in the queen's chamber without anyone noticing her. After they embraced each other affectionately— there is not much difference between a queen and a fairy, since they have almost the same power—the fairy Tu-tu told her that she would see her son very soon. She begged her not to become upset by anything that might happen, for if she was not very mistaken, she could promise her something delightful and quite unexpected. "One day you will be the happiest of mortals."

After making many inquiries about the prince and searching for him carefully, the king's men finally found him at the House of Roses. Then they escorted him back to the king, who scolded him brutally, as though he were not the most handsome young man in the world. The prince remained very sad at his father's court and kept thinking about his beautiful Mirtis. Finally he could no longer contain his grief and took his mother into his confidence, who offered him a good deal of consolation.

"If you'll mount your beautiful palfrey, and go to the House of Roses," he said, "you'll be charmed by what you see."

The queen gladly agreed to do this and took her son with her, who was enchanted by the prospect of seeing his dear mistress again. The queen was astonished by Mirtis's great beauty and also by that of Lirette and Finfin. She embraced them with as much tenderness as she would her own children. Moreover, she immediately developed an immense liking for the Good

Woman. In fact, she admired the house, the garden, and all the rare things she saw there.

When she returned, the king asked her to give an account of her journey. Naturally, she did this, and he felt a desire to go as well and see the wonders that she had described. His son asked permission to accompany him, and he consented with a sullen air: he never did anything graciously.

As soon as he saw the House of Roses, he coveted it. Paying not the least attention to the charming inhabitants of this beautiful place, he exercised his royal prerogative and began taking possession of their property by announcing that he would sleep there that evening. The Good Woman was very annoyed by his decision, for she sensed uproar and disarray, and this frightened her. "What's happened to the happy tranquillity I once enjoyed here!" she exclaimed. "The slightest change in fortune's ways always appears to destroy the calm in my life!"

She gave the king an excellent bed and withdrew to her little family. The wicked king went to bed, but found it impossible to fall asleep. Opening his eyes, he saw a little old woman at the foot of his bed. She was perhaps a yard high and about as wide, and she made frightful grimaces at him. Since cowards are generally fearful, he was in a terrible fright. A thousand needles he felt pricking him all over. In this tormented state of mind and body was he kept awake the whole night. Furious about it, he stormed and swore in language that was not at all in keeping with his dignity.

"Sleep, sleep, sire," the partridge said, who was roosting in a porcelain vase, "or at least let us sleep. If being king means that one must always be so anxious, I prefer being a partridge to being a king."

The king was even more alarmed at these words. He commanded his men to seize the partridge, but she flew up when she heard this order and beat his face with her wings. Since he still saw the same vision and felt the same prickings, he was dreadfully frightened and became more furious. "Ah!" he said. "It's a spell that this sorceress whom they call the Good Woman has cast. I'll get rid of her and all her kin by putting them to death!"

Since he was unable to sleep, he got up, and as soon as it was dawn, he commanded his guards to seize the innocent little family and fling them into dungeons. What's more, he had them dragged before him so that he might witness their despair. Though those charming faces were wet with tears, he was not at all moved. On the contrary, he felt a malignant joy at the sight. His son, whose tender heart was torn apart by such a sad spectacle, could not look at Mirtis without agony. On such occasions a true lover suffers more than the person loved.

Just as they grabbed hold of those poor innocents and began leading them away, the young Finfin, who was unarmed and thus could not fight these barbarians, suddenly touched the ribbon on his neck and cried, "Little almond, I wish that we were freed from the king's power!"

"And with his greatest enemies, my dear cherry!" Lirette continued.

"And let's take the handsome prince with us, my dear medlar!" added Mirtis.

No sooner had they uttered these words than they found themselves with the prince, partridge, and fawn, all in a chariot that rose into the air, and they soon lost sight of the king and the House of Roses.

However, Mirtis soon repented her wish. She was aware that she had been inconsiderate in allowing herself to be carried away by an impulse that she could not control. Therefore, she kept her eyes lowered during the entire journey and felt very much abashed. The Good Woman gave her a severe glance and said, "My daughter, you've not done a good thing to separate the prince from his father. No matter how unjust he may be, the prince shouldn't leave him."

"Ah, madam," the prince replied, "please don't think it ill that I've been given the pleasure of traveling with you. I respect my father, but I would have left him a hundred times before this if not for the virtue, kindness, and tenderness of my mother that always detained me."

As he finished speaking, they found themselves descending in front of a beautiful palace. They stepped from the chariot and were welcomed by Madame Tu-tu. She was the most lovely person in the world—young, lively, and gay. She paid them a hundred compliments and confessed that it was she who had given them all the pleasures that they had enjoyed in their lives and had also given them the cherry, almond, and medlar, whose powers were at an end since they had now arrived in her realm. Then, addressing the prince in private, she told him that she had heard more than a thousand times that his father had made his life miserable. "I'm telling you all this in advance so that you will not accuse me of doing evil things to the king." Indeed, she had played some tricks on him, but that was the full extent of her vengeance.

After that she assured them that they would all be very happy with her: "You will have flocks to keep, crooks, bows, arrows, and fishing rods so that you can amuse yourselves in a hundred different ways." She gave all of them, including the prince, the most elegant kind of shepherds' clothes. Their names and emblems were on their crooks, and that very evening the young prince exchanged crooks with the charming Mirtis. The next day Madame Tu-tu led them to the most delightful promenade in the world and showed them the best pastures for their sheep and a fine countryside for hunting.

"You can go as far as that beautiful river," she said, "but never go to the opposite shore. You may hunt in this wood, but beware of passing a great oak tree in the middle of the forest. It's very remarkable, for it has a trunk and roots of iron. If you go beyond it, you may experience a catastrophe, and I won't be able to protect you. Besides, I wouldn't be in a position to assist you right away because a fairy has plenty of things to keep her busy."

The young shepherds assured her that they would do exactly as she said, and all four led their flocks into the meadows. That left Madame Tu-tu alone with the Good Woman, who appeared to be somewhat anxious.

"What's the matter, madam?" the fairy asked. "What cloud has come over your mind?"

"I won't deny it," the Good Woman said. "I'm uneasy at leaving them together like that. For some time now I've noticed with sorrow that Finfin and Lirette love each other more than is decent, and to add to my trouble, another attachment has developed—the prince and Mirtis are fond of each other. Their youth, I'm afraid, makes them susceptible to their feelings."

"You've brought up these two young girls so well," Madame Tu-tu replied, "that you needn't fear anything. I'll answer for their discretion, and I'll clear up the matter about their destiny."

Then she informed her that Finfin was the son of the wicked king and brother of the young prince. In turn, Mirtis and Lirette were sisters and daughters of the king whom the cruel usurper had murdered. The wicked king had ascended the throne after having committed a hundred atrocities, which he wished to crown by the murder of the two infant princesses. The queen had done all she could to dissuade him, but since she had not succeeded, she had called upon the fairy to help her. She then told the queen that she would save them, but she could only do so by taking her eldest son with them. But she promised the queen she would see them again someday under happier circumstances. "Given those conditions, the queen consented to a separation, which of course, appeared at first very hard. And I carried all three off and confided them to your care as the person most worthy of such a task."

After telling her this, the fairy begged the Good Woman to be at ease and assured her that the union of these young princes would restore peace to the kingdom and Finfin would reign with Lirette. The Good Woman listened to this talk with great interest, but not without letting some tears fall. Surprised, Madame Tu-tu asked why she was crying.

"Alas!" she said. "I fear they'll lose their innocence due to the grandeur to which they'll be elevated. Such a splendid future is certain to corrupt their virtue."

"No," replied the fairy. "You needn't fear such a great misfortune. The principles you've instilled in them are too excellent. It's possible to be a king and yet an honest man. You know that there's already one in this world who's the model of a perfect monarch. Therefore, set your mind at rest. I'll be with you as much as possible, and I hope you won't be melancholy here."

The Good Woman believed her, and after a short time she

felt completely satisfied. The young shepherds were also very happy and did not ask for anything but to continue living as they were. Everything was tranquil; they found pleasure in one another's company each day; and the time passed only too quickly.

The wicked king learned that they were with Madame Tu-tu, but despite all his power he could not get them away from her. He knew that she used magic to protect them and could not deceive her with his tactics. Indeed, he had not been able to take possession of the House of Roses due to the continual tricks played on him by Madame Tu-tu, and he hated her as well as the Good Woman more than ever. And now his hatred extended to his own son as well.

The king used all sorts of stratagems in order to get one of the four young shepherds into his power, but his power did not extend to the realm of Madame Tu-tu. Then one unlucky day (there are some which we cannot avoid), these charming shepherds were nearing the fatal oak when the beautiful Lirette noticed a bird with unusual feathers on a tree about twenty yards away. She impulsively shot an arrow, and when she saw the bird fall dead, she ran to pick it up. All this was done within a moment and without reflection. Consequently, poor Lirette found herself transfixed to the spot. It was impossible for her to return. She wanted to but could not manage it. She discovered her mistake, and all she could do was to reach out with her arms for pity to her brothers and sisters. Mirtis began to cry, and Finfin ran to her without a moment's hesitation.

"I'll perish with you," he cried as he joined her.

Mirtis wanted to follow them, but the young prince held her back. "Let's go and tell Madame Tu-tu what has happened," he said. "That's the best way to help them."

Suddenly they saw the wicked king's men seize them, and all they could do was to cry adieu to one another. The king had arranged to have this beautiful bird placed there by his hunters as a snare for the shepherds. Indeed, he had fully expected everything to happen as it did. They led Lirette and Finfin before the cruel monarch, who abused them terribly and had them confined in a dark, strong prison. It was then they began to lament the fact that their little cherry and almond had lost their powers. The fawn and the partridge looked for them, but when the fawn was not able to espy them, she shed some tears of grief and heard orders shouted to have her seized and burned alive. So she saved herself by running quickly to Mirtis. The partridge was luckier since she saw Lirette and Finfin every day through the grating of their prison. Fortunately for them, the king had not thought of separating them. When one is in love with someone, suffering together is a pleasure.

The partridge flew back every day and brought news to Madame Tu-tu, the Good Woman, and Mirtis. Mirtis was very unhappy, and if she had not had the handsome prince, she would have been inconsolable. She decided to write to the poor captives via the faithful partridge and hung a little bottle of ink around her neck with some paper and put a pen in her beak. The good partridge carried all this to the bars of the prison, and our young shepherds were delighted to see her again. Finfin extended his hand and took from her everything she brought. Afterward they began to read as follows:

Mirtis and the Prince to Lirette and Finfin

We want you to know that we're languishing during this cruel separation. We keep sighing, and this separation may perhaps kill us. We would already have died if we had not been sustained by hope. That hope has supported us ever since Madame Tu-tu assured us that you were still alive. Believe us, dear Lirette and Finfin, we shall meet again and be happy despite the malice we have encountered.

Lirette and Finfin to Mirtis and the Prince

We've received your letter with great pleasure. It made us happier than we had anticipated. In these regions of horror our torments would be insufferable but for the sweet consolation we derive from each other's presence. Since we are close to each other, we don't feel pain, and love renders everything delightful. Adieu, dear prince, adieu, dear Mirtis. Encourage your mutual feelings. Keep alive your tender fidelity. You hold out a hope to us that we can share. The greatest blessing which can happen to us is being once again in your company.

After Finfin attached this note to the partridge's neck, she swiftly flew away with it. The young shepherds received great consolation from it, but the Good Woman had not been comforted from the moment she had been separated from her dear ones, whom she knew to be in so much danger. "How quickly my happiness has changed!" she said to Madame Tu-tu. "I seem to have been born only to be continually disturbed. I thought I had taken the proper steps to guarantee my peace of mind. How short-sighted I was!"

"Don't you know," the fairy replied, "that there's no place in this world in which one can live happily?"

"I do," the Good Woman replied mournfully. "If one can't find happiness in one's self, it's seldom found anywhere else. But, madam, please have consideration for the fate of my children!"

"They didn't remember the orders I gave them," Madame Tu-tu remarked. "But let's think of a way to help them."

Madame Tu-tu entered her library with the Good Woman. She read nearly the entire night, and after opening a large gold-trimmed book that she had frequently passed over despite its beauty, she was suddenly plunged into a state of extreme sadness. After some time passed and day was breaking, the Good Woman observed a few tears fall on the book and took the liberty of asking why the fairy was so sad.

"I'm saddened by the irrevocable decree of fate that these pages have revealed," she said, "and I shudder to tell you what I've learned."

"Are they dead?" the Good Woman cried.

"No," Madame Tu-tu responded, "but nothing can save them unless you or I appear before the king and satisfy his vengeance. I must confess to you, madam, that I don't have enough affection for them, nor enough courage to expose myself to his fury. Indeed, it is too much to ask anyone to make such a sacrifice."

"Pardon me, madam," the Good Woman said with great firmness. "I'll go to this king. No sacrifice is too great for me if it will save my children. I'll gladly pour out every drop of blood that I have in my veins for them."

Madame Tu-tu was struck with admiration by such a grand gesture. "I promise to help you in any way I can, but I find myself limited in this instance due to the mistakes the young people have made." The Good Woman then took leave of her, refusing to tell Mirtis or the prince about her plans, for fear she would distress them and weaken her own determination.

She set out, the partridge flying by her side, and as they passed the iron oak, the bird snatched a little moss from its trunk with her beak and placed it into the Good Woman's hands. "When you are in the greatest danger," she said to her, "throw this moss at the feet of the king."

The Good Woman had barely time to treasure these words when she was seized by some of the wicked king's soldiers, who were always stationed on the borders of Madame Tu-tu's domain. When they led her before the king, he said, "I've got you at last, you wicked creature, and I'm going to put you to death by the most cruel torture!"

"I came expressly for that purpose," she replied. "You may exercise your cruelty on me anyway you want. Only spare my children, who are so young and incapable of having offended you. I offer my life for theirs."

All who heard these words were filled with pity at her magnanimity. The king alone was unmoved. Seeing his queen shedding a flood of tears, he became so angry with her that he would have killed her if her attendants had not interposed themselves between them. With piercing shrieks she fled the room.

The barbarous king had the Good Woman locked up and ordered his men to feed her well to make her approaching death more frightful to her. He commanded them to fill a pit with snakes, vipers, and adders, looking forward keenly to having the pleasure of pushing the Good Woman into it. What a horrible kind of execution! It makes me shudder to think of it!

Regretfully the unjust king's officers obeyed him, and after they had carried out this frightful order, the king advanced to the spot. They were about to bind the Good Woman when she begged them not to, assuring them that she had sufficient courage to meet death with her hands free. Feeling that she had no time to lose, she approached the king and threw the moss at his feet. At that very moment he was stepping forward to inspect the dreadful pit. His feet slipped on the moss, and he fell in. No sooner did he reach the bottom than the bloodthirsty reptiles pounced on him and stung him to death. Meanwhile, the Good Woman found herself transported instantly in the company of her dear partridge to the House of Roses.

While these things were taking place, Finfin and Lirette were almost dead with misery in their frightful prison. Their innocent affection alone kept them alive. They were saying sad, touching things to each other when they noticed the doors of the dungeon open all of a sudden and admit Mirtis, the handsome prince, and Madame Tu-tu. Embracing, they all spoke at the same time, but the fairy did not neglect in the midst of this joyful confusion to announce the death of the king.

"He was your father as well as the prince's," she said. "But he was unnatural and tyrannical and would have put the queen, your dear mother, to death a hundred times. Let us now go and find her."

They did this, and on hearing about the king's death her good nature made her feel some regret because he had been her husband. Finfin and the prince also paid their honorable respects to his memory. Thereafter, Finfin was acknowledged king, and Mirtis and Lirette princesses. Then they all went to the House of the Roses to see the generous Good Woman, who thought she would die from joy as she embraced them. They all stated that they owed their lives to her, and more than their lives, since they were also obliged to her for their happiness.

From that moment on, they considered themselves perfectly happy. The marriages were celebrated with great pomp. King Finfin wed Princess Lirette, and Mirtis, the prince. When these splendid marriages were over, the Good Woman asked permission to retire to the House of Roses. They were very unwilling to consent to this, but yielded since she wished it so sincerely. The widowed queen also desired to spend the rest of her life with the Good Woman, along with the partridge and the fawn. They were quite disgusted with the world and found peace and quiet in that charming retreat. Madame Tu-tu often went to visit them, as did the king and queen and the prince and princess.

> Happy are those who can imitate
> The deeds the Good Woman accomplished.
> Such magnanimity is truly great
> And deserves its rewards at the finish.
>
> Perilous rocks can be avoided
> If only one learns how to navigate
> And steer wisely with great courage.
> Moreover, virtue and common sense necessitate
> That they too receive their due homage.

HENRIETTE JULIE
DE MURAT

THE PALACE OF REVENGE

THERE was once a king and queen of Iceland, who had a daughter after twenty years of married life. Her birth gave them the greatest pleasure, since they had given up hope of having a successor to the throne. The young princess was named Imis, and from the very beginning her budding charms promised that she would be marvelously beautiful and radiant when she grew older.

No one in the universe would have ever been worthy of her if Cupid had not thought it a point of honor to bring such a wonderful person under his sway. Therefore, he arranged to have a prince born in the same court who was just as charming as the lovely princess. He was called Philax and was the son of a brother of the King of Iceland. He was two years older than the princess, and they were brought up together with all the freedom natural to childhood and close relatives. The first sensations of their hearts were mutual admiration and affection, and both found nothing more beautiful in their eyes as the other. Consequently, they could not find a single attraction in the world that interfered with the feeling each had for the other, even though they had yet to discover its name.

The king and queen were pleased to see the children's mutual affection grow. They loved young Philax, for he was a prince of their blood, and no child had ever wakened fairer hopes. Everything seemed to favor Cupid's plans to make Prince Philax the happiest of men.

The princess was about twelve years old when the queen, who was extremely fond of her, wanted to have her daughter's fortune told by a fairy whose extraordinary powers had created a sensation at that time. The queen set out in search of this fairy and took along Imis, who was despondent because she had to separate from Philax. Moreover, she wondered time and again why people troubled themselves about the future when the present was so pleasant. Philax remained with the king, and there was nothing at the court that could compensate for the absence of the princess.

Arriving at the fairy's castle, the queen was magnificently received, but the fairy was not at home. Her usual residence was on the summit of a mountain some distance away, where she absorbed herself in the profound study that had made her famous throughout the world. As soon as she heard about the queen's arrival, she returned to the castle. The queen presented the princess to her, told her her name and the hour of her birth, which the fairy already knew quite well even though she had not been there. The fairy of the mountain knew everything. She promised the queen an answer in two days and then returned to the summit of the mountain. On the morning of the third day she came back to the castle, requested that the queen descend into the garden, and gave her some tablets of palm leaves closely shut, which she was ordered not to open except in the presence of the king. To satisfy her curiosity to some degree, the queen asked her several questions in regard to the fate of her daughter.

"Great queen," the fairy of the mountain replied, "I can't tell you precisely what sort of catastrophe threatens the princess. I see only that love will have a large share in the events of her life, and that no beauty will ever arouse such passionate emotions as that of Imis will do."

One didn't have to be a fairy to foresee that the princess would have admirers. Her eyes already seemed to demand love from everyone's heart that the fairy assured the queen most people would feel for her. In the meantime, Imis, much less uneasy about her destiny than about her separation from Philax, amused herself by gathering flowers. Because she was only thinking about his love and was impatient to depart, however, she forgot the bouquet she had begun to make and unthinkingly threw them away. Then she hastened to rejoin the queen, who was taking her leave of the fairy of the mountain. The fairy also embraced Imis and gazed at her with the admiration she deserved.

"Since it's impossible for me, beautiful princess, to change the decree of destiny in your favor, I'll at least try to let you escape the disasters that it's preparing for you." Upon saying this, she gathered a bunch of lilies of the valley and addressed the youthful Imis again. "Always wear these flowers that I'm giving you," she said. "They'll never fade, and as long as you wear them, they'll protect you from all the evils with which fate threatens you."

Then she fastened the bouquet on the headdress of Imis. The flowers, obedient to the fairy's wishes, were no sooner placed in the princess's hair than they adjusted themselves and formed a sort of aigrette, whose whiteness seemed to prove only that nothing could eclipse Imis's fair complexion.

After thanking the fairy a thousand times, the queen bade her farewell and went back to Iceland, where the entire court impatiently awaited the princess's return. The eyes of Imis and her lover sparkled radiantly and beautifully with a joy that has never been seen before. The mystery of the lilies of the valley was revealed to the king alone. It had such a pleasing effect in the princess's beautiful brown hair that everyone assumed that it was simply an ornament that she herself had culled in the fairy's gardens.

The princess told Philax much more about the grief she felt at her separation from him than about the misfortunes that the fates had in store for her. Although Philax was worried by them, he was happy just to be with her in the present; the evils of the future were as yet uncertain. In fact, they forgot them and abandoned themselves to the delight of seeing each other again.

In the meantime, the queen recounted the events of the journey to the king and gave him the fairy's tablets. The king opened them and found the following words written in letters of gold:

> Fate for Imis hides despair
> Under hopes that seem most fair.
> She'll be miserable as can be
> Because of too much felicity.

The king and queen were very disturbed by this oracle and vainly tried to interpret it. They said nothing about it to the princess in order to spare her unnecessary sorrow.

One day, while Philax was hunting, a pleasure he indulged in frequently, Imis went walking by herself in a labyrinth of myrtles. She was melancholy because Philax had been gone so long, and she reproached herself for succumbing to an impatience that he evidently did not share. She was absorbed in her thoughts when she heard a voice:

"Why do you torment yourself, beautiful princess? If Philax does not appreciate the happiness of being loved by you, I've come to offer you a heart a thousand times more grateful—a heart deeply smitten by your charms—and a fortune remarkable enough to be the object of desire of everyone in the world except yourself."

The princess was astonished when she heard this voice. She had imagined herself alone in the labyrinth, and since she had not uttered a word, she was even more surprised that this voice had responded to her thoughts. She looked around and saw a little man appear in the air, seated upon a cockchafer.

"Fear not, fair Imis," he said to her. "You have no lover more submissive than I, and although this is the first time I've appeared to you, I've loved you for a long time and have gazed upon you every day."

"You astonish me!" the princess replied. "What's that you said? You've watched me and know my thoughts? If so, you must be aware that it's useless to love me. Philax, to whom I've given my heart, will continue to rule over it because of his charm, and although I'm unhappy with him, I've never loved him so much as I do at this moment. But tell me who you are, and where you first saw me."

"I'm Pagan the Enchanter," he replied, "and I have power over everyone but you. I saw you first in the gardens of the fairy of the mountain. I was hidden in one of the tulips you had gathered, and I took it as a good sign that you were induced to choose the flower I was concealed in. I had hoped you would carry me away with you, but you were too pleasantly occupied by thinking about Philax. You threw away the flowers as soon as you had gathered them and left me in the garden the most enamored of creatures. From that moment on, I've felt that nothing could make me happy except the hope of being loved by you. Think favorably of me, fair Imis, if this be possible, and permit me occasionally to remind you of my affection."

With these words he disappeared. The princess returned to the palace, where the sight of Philax dissipated the alarm she felt. She was so eager to hear him apologize for the length of time he had spent hunting that she nearly forgot to tell him what had occurred. But at last, she told him what she had seen in the labyrinth of myrtles. Despite his courage the young prince was alarmed at the idea of a winged rival because he could not fight with him for the hand of the princess on equal terms. Still, the plume of the lilies of the valley protected her against enchantments, and the affection Imis had for him gave him no cause to fear any change in her heart.

The day after this incident in the labyrinth, the princess woke and saw twelve tiny nymphs seated on honey bees fly into her room. They carried minuscule golden baskets in their hands and approached Imis's bed, where they greeted her, and then placed their baskets on a table of white marble that was standing in the center of the room. As soon as the baskets were placed on it, they grew to an ordinary size. The nymphs left them there and greeted Imis again. One approached the bed nearer than the rest, let something fall on it, and then flew away.

Although she was astonished by such a strange sight, she picked up the object that the nymph had dropped beside her. It was a marvelously beautiful emerald, and the moment the princess touched it, the emerald opened and revealed a rose leaf on which she read these verses:

> Let the world learn to its surprise
> The wondrous power of your eyes.
> Such is the love I bear, you'll see,
> It makes even torture dear to me.

The princess had difficulty recovering from her surprise, and at last she called her attendants, who were just as surprised at the sight of the baskets. The king, queen, and Philax rushed to her chamber on hearing the news of this extraordinary event.

When the princess revealed to them what had happened, she told them about everything except the letter of her lover. She thought she was not bound to say anything about it except to Philax. The baskets were carefully examined and found to be filled with extraordinarily beautiful jewels of such great value that everyone's astonishment increased.

The princess would not touch anything, and when she found a moment when nobody was listening, she drew close to Philax and gave him the emerald and the rose leaf. He read his rival's letter with much disquietude, and Imis consoled him by tearing the rose leaf to pieces before his eyes. Alas, how dearly were they to pay for that act!

Some days elapsed without the princess hearing anything from Pagan. She thought that her contempt for him would put an end to his passion, and Philax expected the same thing. So he returned to his hunting as usual. When he stopped beside a fountain to refresh himself, he had the emerald with him that the princess had given him. Recalling with pleasure how little value she had placed on it, he drew it from his pocket to look at it. But no sooner was it in his hand than it slipped through his fingers, and no sooner did it touch the ground than it changed into a chariot. Two winged monsters emerged from the fountain and harnessed themselves to it. Philax gazed at them without alarm, for he was incapable of fear. Nevertheless, he could not avoid feeling some distress when he found himself being transported into the chariot by an irresistible power, and at the same moment raised into the air by the winged monsters, who pulled the chariot along with alarming speed.

Night fell, and the huntsmen, after searching for Philax in vain throughout the wood, went back to the palace, where they imagined he had returned alone. But he was not to be found there, nor had anyone seen him since he had set out with them for the chase.

The king commanded them to renew their search. The entire court shared his majesty's anxiety. They returned to the wood and ran all over looking for him. It was daybreak before they retraced their steps to the palace; however, they had been unable to obtain any news about the prince's whereabouts. Imis had spent the night despairing of her lover's absence, which she could not comprehend. She had ascended to the battlements of the palace to watch for the return of the search party, hoping she would see him arrive in their company. No words can express her grief when Philax did not appear, and when she was informed that it had been impossible to discover what had happened to him, she fainted. Carrying her into the palace, one of her women undressed her and put her to bed. In her haste, however, she took the plume of the lilies of the valley out of the princess's hair that guarded her against the power of enchantment. The instant it was removed, a dark cloud filled the apartment, into which Imis vanished. The king and queen fell into deep despair when they learned about her disappearance, and there was nothing that could console them.

On recovering from her swoon, the princess found herself in a chamber of multicolored coral with a floor made of pearls. She was surrounded by nymphs, who waited on her with the most profound respect. They were very beautiful and dressed in a magnificent and tasteful manner. Imis first asked them where she was.

"You're in a place where you're adored," one of the nymphs said to her. "Fear nothing, fair princess, you'll find everything you can desire here."

"Then Philax is here!" the princess exclaimed, her eyes sparkling with joy. "My only desire is to be fortunate enough to see him again."

"You cherish the memory of an ungrateful lover too long," Pagan said, making himself visible to the princess. "Since that prince has deserted you, he's no longer worthy of your affection. Let resentment and respect for your own pride combine with the feelings I have for you. Reign forever in these regions, lovely princess. You'll find immense treasures in them, and every kind of conceivable delight will accompany your steps."

Imis replied to Pagan's words with tears alone, and since he was afraid to embitter these tears, he left her. The nymphs remained with her and used everything within their power to console her. They served her a magnificent meal, but she refused to eat. By the following morning, though, her desire to see Philax once more made her determined to live. She took some food, and the nymphs conducted her through various parts of the palace to take her mind off her sorrow. It was built entirely of shiny shells mixed with precious stones of different colors that produced the finest effect in the world. All the furniture was made of gold, and it was clear from such wonderful craftsmanship that only fairies could have made it.

After they had shown Imis the palace, the nymphs led her into the gardens, which were indescribably beautiful. She found a splendid chariot drawn by six stags and led by a dwarf, who requested that she get in. Imis complied, and the nymphs seated themselves at her feet. They were driven to the seaside, where a nymph informed the princess that Pagan, who reigned on this island, had used the power of his art to make it the most beautiful in the universe. The sound of instruments interrupted the nymph's talk. The sea appeared to be entirely covered with little boats built of scarlet coral and filled with everything necessary to create a splendid aquatic entertainment. In the middle of the small craft was a much larger barque on which Imis's initials, formed by pearls, could be seen everywhere. Drawn by two dolphins, the barque approached the shore. The princess got in, accompanied by her nymphs. As soon as she was on board, a superb meal appeared before her, and her ears were entertained at the same time by exquisite music that emanated from the boats around her. Songs lauding her were sung, but Imis did not pay any attention. She remounted her chariot and returned to the palace overcome with sadness.

In the evening Pagan appeared again, and he found her more inappreciative of his love than ever before, but he was not discouraged and was confident that his constancy would have an effect. He had yet to learn that the most faithful are not always the most happy when it comes to love.

Every day he offered the princess entertainments worthy of arousing the admiration of the entire world, but they were lost upon the person for whom they were invented. Imis thought of nothing but her missing lover.

In the meantime, that unfortunate prince had been transported by the winged monsters to a forest belonging to Pagan, called the Dismal Forest. As soon as Philax arrived there, the emerald chariot and monsters disappeared. Surprised by this miracle, the prince summoned all his courage to help himself. It was the only aid on which he could count in that place. He first explored several of the roads through the forest. They were dreadful, and the sun could not illuminate a way out of the gloomy forest. There was not a soul to be found, not even an animal of any kind. It seemed as though the beasts themselves were horrified of this dreary abode.

Philax lived on wild fruit and spent his days in the deepest sorrow. His separation from the princess caused him great despair, and sometimes he occupied himself by using his sword to carve the name of Imis on the tree trunks. Although these rank growths were hardly befitting for such a tender purpose, when we are truly in love, we frequently make the least suitable things express our feelings.

Continuing to advance through the forest every day, the prince had been journeying nearly a year when one night he heard some plaintive voices. Try as he might, he could not distinguish any words. Alarming as these wailing sounds were at such a dark hour—in a place where the prince had not encountered a soul—he desperately sought some kind of company. "If I could at least find someone as wretched as I," he said to himself, "he could console me for the misfortunes I have experienced." Thus he waited impatiently for morning, when he could search for the people whose voices he had heard. He walked toward that part of the forest where he thought the sounds had come from, but he searched all day in vain. At last, however, toward evening he discovered a spot barren of trees. There sprawled the ruins of a castle that appeared to have been enormous at one time. He entered a courtyard that had walls made of green marble and still seemed somewhat splendid. Yet he found nothing but huge trees standing irregularly in various spots of the enclosure. Noticing something elevated on a pedestal of black marble, he found on closer inspection a jumbled pile of armor and weapons, heaped one on top of the other. Ancient helmets, shields, and swords formed a sort of motley trophy. He had been looking for some inscription that might tell him who had been the former owners, and he found one engraved on the pedestal. Time had nearly effaced the characters, and he had great difficulty in deciphering these words:

TO THE IMMORTAL MEMORY OF THE GLORY
OF THE FAIRY CÉORÉ
IT WAS HERE
THAT ON THE SAME DAY
SHE TRIUMPHED OVER CUPID
AND PUNISHED HER UNFAITHFUL LOVERS

This inscription did not provide Philax with nearly enough information to solve the mystery. Therefore, he was about to continue his search through the forest when night overtook him. He sat down at the foot of a cypress, and no sooner did he begin to relax than he heard the same voices that had attracted his attention the previous evening. He was not so much surprised by this as when he noticed that it was the trees themselves that uttered these complaints just as if they had been human beings. The prince rose, drew his sword, and struck the cypress nearest him. He was about to repeat the blow when the tree exclaimed, "Stop! Stop! Don't insult an unfortunate prince who's no longer in a position to defend himself!"

Philax stopped, and as he adjusted to the extraordinary nature of this happenstance, he asked the cypress what miracle had transformed it into a man and a tree at the same time.

"I'll gladly tell you," the cypress replied, "especially since this is the first opportunity in two thousand years that fate has afforded me the chance of relating my misfortunes and I don't want to lose it. All the trees you see in this courtyard were princes, renowned in their time for their rank and valor. The fairy Céoré reigned in this country. Beautiful though she was, her powers made her more famous than her beauty. These other charms she used to bring us under her spell. She had become enamored of the young Orizée, a prince whose remarkable qualities made him worthy of a better fate—I should tell you," the cypress added, "he's the oak you see beside me."

Philax looked at the oak and heard it breathe a heavy sigh as it recalled its misfortune.

"To attract this prince to her court," the cypress continued, "the fairy had a tournament proclaimed. We were all quick to seize this opportunity to acquire glory, and Orizée was one of the princes who contended. The prize consisted of a fairy armor that made the wearer invulnerable. Unfortunately, I was the winner. Céoré was annoyed that fate had not favored her inclinations and, deciding to avenge herself on us, she enchanted all the mirrors that lined a gallery in her castle. Those who saw her reflection in these fatal mirrors just once could not resist having the most passionate feelings for her. It was in this gallery that she received us the day after the tournament. We all saw her in these mirrors, and she appeared so beautiful that those among us who had been indifferent to love up until then stopped being so from that point on, and those who were in love with others became unfaithful all at once. We no longer thought of leaving the fairy's palace. Our only concern was to please her. The affairs of our realms no longer mattered to us. Nothing seemed of consequence except the hope of being loved by Céoré. Orizée was the only one she favored, and the passion of the other princes merely gave the fairy opportunities of sacrificing them to this lover who was so dear to her, and causing the fame of her beauty to spread throughout the world. Love appeared for some time to soften Céoré's cruel nature, but at the end of four or five years she displayed her former ferocity. Abusing the power of her enchantment over us, she used us to avenge herself on neighboring kings for the slightest offense by the most horrible murders. Orizée tried in vain to prevent her cruel acts. She loved him but would not obey him. Having returned one day from subduing a giant whom I had challenged on her orders, I had the vanquished giant's arms brought before her. She was alone in the gallery of mirrors. I laid the giant's spoils at her feet and declared my feelings for her with indescribable ardor, augmented no doubt by the power of the enchantment that surrounded me. But far from showing the least gratitude for my triumph or for the love I felt for her, Céoré treated me with utmost contempt. Into a boudoir she withdrew and left me alone in the gallery in a state of utter despair and rage. I remained there for some time, not knowing what to do because the fairy's enchantments did not permit us to fight with Orizée. Since she was concerned about the life of her lover, the cruel Céoré had deprived us of the natural desire to avenge ourselves on a fortunate rival when she aroused our jealousy. Finally, after pacing the gallery for some time, I remembered that it was in this place that I had first fallen in love with the fairy and exclaimed, 'It's here that I first felt that fatal passion which now fills me with despair. You wretched mirrors that have pictured the unjust Céoré to me so often with a beauty that enslaved my heart and reason, I'm going to punish you for the crime of making her too appealing to me.' Upon saying this, I snatched the giant's club that I had brought to give the fairy as a present, and I dashed the mirrors to pieces. No sooner were they broken than I felt an even greater hatred for Céoré than my former love. At the same time, the other princes who had been my rivals felt their spells broken, and Orizée himself became ashamed of the love the fairy had for him. Céoré vainly tried to retain her lover by her tears, but he did not respond to her grief. Despite her cries, we set out all together, determined to flee from the terrible place. Yet as we passed through the courtyard, the sky appeared to be on fire. A frightful clap of thunder was heard, and we found we could not move. The fairy appeared in the air, riding on a large serpent, and she addressed us in a tone that revealed her rage. 'Faithless princes,' she said, I'm about to punish you by a torture that will never end because of the crime you've committed in breaking my chains, which were too great an honor for you to bear. As for you, ungrateful Orizée, I'll triumph after all in the love you've felt for me. I'm going to plague you with the same misfortune that your rivals will experience. Now, I command in memory of this incident that when mirrors become commonly used throughout the world, it will always be a definite sign of infidelity whenever a lover breaks one.' The fairy vanished after having uttered these words. We were changed into trees, but cruel Céoré left us our reason, undoubtedly with the intention to increase our suffering. Time has destroyed the superb castle that was the avenue of our misfortune, and you're the only man we've seen during the two thousand years that we've been in this frightful forest."

Philax was about to reply to the cypress tree's story when he was suddenly transported into a beautiful garden. There he found a lovely nymph who approached him with a gracious air and said. "If you wish, Philax, I'll allow you to see Princess Imis in three days."

The prince was ecstatic when heard such an unexpected offer and threw himself at her feet to express his gratitude. At that same moment Pagan was aloft, concealed in a cloud with the Princess Imis. He had told her a thousand times that Philax was unfaithful, but she had always refused to believe a word of this jealous lover. He now conducted her to this spot, he said, to convince her of the fickleness of the prince. The princess saw Philax throw himself at the nymph's feet with an air of extreme delight, and she became despondent. No longer did she deceive herself of something that she was afraid to believe more than anything in the world. Pagan had placed her at a distance from the earth that prevented her from hearing what Philax and the nymph had said—it was by his orders that the nymph had appeared before Philax.

Pagan led Imis back to his island, where, after having convinced her of Philax's infidelity, he found that he had only increased the beautiful princess's grief without making her any more positive toward him. To his despair he found that his plan of alleged infidelity had failed despite the fact that it had seemed so promising. Therefore, he was now determined to avenge himself for the constancy of these lovers. He was not cruel like the fairy Céoré, his ancestress, so he conceived a different kind of punishment from the one she had used to torment her unfortunate lovers. He did not wish to destroy either the princess, whom he had loved so tenderly, or even Philax, whom he had already made suffer so much. Consequently he limited his revenge to the destruction of a feeling that had opposed his own.

Erecting a crystal palace on his island, he took great care to put everything in it that would make life pleasant. However, there would be no way to leave this castle. He enclosed nymphs and dwarfs to wait on Imis and her lover, and when everything was ready for their reception, he transported the two of them there. At first they thought themselves at the height of happiness and blessed Pagan a thousand times for softening his anger. As for Pagan, although he at first could not bear to see them together, he hoped that this spectacle would one day prove less painful. In the meantime, he left the crystal palace after engraving this inscription on it with a stroke of his wand:

> Absence, danger, pleasure, pain,
> Were all employed, and all in vain.
> Imis and Philax could not be severed.
> Pagan, whose power they dared defy,
> Condemned them for their constant tie
> To dwell in this place together forever.

They say that at the end of some years, Pagan was as much avenged as he had hoped and that the beautiful Imis and Philax fulfilled the prediction of the fairy of the mountain. Indeed, they fervently kept seeking to recover the aigrette of the lilies to destroy their enchanted palace in the exact same way that they had previously used the lilies to protect themselves against the evil that had been predicted for them.

> Until that moment a fond pair had been blessed
> And cherished in their hearts love's constant fire.
> But Pagan taught them by that fatal test
> That even of bliss human hearts could tire.

JEAN-PAUL
BIGNON

PRINCESS ZEINEB
AND KING LEOPARD

I AM the daughter of King Batoche, who rules over the eastern-most part of the Island of Gilolo. My name is Zeineb, and I have five older sisters. One day my father went hunting in the mountains, and after he had gone a long way, he eventually reached a desolate spot and was extremely surprised to find a beautiful palace that he had never seen before. Anxious to find out more about this unknown mansion, he started to approach it. Yet he froze as a terrifying voice called him by name and threatened him with immediate death unless he sent one of his daughters within three days. King Batoche raised his eyes and saw a leopard at a window. The fire emanating from the eyes of this beast terrified him. In fact, so great was my father's fright that he fled the spot with his men without daring to reply.

My sisters and I were all upset by the sadness that overcame our father, especially since it was quite visible on his face. We hugged him and urged him to tell us what was troubling his heart. After we had persisted for a long time, he finally told us.

"It's a matter of my life or yours," he said. "Ah, I'd much rather die than lose the children I so dearly love."

Tears were in his eyes as he began telling us what he had seen and how he had been threatened in such a terrible way.

"If that's the only dreadful thing that's been disturbing you, my dear father," our eldest sister said, "console yourself. I'll depart tomorrow. Perhaps this leopard won't be as merciless as you think."

The king vainly tried to oppose her plan, for she let herself be guided to the secluded palace. But when the doors opened and the leopard showed himself, my sister found him so horrible that she forgot all her good resolutions, turned around, and fled. When my four other sisters saw her return, they scolded her harshly for having so little courage, and the next day they all tried their luck together. But their courage failed them in the same way that it had failed our eldest sister. As a result, the king's life depended solely on me.

When I took my turn, I was more fearless than they. Not only did I withstand the dreadful gaze of the leopard at the window when I arrived, but I also had the courage to enter the marvelous palace with my mind firmly made up not to leave until I had completely brought everything to light. As soon as I was in the courtyard, the doors closed. A group of nymphs who were quite comely but, due to some miracle, could not talk, appeared before me and began serving me. I was led into a magnificent apartment and spent the entire day regarding the beautiful features of the palace and its gardens. My evening repast was delicious, and I went to sleep in a bed that was better than any in King Batoche's palace. But a thousand troubling things were soon to follow.

Shortly after I was in bed, I heard his steps, and it would not have taken much to have frightened me to death. He rushed into my room and made a terrible noise, brandishing teeth, claws, and tail. Then he stretched his whole body alongside me. I had left him plenty of space because, believe me, I did not occupy much myself. The beast behaved himself in an astonishingly discreet way: he did not touch me at all and left before daybreak. I would have liked to take advantage of this time to sleep, but my fear was much too overwhelming. The same nymphs who had served me the day before came to wake me and get me dressed. They did not neglect a thing to make me comfortable. I had a royal lunch and heard a musical concert during the afternoon. My pleasure was made complete when I observed that the leopard did not appear during the entire day. Indeed, this day set the tone for all the days that followed, but, to tell the truth, I spent many nights without daring to sleep. Finally, the discretion demonstrated by the leopard enabled me to regain my tranquillity.

Ten months went by like this, and at the end of this time, I succumbed to a curious desire that had possessed me from the start and one I had continually resisted: I wanted to know whether the leopard by day was also a leopard by night.

I rose from the bed while he slept, avoiding any contact with him. Then I tiptoed all around the room, searching for something to light it. I suspected that the beast's skin was lying on the ground. In fact, I found it and was then overcome by a mad whim—for what else could I call my behavior? I boldly tore the skin to pieces without considering what might happen. After this rash act I lay down again on my edge of the bed as if nothing had happened.

My companion got up at his usual time, and when he discovered that his skin was gone, he began to wail. I responded by coughing to make him aware that I was awake.

"It's superfluous now to continue taking precautions," the groaning man said to me sadly. "I'm a powerful king who was placed under a magic spell by a magician serving my enemies. My enchantment would have been over now, and I had decided to share my throne and my bed with you. But alas, your curiosity has set me back, and it is now as if I had never suffered anything! Why did you act against your better judgment? Common sense should have told you that you can't act recklessly in a place where you don't know the laws."

I frankly confessed my mistake and begged him to consider that girls are naturally curious. I told him he should be grateful to me for not having looked sooner for the answer to his mysterious appearance. This excuse spoiled everything, and he heaped upon me a new flood of reproaches. Finally, the enchanted king calmed down and momentarily revealed his splendid face, which radiated a sudden light. But as he felt dark forces about to act on him again, he bade farewell and taught me some words that I was to pronounce against anyone I wanted to restrain from doing something until I pronounced some other words that would free that person to continue his actions. No sooner did I learn them than the palace disappeared along with all its pleasant things, and I found myself alone and completely naked lying on a rock.

Tears poured from my eyes as I cursed my curiosity and imprudence. Daylight came, and I was obliged out of shame to look around for something to cover me. I noticed some clothes near the spot where I was lying and went over to pick them up. They were my own clothes, which had been almost worn out over those ten months by all the abuses of exposure. I put on those sad rags as best I could and, fearing that my mistake had caused my father's death, I thought it wiser to leave my country and to go begging rather than to appear before my sisters in my sorry condition. Smearing my face with dirt, I summoned up my courage to begin my wandering.

After a long and fatiguing journey I arrived at a seaport where an old Moslem who was heading to Borneo to do some trading took pity on me and took me on board his ship. We had a safe voyage and let down the anchor in a bay of that large island, even though I was not sure why. After descending with many other people weary of the sea, I left their company without anyone noticing, since I had no desire to go with their leader, who was on his way to the coastal cities where business called him. Instead, I went into the interior of the island, which was very populous, and in three months I reached the pretty city of Soucad, which got its name from the large river that crosses it.

I noticed from the very first that the embroidery decorating the clothes of the women was extremely coarse, and I was convinced that I was more skillful in doing this simple work than the women of Borneo, and that I had found a source that would provide me with work. Once my skill became known, I soon had success beyond my greatest expectations. I rented a small cottage and in a short time established an honest business for myself. I did not have any difficulty learning the language because people use approximately the same language in Soucad as they do in Gilolo. For six or seven months I was able to work in peace and gradually regained the beauty that people had flattered me with having—good looks that had almost entirely disappeared due to the exhaustion and misery I had suffered. I drew the attention of many people. Among them were three of the most distinguished young men of the city, who conspired together to discover whether I was a cruel beauty. They agreed among themselves that one of them, who was considered an artful seducer, would make the first attempt. He came to my house that very evening and began the conversation by asking me to make an embroidered belt for him. Then he talked about his feelings for me: no beauty intended for easy conquest has ever heard so many professions of friendship and favors all at once. When dinnertime arrived, he wanted to entertain me, and though he saw I was repulsed by the idea, he insisted, and I consented. The meal was exquisite, and he did not forget little sweet songs to accompany it. In fact, my lover made it quite clear from several brazen looks that he expected me to be most obliging to him.

Since an open window in my room made him feel uncomfortable, he went over to shut it. While he was closing it, however, I pronounced those powerful words King Leopard had taught me. I put him into a trance so that he had to keep closing and reclosing the window. As for me, I went to bed as I ordinarily did without any difficulties. The poor spellbound man spent the entire night closing that window. The next morning I released him and let him go with a good warning to behave better in the future.

His comrades, who had been waiting impatiently for him in a street since daybreak, ran toward him as soon as he appeared. He cleverly led them to believe that he had been perfectly well received and described his good fortune to them in glowing colors that set them afire. They drew lots to see which one would enjoy the expected happiness next, and the day seemed long to the one who won. However, the night was much more tedious for him because he was obliged to wind a reel of silk for the exact same time that the other had spent closing the window. The third young man was tricked just like his friends, and he had to comb my hair the entire night because of my orders.

These young men did not have the strength to conceal their misadventures for long. All three were outraged, and their tenderness changed into obsessive hate. Therefore, they agreed to denounce me to the judges as the most despicable sorceress in the world. As a result, I was taken from my house and imprisoned. My powerful and motivated adversaries worked feverishly at getting ready for my trial. Since I did not deny a single fact they accused me of, the affair would not have lasted four days if I had not distributed some money among several of the judges through the help of a good friend who was kind enough to do this. The decision was postponed for three whole months due in part to the money and in part to the fact that two of the other judges were appreciative of my charms. They did everything they could to save me, convinced that I would not be ungrateful after such a great service. Nevertheless, in the end my persecutors won, and I was condemned to be burned alive.

After this cruel sentence had been pronounced, I was led to the stake set up in the most beautiful square in Soucad. When I arrived there, they told me what to expect when one is to be executed in a public ceremony, and they bound me to the stake with a large chain. The people hurled insults at me: "She's a sorceress!" "She's an enemy of the human race!" They accused me of all the bad things that had happened naturally or accidentally to all those people who had bought my work. They were delighted to see the executioner advance toward the stake with a flaming torch in his hand, but this unsuspecting crowd was greatly surprised a moment later to see this same executioner become immobile and entranced. The only thing he could do was to hold his burning torch. This effect had been induced by the words that I had secretly pronounced against him. Everyone was in suspense due to this strange incident. Then their mood changed all at once, and they could not stop themselves from laughing as they watched how ridiculous a figure the executioner cut.

The three young men were present and had a large number of partisans in the crowd. They became extraordinarily furious at seeing an event that reminded them of what had happened to them. They cried out that this was public proof of my guilt and that they should quickly reduce to ashes a woman who even at the point of death had abominable ties with evil spirits. The mob was moved by these words and ran to the nearby houses to fetch firebrands. I prepared again to stop this riot when an uproar mixed with acclamations caught their attention in the main street that emptied into the square.

The King of Soucad himself had caused this pleasant commotion. After a long absence he had wanted to surprise his people by making a sudden appearance. Since he was greatly beloved, everyone's attention was drawn to him and away from the stake, executioner, victim, and judges.

The king had gotten out of his carriage and was riding slowly on horseback in order to be better seen. He advanced right into the middle of the square and saw a spectacle that he found rather strange, since it did not fit the public joy that had been aroused by his happy return. When he turned toward the stake, he granted me the reprieve that only he could give and had me untied. Immediately I ran to embrace the knees of my liberator, who looked at me very attentively. He dismounted and embraced me with a joy that equaled the amazement of all the spectators. I did not dare to raise my eyes, but finally, once I glimpsed the person from whom I had received such a surprising reprieve, I recognized King Leopard, whose image had remained deeply engraved in my mind.

It is impossible to express the feelings of my heart, my thoughts, and what I wanted to say. I could not form a single coherent sentence. My gratitude and joy took away all the words that came to my mind. The king had me climb into his carriage without getting in himself and conducted me to his palace in triumph. Some days later, he married me in a solemn ceremony and empowered me to reign in his dominions. The first merciful act I asked him to perform was to pardon my accusers. Then I gave the judges who had let themselves be bribed by my money the punishment they deserved. On the other hand, those judges who had been moved by my beauty were punished in a more lenient way.

JEANNE-MARIE LEPRINCE DE BEAUMONT

BEAUTY AND THE BEAST

ONCE upon a time there was an extremely rich merchant who had six children, three boys and three girls. Since he was a sensible man, the merchant spared no expense in educating them, hiring all kinds of tutors for their benefit.

His daughters were very pretty, but everyone admired the youngest one in particular. When she was a small child, they called her simply "Little Beauty." The name stuck and as a result it led to a great deal of envy on the part of her sisters. Not only was the youngest girl prettier, she was also better natured. The two elder girls were very arrogant because their family was rich. They pretended to be ladies and refused to receive visits of daughters who belonged to merchant families. They chose only people of quality for their companions. Every day they went to the balls, the theater, and the park, and they made fun of their younger sister, who spent most of her time reading books.

Since these girls were known to be rich, many important merchants sought their hand in marriage. But the two elder sisters maintained that they would never marry unless they found a duke, or at the very least, a count. But Beauty—as I have mentioned, this was the name of the youngest daughter—thanked all those who proposed marriage to her and said that she was too young and that she wanted to keep her father company for some years to come.

Suddenly the merchant lost his fortune, and the only property he had left was a small country house quite far from the city. With tears in his eyes he told his children that they would have to go and live in this house and work like farmers to support themselves. His two elder daughters replied that they did not want to leave the city and that they had many admirers who would be only too happy to marry them even though they no longer had a fortune. But these fine young ladies were mistaken. Their admirers no longer paid them any attention now that they were poor. Moreover, since they were so arrogant, everyone disliked them and said, "They don't deserve to be pitied. It's quite nice to see pride take a fall. Now let's see them pretend to be ladies while minding sheep in the country."

Yet at the same time people said, "As for Beauty, we're distressed by her misfortune. She's such a good girl. She has always been kind to poor people. She's so sweet and forthright!"

Several gentlemen still wanted to marry her, despite the fact that she told them that she could not abandon her poor father in his distress. She was going to follow him to the country to console him and help him in his work. Poor Beauty had been greatly upset by the loss of her fortune, but she said to herself, "My tears will not bring back my fortune. So I must try to be happy without it."

When they arrived at the country house, the merchant and his three sons began farming the land. Beauty rose at four o'clock every morning and occupied herself by cleaning the house and preparing breakfast for the family. At first she had a great deal of difficulty because she was not accustomed to working like a servant. But after two months she became stronger, and the hard work improved her health. After finishing her chores, she generally read, played the harpsichord, or sung while spinning. On the other hand, her two sisters were bored to death. They rose at ten, took walks the entire day, and entertained themselves by bemoaning the loss of their beautiful clothes and the fine company they used to have.

"Look at our little sister," they would say to each other. "She's so thick and stupid that she's quite content in this miserable situation."

The good merchant did not agree with them. He knew that Beauty was more suited to stand out in company than they were. He admired the virtues of this young girl—especially her patience, for her sisters were not content merely to let her do all the work in the house, but also insulted her every chance they had.

After living a year in this secluded spot, the merchant received a letter informing him that a ship containing his merchandise had just arrived safely. This news turned the heads of the two elder girls, for they thought that they might put an end to their boredom and would finally be able to leave the countryside. When they saw their father getting ready to depart for the city, they begged him to bring them back dresses, furs, caps, and all sorts of finery. Beauty asked for nothing because she thought that all the profit from the merchandise would not be sufficient to buy what her sisters had requested.

"Don't you want me to buy you something?" her father asked her.

"Since you are so kind to think of me," she replied, "please bring me a rose, for there are none here."

Beauty was not really anxious to have a rose, but she did not want to set an example that would disparage her sisters, who would have said that she had requested nothing to show how much better she was.

The good man set out for the city, but when he arrived, he found there was a lawsuit concerning his merchandise, and after a great deal of trouble, he began his return journey poorer than before.

He had only thirty miles to go before he would reach his house and was already looking forward to seeing his children again, but in passing through a large forest to get to his house, he got lost in a raging snowstorm. The wind was so strong that he was twice knocked from his horse. When night fell, he was convinced that he would die of hunger and cold, or else be eaten by the wolves that were howling all around him. Suddenly he saw a light at the end of a long avenue of trees. It appeared to be quite some distance away, and he began walking in that direction. Soon he realized that the light was coming from a huge palace that was totally illuminated. Thanking God for sending this help, the merchant hurried toward the castle. Imagine his surprise, though, when he found nobody in the courtyards! His horse, which had followed him, saw a large, open stable and walked inside. Upon finding hay and oats, the poor animal, which was dying of hunger, began eating with a rapacious appetite. The merchant tied the horse up in the stable and walked toward the palace without encountering a soul. When he entered a large hall, however, he discovered a good fire and a table set with food for one. Since the sleet and snow had soaked him from head to foot, he approached the fire to dry himself. "The master of this house will forgive the liberty I'm taking," he said to himself, "and I'm sure that he'll be here soon."

He waited a considerable time, but when the clock struck eleven and he still did not see anyone, he could not resist his pangs of hunger anymore. Trembling all over, he took a chicken and devoured it in two mouthfuls. As he became more hardy, he left the hall and wandered through several large, magnificently furnished apartments. Finally he found a room with a good bed, and since it was past midnight and he was tired, he decided to shut the door and go to bed. It was ten o'clock when he woke the next day, and he was greatly surprised to find clean clothes in place of his own, which had been completely muddied.

"Surely," he said to himself, "this palace belongs to some good fairy who has taken pity on my predicament."

He looked out the window and no longer saw snow but an enchanting vista of arbors of flowers. He returned to the large hall where he had dined the night before and saw a small table with a cup of chocolate on it.

"I want to thank you, madam fairy," he said aloud, "for being so kind to think of breakfast for me."

After drinking his chocolate, the good man went to look for his horse. As he passed under an arbor of roses, he remembered Beauty's request, and he plucked a rose from a branch heavy with those flowers. All of a sudden he heard a loud noise and saw a beast coming toward him. It looked so horrible that he almost fainted.

"You're very ungrateful," the beast said in a ferocious voice. "I saved your life by receiving you in my castle, and then you steal my roses, which I love more than anything else in the world. You will have to die for this mistake. I'll give you a quarter of an hour to ask for God's forgiveness."

The merchant threw himself on his knees and pleaded with clasped hands: "Pardon me, my lord. I didn't think that I'd offend you by plucking a rose. One of my daughters had asked me to bring her one."

"I'm not called 'lord' but Beast. I prefer that people speak their minds, so don't think that you can move me by flattery," replied the monster. "But are you telling me that you have daughters . . . ? I'll pardon you on one condition, that one of your daughters comes here voluntarily to die in your place. Don't try to reason with me. Just go. And if your daughters refuse to die for you, swear to me that you'll return within three months."

The good man did not intend to sacrifice one of his daughters to this hideous monster, but he thought, "At least I'll have the pleasure of embracing them one more time."

So he swore he would return, and the Beast told him he could leave whenever he liked. "But," he added, "I don't want you to part empty-handed. Go back to the room where you slept. There you'll find a large, empty chest. You may fill it with whatever you like, and I shall have it carried home for you."

The Beast withdrew, and the good man said to himself, "If I must die, I shall still have the consolation of leaving my children with something to sustain themselves."

He returned to the room where he had slept, and upon finding a large quantity of gold pieces, he filled the chest that the Beast had mentioned. After closing it, he went to his horse in the stable, and left the palace with a sadness that matched the joy that he had experienced upon entering it. His horse took one of the forest roads on its own, and within a few hours the good man arrived at his small house, where his children gathered around him. But instead of returning their caresses, the merchant burst into tears at the sight of them. He held the branch of roses that he had brought for Beauty, and he gave it to her, saying, "Beauty, take these roses. They will cost your poor father dearly."

Immediately thereafter he told his family about the tempestuous adventure that he had experienced. On hearing the tale, the two elder daughters uttered loud cries and berated Beauty, since she did not weep.

"See what this measly creature's arrogance has caused!"

they said. "Why didn't she settle for the same gifts as ours? But no, our lady had to be different. Now she's going to be the cause of our father's death, and she doesn't even cry."

"That would be quite senseless," replied Beauty. "Why should I lament my father's death when he is not going to perish? Since the monster is willing to accept one of his daughters, I intend to offer myself to placate his fury, and I feel very fortunate to be in a position to save my father and prove my affection for him."

"No, sister," said her three brothers, "you won't die. We shall go and find this monster, and we'll die under his blows if we can't kill him."

"Don't harbor any such hopes, my children," said the merchant. "The Beast's power is so great that I don't have the slightest hope of killing him. And I'm delighted by the goodness of Beauty's heart, but I won't expose her to death. I'm old, and I don't have much longer to live. Therefore, I'll lose only a few years of my life that I won't regret losing on account of you, my dear children."

"Rest assured, Father," said Beauty, "you won't go to this palace without me. You can't prevent me from following you. Even though I'm young, I'm not so strongly tied to life, and I'd rather be devoured by this monster than to die of the grief that your loss would cause me."

Arguments were in vain: Beauty was determined to depart for this beautiful palace. And her sisters were delighted because the virtues of their younger sister had filled them with a good deal of envy. The merchant was so concerned by the torment of losing his daughter that he forgot all about the chest that he had filled with gold. But as soon as he retired to his room to sleep, he was quite astonished to find it by the side of his bed. He decided not to tell his children that he had become rich, for his daughters would want to return to the city and he was resolved to die in the country. But he confided his secret to Beauty, who informed him that several gentlemen had come during his absence and that two of them loved her sisters. She pleaded with her father to let her sisters get married, for she was of such a kind nature that she loved them and forgave with all her heart the evil they had done her.

When Beauty departed with her father, the two nasty sisters rubbed their eyes with onions to weep. But her brothers wept in truth, as did the merchant. The only one who did not cry was Beauty, because she did not want to increase their distress.

The horse took the road to the palace, and by nightfall they spotted it all alight as before. The horse was installed in the stable, and the good man entered the large hall with his daughter. There they found a table magnificently set for two people. However, the merchant did not have the heart to eat. On the other hand, Beauty forced herself to appear calm, and she sat down at the table and served him. Then she said to herself, "It's clear that the Beast is providing such a lovely feast to fatten me up before eating me."

After they had finished supper, they heard a loud roar, and the merchant tearfully said good-bye to his daughter, for he knew it was the Beast. Beauty could not help trembling at the sight of this horrible figure, but she summoned her courage. The monster asked if she had come of her own accord and, continuing to shake, she responded yes.

"You are, indeed, quite good," said the Beast, "and I am very much obliged to you. As for you, my good man, you are to depart tomorrow, and never think of returning here. Good-bye, Beauty."

"Good-bye, Beast," she responded.

Suddenly the Beast disappeared.

"Oh, my daughter!" said the merchant, embracing Beauty. "I'm half dead with fear. Believe me, it's best if I stay."

"No, my father," Beauty said firmly. "You're to depart tomorrow morning, and you'll leave me to the mercy of Heaven. Perhaps Heaven will take pity on me."

When they went to bed, they thought they would not be able to sleep the entire night. But they were hardly in their beds before their eyes closed shut. During her sleep Beauty envisioned a lady who said to her, "Your kind heart pleases me, Beauty. The good deed you're performing to save your father's life will not go unrewarded."

When Beauty woke the next morning, she told her father about the dream, and though this consoled him somewhat, it did not prevent him from sobbing loudly when he had to tear himself away from his dear child. After he departed, Beauty sat down in the great hall and began to weep as well. Yet since she had a great deal of courage, she asked God to protect her and resolved not to grieve anymore during the short time she had to live. Convinced that the Beast was going to eat her that night, she decided to take a walk in the meantime and explore the splendid castle. She could not help but admire its beauty, and was quite surprised when she found a door on which was written: "BEAUTY'S ROOM." She opened the door quickly and was dazzled by the magnificence that radiated throughout the room. But what struck her most of all was a glass-walled bookcase, a harpsichord, and numerous books of music. "He doesn't want me to get bored," she whispered to herself. "If I'm only supposed to spend one day here, he wouldn't have made all these preparations."

This thought renewed her courage. She opened the library, chose a book, and read these words on it: "Your wish is our command. You are queen and mistress here."

"Alas!" she said with a sigh. "My only wish is to see my poor father again and to know what he's doing at this very moment."

She had said this to herself, so you can imagine her surprise when she glanced at a large mirror and saw her house, where her father was arriving with an extremely sorrowful face. Her sisters went out to meet him, and despite the grimaces they made in pretending to be distressed, the joy on their faces at the absence of their sister was visible. A moment later, everything in the mirror disappeared, and Beauty could not but think that the Beast had been most compliant and that she had nothing to fear from him.

At noon she found the table set, and during her meal she heard an excellent concert, even though she did not see a soul. That evening as she was about to sit down at the table, she heard the noise made by the Beast. She could not keep herself from trembling.

"Beauty," the monster said to her, "would you mind if I watch you dine?"

"You're the master," replied Beauty, trembling.

"No," responded the Beast. "You are the mistress here, and you only have to tell me to go if I bother you. Then I'll leave immediately. Tell me, do you find me very ugly?"

"Yes, I do," said Beauty. "I don't know how to lie. But I believe that you're very good."

"You're right," said the monster. "But besides being ugly, I'm not intelligent at all. I know quite well that I'm just a beast."

"A stupid person doesn't realize that he lacks intelligence," Beauty replied. "Fools never know what they're lacking."

"Enjoy your meal, Beauty," the monster said to her, "and try to amuse yourself in your house, for everything here is yours. I'd feel upset if you were not happy."

"You're quite kind," Beauty said. "I assure you that I am most pleased with your kind heart. When I think of that, you no longer seem ugly to me."

"Oh, yes," the Beast answered, "I have a kind heart, but I'm still a monster."

"There are many men who are more monstrous than you," Beauty said, "and I prefer you with your looks rather than those who have pleasing faces but conceal false, ungrateful, and corrupt hearts."

"If I had the intelligence," the Beast responded, "I'd make a fine compliment to thank you. But I'm so stupid that I can only say that I'm greatly obliged to you."

Beauty ate with a good appetite, for she was no longer afraid of the Beast. She nearly died of fright, though, when he asked, "Beauty, will you be my wife?"

She did not answer right away, for she feared enraging the monster by refusing him. At last, however, she said with a quaver, "No, Beast."

The poor monster meant merely to sigh, but he made such a frightful whistle that it echoed through the entire palace. Beauty soon regained her composure, for the Beast said to her in a sad voice, "Farewell, then, Beauty."

He left the room, turning from time to time to look at her as he went. When Beauty was alone, she felt a great deal of compassion for the Beast. "It's quite a shame," she said, "that he's so ugly, for he's so good."

Three months Beauty spent in great tranquillity. Every evening at supper the Beast paid her a visit and entertained her in conversation with plain good sense, but not what the world calls wit. Every day Beauty discovered new qualities in the monster. She became so accustomed to seeing him that she adjusted to his ugliness, and far from dreading the moment of his visit, she often looked at her watch to see if it was nine o'clock yet, for the Beast never failed to appear at that hour.

Only one thing troubled Beauty. Before she went to bed every night, the Beast would ask her if she would be his wife, and he seemed deeply wounded when she refused.

"You're making me uncomfortable, Beast," she said one day. "I'd like to say I'll marry you, but I'm too frank to allow you to believe that this could ever happen. I'll always be your friend. Try to be content with that."

"I'll have to," responded the Beast. "I am honest with myself, and I know I'm quite horrid-looking. But I love you very much. However, I'm happy enough with the knowledge that you want to stay here. Promise me that you'll never leave me."

Beauty blushed at these words, for she had seen in her mirror that her father was sick with remorse for having lost her, and she wished to see him again.

"I could easily promise never to leave you," she said. "But I have such a desire to see my father again that I would die of grief if you were to refuse me this request."

"I'd rather die myself than distress you," the monster said. "I'll send you to your father's home. You will stay with him, and your poor beast will die of grief."

"No," Beauty said. "I love you too much to want to cause your death. I promise to return in a week's time. You've shown me that my sisters are married and my brothers have left home to join the army. Just let me stay a week with my father since he's all alone."

"You will be there tomorrow morning," the Beast said. "But remember your promise. You only have to place your ring on the table before going to bed if you want to return. Farewell, Beauty."

As was his custom, the Beast sighed when he said these

words, and Beauty went to bed very sad at having troubled him. When she awoke the next morning, she found herself in her father's house, and when she rang a bell at her bedside, it was answered by a servant who uttered a great cry upon seeing her. Her good father came running when he heard the noise and almost died of joy at seeing his dear daughter again. They kept hugging each other for more than a quarter of an hour. After their excitement subsided, Beauty recalled that she did not have any clothes to wear. But the servant told her that he had just found a chest in the next room, and it was full of dresses trimmed with gold and diamonds. Beauty thanked the good Beast for looking after her. She took the least sumptuous of the dresses and told the servant to lock up the others, for she wanted to send them as gifts to her sisters. But no sooner had she spoken those words than the chest disappeared. Her father remarked, "The Beast probably wants you to keep them for yourself." Within seconds the dresses and the chests came back again.

As Beauty proceeded to get dressed, a message was sent to inform her sisters of her arrival, and they came running with their husbands. Both sisters were exceedingly unhappy. The oldest had married a young gentleman who was remarkably handsome, but was so enamored of his own looks that he occupied himself with nothing but his appearance from morning until night and despised his wife's beauty. The second sister had married a man who was very intelligent, but he used his wit only to enrage everyone, first and foremost his wife. The sisters almost died of grief when they saw Beauty dressed like a princess and more beautiful than daylight. It was in vain that she hugged them, for nothing could stifle their envy, which increased when she told them how happy she was.

The two envious sisters descended into the garden to vent their feelings in tears. "Why is this little prig happier than we are?" they asked each other. "Aren't we just as pleasing as she?"

"Sister," said the oldest, "I've just had an idea. Let's try to keep her here more than a week. That stupid beast will become enraged when he finds out that she's broken her word, and perhaps he'll devour her."

"Right you are, sister," responded the other. "But we must show her a great deal of affection to succeed."

Having made this decision, they returned to the house and showed Beauty so much attention that she wept with joy. Once the week had passed, the two sisters tore their hair and seemed so distressed by her departure that she promised to remain another week. Even so, Beauty reproached herself for the grief she was causing her poor Beast, whom she loved with all her heart. In addition, she missed not being able to see him any longer. On the tenth night she spent in her father's house, she dreamt that she was in the palace garden and saw the Beast lying on the grass nearly dead and reprimanding her for her ingratitude. Beauty woke with a start and burst into tears.

"Aren't I very wicked for causing grief to a beast who's gone out of his way to please me?" she said. "Is it his fault that he's so ugly and has so little intelligence? He's so kind, and that's worth more than anything else. Why haven't I wanted to marry him? I'm more happy with him than my sisters are with their husbands. It is neither handsome looks nor intelligence that makes a woman happy. It is good character, virtue, and kindness, and the Beast has all these good qualities. It's clear that I don't love him, but I have respect, friendship, and gratitude for him. So there's no reason to make him miserable, and if I'm ungrateful, I'll reproach myself for the rest of my life."

With these words Beauty placed her ring on the table and lay down again. No sooner did her head hit the pillow than she fell asleep, and when she woke the next morning, she saw with joy that she was in the Beast's palace. She put on her most magnificent dress to please him and spent a boring day waiting for the evening to arrive. But the clock struck nine, and Beast did not appear.

Now Beauty feared that she had caused his death. She ran throughout the palace, sobbing loudly. After searching everywhere, she recalled her dream and ran into the garden toward the canal, where she had seen him in her sleep. There she found the poor Beast stretched out unconscious. She thought he was dead. Without concern for his horrifying looks, she threw herself on his body and felt his heart still beating. So she fetched some water from the canal and threw it on his face.

Beast opened his eyes and said, "You forgot your promise, Beauty. The grief I felt upon having lost you made me decide to fast to death. But I shall die content since I have the pleasure of seeing you one more time."

"No, my dear Beast, you shall not die," said Beauty. "You will live to become my husband. I give you my hand and swear that I belong only to you from this moment on. Alas! I thought that I only felt friendship for you, but the torment I am feeling makes me realize that I cannot live without you."

Beauty had scarcely uttered these words when the castle radiated with light. Fireworks and music announced a feast. These attractions did not hold her attention, though. She returned her gaze to her dear Beast, whose dangerous condition made her tremble. How great was her surprise when she discovered that the Beast had disappeared, and at her feet was a prince more handsome than Eros himself, who thanked her for having put an end to his enchantment. Although she should have been only concerned about the prince, she could not refrain from asking what had happened to the Beast.

"You're looking at him right at your feet," the prince said. "A wicked fairy condemned me to remain in this form until a beautiful girl consented to marry me, and she prohibited me from revealing my intelligence. You were the only person in the world kind enough to allow the goodness of my character to touch you. In offering you my crown, I'm only discharging the debt I owe you."

Beauty was most pleasantly surprised and assisted the handsome prince in rising by offering her hand. Together they went to the castle, where Beauty was overwhelmed by joy in finding her father and entire family in the hall, for the beautiful lady who had appeared to her in her dream had transported them to the castle.

"Beauty," said this lady, who was a grand fairy, "come and receive the reward for your good choice. You've preferred virtue over beauty and wit, and you deserve to find these qualities combined in one and the same person. You're going to become a great queen, and I hope that a throne will not destroy your virtuous qualities. As for you, my young ladies," the fairy said to Beauty's two sisters, "I know your hearts and all the malice they contain. You shall become statues while retaining your ability to think beneath the stone that encompasses you. You will stand at the portal of your sister's palace, and I can think of no better punishment to impose on you than to witness her happiness. I'll allow you to return to your original shape only when you recognize your faults, but I fear that you'll remain statues forever. Pride, anger, gluttony, and laziness can all be corrected, but some sort of miracle is needed to convert a wicked and envious heart."

The fairy waved her wand and all at once transported everyone in the hall to the prince's realm, where his subjects rejoiced upon seeing him again. Then he married Beauty, who lived with him a long time in perfect happiness because their relationship was founded on virtue.

PRINCE DÉSIR AND
PRINCESS MIGNONE

ONCE upon a time there was a king who was passionately in love with a princess, but she could not marry because she was under a magic spell. When he went in search of a fairy to learn what he could do to win this princess's hand, the fairy said to him, "This princess has a large cat that she's very fond of, and she's destined to marry the man who's nimble enough to tread on her cat's tail."

Saying to himself, "That won't be difficult," the king left the fairy determined to crush the cat's tail without fail. So he ran to the princess's palace, and Minon came toward him, raising its back as it was accustomed to do. The king responded by lifting his foot, and just as he was sure he would step on the cat's tail, Minon turned around so quickly that his majesty trod on nothing but the floor. For a week he tried to step on this fatal tail, but it seemed to be full of quicksilver, so continually was it in motion. At last the king had the good fortune of surprising Minon while he was sleeping, and he stamped on its tail with all his might. Minon awoke with a horrible squeal. Suddenly it took the form of a huge man and looked at the king with eyes full of rage.

"You will wed the princess," he said, "because you've destroyed the enchantment that prevented you from doing so. But I'll be avenged. You will have a son who'll turn unhappy once he discovers that he has a nose that's too long. And if you dare reveal this curse, you will die immediately."

Although the king was very frightened by the sight of this giant, who was a sorcerer, he could not help but laugh at this threat. "If my son has a nose that's too long," he said to himself, "he'll always be able to see or feel it, unless he's either blind or has no hands."

Since the sorcerer had disappeared, the king went looking for the princess. She consented to marry him, but his happiness was brief, for he died at the end of eight months. A month later, the queen gave birth to a little prince, who was named Désir. He had the most beautiful blue eyes, and a pretty little mouth, but his nose was so big that it covered half his face.

When she saw this great nose, the queen was inconsolable, but her ladies in attendance told her that the nose was not as large as it appeared to be. "It's a Roman nose, and if you study history, you'll learn all heroes have large noses." The queen, who doted on her newborn, was charmed by these words, and after continually looking at Désir, his nose did not appear so large after all.

The prince was carefully reared, and as soon as he could talk, they told all sorts of shocking stories in front of him about people with short noses. They allowed no one to come near him, but those whose noses in some degree resembled his own. Indeed, all the courtiers pulled the noses of their children several times a day to make them long enough to pay their respects to the queen and her son. (It was no use pulling, though, because they appeared snub-nosed beside Prince Désir.) As soon as he could read, they taught him history, and when they spoke of any great prince or beautiful princess, they always spoke of their long noses. Désir became so accustomed to regarding the length of a nose as a mark of beauty that he would not have wished his smaller even for a crown.

When he reached the age of twenty, they thought of marrying him and showed him portraits of several princesses. He became captivated by that of Mignone's. She was the daughter of a great king and heiress to several kingdoms, but this did not matter a whit to Désir because he was so enchanted by her beauty.

This princess whom he found so charming had a little turned-up nose, which made her face the prettiest in the world, but which created a predicament for Désir's courtiers. They had acquired the habit of ridiculing little noses, and they could not keep from smiling when they saw the princess's nose.

However, Désir would allow no raillery on the subject and banished two men from his court who dared to disparage Mignone's nose. The other courtiers learned from this example and corrected themselves, and there was one who said to the prince that, in truth, a man could not be handsome without a large nose, but that female beauty was altogether different. "A scholar who speaks Greek told me he read in an old Greek manuscript that the beautiful Cleopatra had the tip of her nose turned up."

The prince gave a magnificent present to the person who told him this good news, and he sent ambassadors to demand Mignone's hand in marriage. They granted his request, and he rode more than three miles to meet her along the way because he was so eager to see her. But when he advanced to kiss her hand, the sorcerer descended, carried off the princess right in front of him, and left him inconsolable. Désir made up his mind not to return to his kingdom until he had rescued Mignone. He would not allow any of his courtiers to follow him, and since he was mounted on his good horse, he put the bridle on his neck and let him lead the way.

The horse entered a large plain, and Désir traveled all day without seeing a single house. The master and his horse were both dying of hunger when toward evening the prince at last saw a cave that appeared to emit light. Entering, he saw a little woman who seemed to be more than a hundred years old. She put on her spectacles to look at the prince, but she took a long time in adjusting them because her nose was too short. The prince and the fairy (for that was what she was) both burst out laughing at seeing each other, and both cried at once, "Ah, what a droll nose!"

"Not so droll as yours," Désir said to the fairy. "But, madam, let's leave our noses as they are, and be so kind as to give me something to eat, for I'm dying of hunger, and so is my poor horse."

"With all my heart," the fairy said. "Although your nose is ridiculous, you're no less the son of my best friend. I loved the king, your father, like my own brother. He had a very handsome nose, that prince!"

"And what's wrong with mine?"

"Oh, there's nothing wrong," the fairy replied. "On the contrary, there's just too much of it. But never mind, one may be a very good man, even with a long nose. I've told you that I was your father's friend. He came to see me often back then, and apropos of those days, let me tell you I was then very pretty, and he used to say so. I must tell you a conversation we had together the first time he saw me—"

"Madam," Désir said, "it will be my pleasure to listen to you once I've had something to eat. Please, remember that I've not eaten all day."

"Poor boy," the fairy said. "You're right. I forgot all about that. I'll give you your supper right away, and while you're eating, I'll tell you my story in as few words as possible. I'm not fond of long stories, you know. Too long a tongue is even more insufferable than a long nose, and I remember when I was young, I was admired because I wasn't a great prattler. They told this to the queen, my mother. In spite of the way you see me now, I'm the daughter of a great king. My father—"

"Your father ate when he was hungry," the prince interrupted.

"Yes, without a doubt," the fairy replied, "and you'll eat also in a moment. I only wanted to tell you that my father—"

"And I'll listen to nothing until I've eaten!" said the prince, beginning to get angry. He calmed down, however, because he needed the fairy, and said to her, "I know the pleasure I'd have in listening to you would make me forget my hunger, but my horse can't listen to you, and he needs food."

The fairy was pleased by this compliment. "You won't wait much longer," she said, calling her servants. "You're very polite, and despite the enormous size of your nose, you're very good-looking."

"May the plague take the old woman for going on so about my nose," the prince said to himself. "You'd think that my mother had stolen that part of her nose that makes hers so deficient. If I didn't want something to eat so badly, I'd leave this chatterbox. Where did she ever get the idea that she's not an incessant talker? You've got to be a great fool not to know your own defects. This must come from being born a princess.

No doubt, flatterers have spoiled her and have convinced her that she talks very little."

While the prince mulled over these thoughts, the servants set the table, and he could not but stare in amazement at the fairy, who asked them a thousand questions merely for the pleasure of talking. Above all he admired the tact of a lady-in-waiting who, no matter what the fairy said, praised her mistress for her discretion.

"Well," he thought while eating, "I'm charmed at having come here. This example makes me see how wisely I've acted in not listening to flatterers. Such people's praise is shameless. They hide our defects from us and change them into perfections. As for me, I'll never be their dupe. Thank God, I know my faults!"

Poor Désir was thoroughly convinced of this and did not feel that those who had praised his nose mocked him just as the lady-in-waiting mocked the fairy (for the prince saw that she turned aside from time to time to giggle). As for him, he did not say a word.

"Prince," the fairy said when she saw he was satisfying his hunger, "please turn yourself a little. Your nose is casting a shadow that prevents me from seeing what's on my plate. Now, come, let's talk about your father. I went to his court when he was a little boy, but it's forty years since I withdrew to this solitary place. Tell me a little about the way they live at court these days. Do the ladies still love rushing from place to place? In my time they could be seen on the same day at the assembly, the theater, the promenades, and the ball—how long your nose is! I can't get accustomed to the sight of it!"

"Indeed," Désir replied, "I wish you'd stop talking about my nose. It is what it is. What does it matter to you? I'm content with it and don't want it any shorter. Everyone's nose is just as it pleases Providence."

"Oh! I see plainly that you're angry, my poor Désir," the fairy said. "However, it wasn't my intention to annoy you. Quite the contrary. I'm one of your friends, and I'd like to do you a favor. It's just that I can't help being shocked by your nose. I'll try not to talk about it, however. I'll even force myself to think you're snub-nosed, although to tell the truth, there's enough material in that nose of yours to make three reasonable noses."

Désir, who had finished eating, became so impatient with the endless talk the fairy kept up on the subject of his nose that he threw himself on his horse and rode off. He continued his journey and wherever he passed, he thought everybody mad because they talked about his nose. So accustomed had he been to hearing that his nose was handsome that he could never admit to himself that it was too long. The old fairy, who wanted to do him a favor in spite of himself, got it into her head to get Mignone from the sorcerer and lock her up in a crystal palace. Then she placed this palace on Prince Désir's way. Ecstatic, he tried to break the crystal, but he found it impossible to do. In despair he approached so that he could at least speak to the princess. For her part, she pressed her hand close to the glass. He wanted to kiss it, but no matter how he turned, he could not get his lips near it. His nose prevented him. For the first time he realized how extraordinarily long it was, and he grabbed it with his hand to bend it to one side. "I must confess," he said, "that my nose *is* too long."

All at once the crystal palace collapsed, and the old woman, holding Mignone by the hand, said to the prince, "Admit that you're greatly indebted to me. I could have talked myself blue, and you still wouldn't have believed that you had a defect until it became an obstacle that hindered the fulfillment of your wishes."

Thus does self-love conceal the deformities of our soul and body from us. Reason seeks in vain to reveal them to us. We do not admit that we have them until the moment when this same self-love discovers that they oppose its interests. Désir, whose nose now became an ordinary one, had learned his lesson. He married Mignone and lived happily with her for a great number of years.

MADEMOISELLE
DE LUBERT

THE PRINCESS CAMION

ONCE upon a time there was a king and queen who placed all their hopes for a successor in their only son, for the queen did not bear any other children. By the time Prince Zirphil was fourteen, he was marvelously handsome and learned everything taught him with ease. The king and queen were tremendously fond of him, and their subjects adored him, for whereas he was friendly to everyone, he knew how to make distinctions among those who approached him. Since he was an only son, the king and queen decided he should marry as soon as possible in order to secure the succession to the crown.

Therefore, they had their men travel by foot and on horseback to look for a princess worthy of the heir apparent, but they failed to find anyone suitable. At last, after the long, careful search, the queen was informed that a veiled lady requested a private audience regarding an important affair. The queen immediately ascended her throne in the audience chamber and ordered the lady to be admitted. The lady approached without removing her white crepe veil, which hung all the way to the ground. Arriving at the foot of the throne, she said, "Queen, I'm astonished that you thought of marrying your son without consulting me. I'm the fairy Marmotte, and my name is sufficiently well known to have reached your ears."

"Ah, madam," the queen said, quickly descending her throne and embracing the fairy, "I'm sure you'll pardon my fault when I tell you that people related stories to me about your wonders as though they were nursery tales. But now that you've graced this palace by coming here, I no longer doubt your power. I beg you, do me the honor of giving me your advice."

"That's not a sufficient answer for a fairy," Marmotte replied. "Such an excuse might perhaps satisfy a common person, but I'm mortally offended, and to begin your punishment, I command you to have Zirphil marry the person I've brought with me."

Upon saying these words, she felt around in her pocket and took out a toothpick case. When she opened it, out came a little ivory doll, so pretty and well made that the queen could not help admiring it despite her unease.

"This is my goddaughter," the fairy said, "and I had always destined her for Zirphil."

The queen soaked herself in her tears. She implored Marmotte in the most touching terms not to expose her to the ridicule of her people, who would laugh at her if she announced such a marriage.

"Laugh, will they, madam?" the fairy exclaimed. "Indeed, we shall see if they have reason to laugh! We shall see if they laugh at my goddaughter, and if your son doesn't adore her. I can tell you that she deserves to be adored. It's true that she's tiny, but she has more sense than your entire kingdom put together. When you hear her speak, you'll be surprised yourself— for she can talk, I promise you. Now, then, little Princess Camion," she said to the doll, "speak a little to your mother-in-law, and show her what you can do."

Then the pretty Camion jumped on the queen's fur tippet and paid her a little compliment so tender and sensitive that her majesty stopped crying and gave the Princess Camion a hearty kiss.

"Here, Queen, is my toothpick case," the fairy said. "Put your daughter-in-law in it. I want your son to become acquainted with her before marrying her. I don't think it will take long. Your obedience may soften my anger, but if you act contrary to my orders, you, your husband, your son, and your kingdom will all feel the effect of my wrath. Above all, take care to put her back into her case early in the evening because it's important that she doesn't stay out late."

As she finished saying this, the fairy raised her veil, and the queen fainted from fright when she saw an actual marmot— black, sleek, and as large as a human being. Her attendants rushed to her assistance, and when she recovered, she saw nothing but the case that Marmotte had left behind her.

Putting her to bed, they went to inform the king about the accident. He arrived very anxious, and the queen sent everyone away. In a flood of tears she told the king about what had just happened. At first the king did not believe it, not until he saw the doll that the queen drew from the case.

"Heavens!" he cried, and after reflecting a moment, he asked, "Why is it that kings are exposed to such great misfortunes? Ah, we're placed above other men only to feel the cares and sorrows that are part of our existence more acutely."

"And in order to set greater examples of fortitude, sire," added the doll in a small, sweet, distinct voice.

"My dear Camion," the queen said, "you speak like an oracle."

After the three of them had conversed for an hour, they decided not to reveal the impending marriage until Zirphil, who had gone hunting for three days, returned and agreed to obey the fairy's command. In the interim the queen and the king withdrew to the privacy of their rooms in order to talk to little Camion. Since she had a highly cultivated intellect, she spoke well and with an unusual turn of thought that was very pleasing. Although she was vivacious, her eyes had a fixed expression that was not very pleasant. Moreover, it disturbed the queen because she had begun to love Camion and feared the prince might take a dislike toward her.

More than a month passed since Marmotte had appeared, but the queen still had not dared to show Zirphil his intended. One day he entered the room while she was in bed. "Madam," he said, "the most unusual thing happened to me some days ago while I was hunting. I had wanted to keep it from you, but it's come to seem so extraordinary that I must tell you about it no matter what.

"I had followed a wild boar and chased it into the middle of the forest without observing that I was alone. When I saw him jump into a great hole that opened up in the ground, my horse plunged in after it, and I continued falling for half an hour. At last I found myself at the bottom of this hole without having hurt myself. Instead of encountering the boar, which, I confess, I was afraid of facing, I saw a very ugly woman who asked me to dismount and follow her. I didn't hesitate giving her my hand, and she opened a small door that had previously been hidden from view. I entered with her into a salon of green marble, where there was a golden bathtub covered with a curtain of very rich material. The curtain rose, and I saw a person of such marvelous beauty in the tub that I thought I would faint. 'Prince Zirphil,' said the bathing lady, 'the fairy Marmotte has enchanted me, and it's only through your aid that I can be released.'

"'Speak, madam,' I said to her. 'What must I do to help you?'

"'You must either marry me this instant or skin me alive.'

"I was just as surprised by the first alternative as I was alarmed by the second. She read the embarrassment in my eyes and said, 'Don't think I'm jesting, or that I'm proposing something you may regret. No, Zirphil, dismiss your fears. I'm an unfortunate princess who's detested by a fairy. She's made me half woman, half whale because I wouldn't marry her nephew, the King of the Whiting—he's frightful and even more wicked than he is hideous. She's condemned me to remain in my present state until a prince named Zirphil fulfills one of the two conditions that I've just proposed. To expedite this matter, I had my maid of honor take the form of a wild boar, and it was she who led you to this spot, where you'll remain until you fulfill my desire in one way or the other. I'm not mistress here, and Citronette, whom you see with me, will tell you that this is the only way it can be.'

"Imagine, madam," the prince said to the queen, who was listening attentively, "what a state I was in when I heard these words! Although the whale-princess's face was exceedingly pleasing and her charms and misfortunes made her extremely intriguing, the fact that she was half fish horrified me, and the idea of skinning her alive threw me into utter despair. 'But, madam,' I said to her at length (for my silence was as stupid as it was insulting), 'isn't there a third way?' No sooner had I uttered those unfortunate words than the whale-princess and her attendant uttered shrieks and lamentations that were enough to pierce the vaulted roof of the salon. 'Ungrateful wretch! Cruel tiger, and everything that is most ferocious and inhuman!' the whale-princess exclaimed. 'Do you want to condemn me to the torture of seeing you perish as well? If you don't grant my request, the fairy has assured me you'll die, and I'll remain a whale my entire life.'

"Her reproaches pierced my heart. She raised her beautiful arms out of the water and joined her charming hands together to implore me to decide quickly. Citronette fell at my feet and embraced my knees, screaming loud enough to deafen me. 'But how can I marry you?' I asked. 'What sort of ceremony could be performed?' 'Skin me,' she said tenderly, 'and don't marry me. I prefer that.'

"'Skin her!' screamed the other. 'You have nothing to fear.'

"I was in an indescribable state of confusion, and while I was trying to make up my mind, their shrieks and tears increased until I had no idea what would become of me. After a thousand and one struggles, I cast my eyes once more on the beautiful whale. I confess, I found an inexpressible charm in her features. Throwing myself on my knees close to the tub, I took her hand. 'No, divine princess,' I said to her. 'I won't skin you. I'd prefer to marry you!'

"As I said these words, joy lit the princess's countenance, but a modest joy, for she blushed and lowered her beautiful eyes. 'I'll never forget the favor you're doing for me,' she said. 'I'm so overwhelmed with gratitude that you can demand anything from me after this generous act.'

"'Don't waste time,' the insufferable Citronette said. 'Tell him quickly what he must do.'

"'It's sufficient,' said the whale princess blushing again, 'that you give me your ring, and that you take mine. Here's my hand. Receive it as a pledge of my faith.'

"No sooner did I perform this tender exchange and kiss the beautiful hand she held out to me than I found myself on my horse again in the middle of the forest. After calling my attendants, they came to me, and I returned home unable to say a word because I was so completely astounded. Since then I've been transported every night, without knowing how, into the beautiful green salon, where I spend the night near an invisible person. She speaks to me and tells me that the time hasn't come yet for me to know who she is."

"Ah, my son," the queen interrupted, "is it really true that you're married to her?"

"I am, madam," the prince replied. "Yet even though I love

my wife enormously, I would have given her up if I could have escaped the salon without resorting to the marriage."

Upon saying these words, a little voice that came from the queen's purse said, "Prince Zirphil, you should have flayed her. Your pity may perhaps be fatal to you."

Surprised by this voice, the prince was speechless. The queen vainly tried to conceal the cause of his astonishment from him, but he quickly searched the purse hanging on the armchair near the bed and drew out the toothpick case, which the queen took from his hand and opened. Princess Camion immediately emerged, and the dumbfounded prince threw himself onto his knees by the queen's bedside to inspect her more closely.

"I swear, madam," he cried, "this is my dear whale in miniature! Is this some jest? Did you only want to frighten me by allowing me to believe so long that you wouldn't approve of my marriage?"

"No, my son," the queen replied. "My grief is real, and you've exposed us to the most cruel misfortunes by marrying that whale. In fact, you were promised to the Princess Camion, whom you see in my hands."

Then she related to him what had happened between her and the fairy Marmotte. The prince did not interrupt because he was so astonished that she and his father had agreed to a proposal that was so patently ridiculous.

"Heaven forbid, madam," he said when the queen had finished, "that I should ever oppose your majesty's plans, or that I should act contrary to the wishes of my father, even when he commands me to do something impossible as this appears to be. But if I had consented, could I really have fallen in love with this pretty princess? Would your subjects ever have—"

"Time is a great teacher, Prince Zirphil," Camion interrupted. "But what is done is done. You can't marry me now, and my godmother is a person who won't easily tolerate anyone breaking his word to her. Tiny as I am, I feel the unpleasantness of this predicament as acutely as the largest woman would. But since you're not so much to blame, except for having been a mite too hasty, I may be able to persuade the fairy to mitigate the punishment."

After saying these words, Camion fell silent, exhausted from having said so much.

"My darling," the queen said, "I implore you to get some rest. I fear you might become ill, and then you'll be in no condition to speak to the fairy when she comes to torment us. You're our only hope, and no matter how she may punish us, I won't feel it so deeply if Marmotte doesn't take you from us."

Princess Camion felt her little heart beat at these words. Since she was quite exhausted, however, she could only kiss her hand and let some tiny tears drop on it. Moved by this incident, Zirphil begged Camion to permit him to kiss her hand in turn. She gave it to him with much grace and dignity and then reentered her case. After this tender scene the queen rose in order to tell the king what had happened and to take every sensible precaution against the fairy's anger.

In spite of a double guard in front of Zirphil's apartment, he was carried off at midnight and found himself as usual in the company of his invisible wife. But instead of hearing the sweet, touching things she usually said to him, she wept and refused to speak at all.

"What have I done?" he asked after he tired of asking her to confide in him. "You weep, dear princess, when you ought to console me for all the danger I've incurred due to my tender feelings for you."

"I know everything," the princess said, her voice racked by sobs. "I know all the misery that may happen to me. But you, ungrateful man, you're the one I have most to complain about!"

"Oh, heavens!" Zirphil cried. "With what do you reproach me?"

"The love Camion has for you and the tenderness with which you kissed her hand."

"The tenderness!" the prince replied quickly. "You know too little about it if you can accuse me so lightly. Besides, even if Camion could love me—which is impossible, since she only saw me for a moment—how can you worry when you've had proofs of my commitment to you? I should accuse you of injustice. If I looked at her with any attention, it was because her features reminded me of yours, and being deprived of the pleasure of beholding you, anyone who resembles you gives me the greatest satisfaction. Show yourself to me again, my dear princess, and I'll never look at another woman."

The invisible lady appeared to be consoled by these words, and she approached the prince. "Pardon my spate of jealousy," she said. "I have too much reason to fear they'll take me from you not to feel troubled by an incident that seemed to announce the beginning of that separation."

"But," the prince said, "can't I know why you're no longer permitted to show yourself? If I've rescued you from Marmotte's tyranny, how can it be that you can be subjected to it again?"

"Alas!" the invisible princess said. "If you had decided to flay me, we would have been very happy. But you were so horrified by that proposal that I didn't dare push you further."

"Pray, how did Camion chance to learn about this adventure?" the prince interrupted. "She told me nearly the exact same thing."

No sooner did he finish saying these words than the princess uttered a frightful shriek. Surprised, the prince rose hastily. His alarm was enormous when he saw the hideous Marmotte in the middle of the room. She held the beautiful princess, who was now neither half whale nor invisible, by the hair. He was about to grab his sword when the princess tearfully begged him to temper his anger because it would be to no avail against the fairy's power. The horrible Marmotte was grinding her teeth and spewed a blue flame that scorched his beard.

"Prince Zirphil," she said to him, "a fairy protects you and prevents me from exterminating you, your father, your mother, and your kin. But since you've married without consulting me, you'll at least suffer in regard to everything that's dear to you. Neither your torment nor that of your princess will ever end until you've obeyed my commands."

When she finished speaking, the fairy, princess, salon, and palace all disappeared together, and he found himself in his own apartment in his nightdress and with his sword in his hand. So astonished and infuriated was he that he did not feel the severity of the cold, though it was the middle of winter. The cries he made caused his guards to enter the room, and they begged him to go to bed or to allow them to dress him. Deciding to get dressed, he went to the queen's chamber, who, for her part, had spent the night in the cruelest state of anxiety. She had been unable to sleep, and in order to induce slumber she had wanted to talk over her despair with tiny Camion. When she had looked for her toothpick case, though, Camion had disappeared. Afraid she might have lost her in the garden, the queen got up, and after ordering torches to be lit, she searched for her without success. Camion had vanished. Therefore, the queen retired to bed again in an alarming state of sorrow. She was giving fresh vent to her grief as her son entered, but he was so distressed himself that he did not notice her tears. Yet she saw how disturbed he was and exclaimed, "Ah! No doubt you've come to bring some dreadful tidings to me!"

"Yes, madam," the prince replied. "I've come to tell you that I'll die if I don't find my princess."

"What?" the queen cried out. "Do you already love that unfortunate princess, my dear son?"

"Do you mean your Camion?" the prince asked. "Madam, how can you suspect me of such a thing? I'm speaking of my dear whale-princess. She's been torn away from me. It's for her alone that I live, and the cruel Marmotte has carried her away!"

"Ah, my son," the queen said. "I'm far more unhappy than you. They may have taken away your princess, but they've also robbed me of my Camion! She's been missing from her case since last night!"

Then they told each other their respective adventures and wept together over their common misfortunes. The king was informed about the sorrow of the queen and the grief of his son. He entered the apartment in which this tragic scene was taking place, and since he was an extremely clever man, it occurred to him immediately to post a large reward for finding Camion. Everybody agreed that this was a capital idea, and even the queen, in spite of her great grief, confessed that only an extraordinary mind could have thought of such a novel expedient. The handbills were printed and distributed, and the queen became rather calm in the hope of soon hearing some tidings of her little princess. As for Zirphil, Camion's disappearance interested him no more than her presence had. He decided to seek out a fairy about whom he had heard, and after receiving the permission of the king and queen, he departed with a single equerry to accompany him.

A great distance separated his country and that inhabited by the fairy, but neither time nor obstacles checked the ardor of young Zirphil. Through countless countries and kingdoms he passed. Nothing in particular happened to him because he was not looking for any adventures. Since he was as handsome as Cupid and brave as his sword, he could have had plenty of adventures if he had sought them.

After traveling for a year, he arrived at the beginning of the desert in which the fairy had her abode. He dismounted from his horse and left his equerry in a cottage with orders to wait for him there. Into the desert, which was frightful due to its desolation, he entered. Only screech owls inhabited it, but their cries did not alarm the valiant spirit of our prince.

One evening he saw a light at a distance, and this made him think, I must be approaching the famous grotto. Indeed, who but a fairy could live in such a horrible desert? He walked all night long, and finally at daybreak he discovered the grotto, but a lake of fire separated him from it, and all his valor could not protect him from the flames that spread left and right. He searched around for a long time to see what he could do, and his courage nearly failed him when he found not even a bridge.

Despair proved his best friend, for in a frenzy of love and anguish he decided, "I'll end my days in the lake if I cannot cross it." No sooner did he make this strange resolution than he threw himself bodily into the flames. From the first he felt a gentle warmth that hardly inconvenienced him, and he swam to the other side without the least trouble. As soon as he got there, a young and beautiful salamander emerged from the lake and said, "Prince Zirphil, if your love is as great as your courage, you may hope for everything from the fairy Lumineuse. She favors you, but she wants to test you."

Zirphil made a profound bow to the salamander in acknowledgment, for she plunged again into the flames before he had time to speak. He continued on his way, and after a while he arrived at the foot of an enormous rock that glowed so radiantly that it appeared to be on fire. It was such a large carbuncle that the fairy was lodged inside in a very comfortable manner. As soon as the prince approached, Lumineuse emerged from the rock, and he prostrated himself before her. Then she raised him and asked him to enter.

"Prince Zirphil," she said, "a power equal to mine has neutralized the benefits I bestowed on you at birth, but since I am very concerned for your future, I'll do the best I can for you. Indeed, you'll need as much patience as courage to foil the wickedness of Marmotte. I can tell you nothing more."

"At least, madam," the prince replied, "do me the favor of informing me if my beautiful princess is unhappy, and if I may hope to see her again soon."

"She's not unhappy," the fairy responded. "But you won't be able to see her until you've pounded her in the mortar of the King of the Whiting."

"Oh, heavens!" the prince cried. "Is she in his power? Now I'll not only have to dread the consequences of his fury, but also the even greater horror of pounding her with my own hands!"

"Summon your courage," the fairy replied. "Don't hesitate to obey. Your entire happiness, and your wife's as well, depend on it."

"But she'll die if I pound her," the prince said, "and I'd rather die myself."

"Be off," the fairy said, "and don't argue! Each moment you lose adds to Marmotte's fury. Go and look for the King of the Whiting. Tell him you're the page I promised to send him, and rely on my protection."

Then she took a map and pointed out the road that he had to take to reach the dominions of the King of the Whiting. Before she took leave of him, she informed him that the ring that the princess had given him would show him what he should do whenever the king commanded him to perform a difficult task. He departed, and after traveling some days, he arrived in a meadow that stretched down to the seashore, where a small sailing vessel made of mother-of-pearl and gold was moored. Looking at his ruby, he saw himself in it going on board the vessel. Therefore, he embarked and cast off, whereupon the wind took the boat out to sea. He had been sailing for several hours when the vessel finally docked at the foot of a crystal castle built upon wooden piles. He jumped ashore and entered a courtyard that led to a magnificent vestibule and countless apartments whose walls were remarkably cut from rock crystal, producing the most beautiful effect in the world. The castle appeared to be inhabited only by people with heads of all sorts of fish. Convinced this was the dwelling of the King of the Whiting, he shuddered with rage. However, he restrained himself so he could ask a turbot, who had the manner of a captain of the guard, how he could manage to see the King of the Whiting. The man-turbot made a grave signal for him to advance, and he entered the guard chamber, where he saw a thousand armed men with pike heads formed in rows through which he was to pass.

Making his way through this infinite crowd of fish-men, he came to the throne room. There was not much noise, for the courtiers could not speak since the greater number of them had whitings' heads. He saw several who appeared to be of a higher rank than the rest due to the air they assumed with the crowd surrounding them. Once he arrived at the king's room, he saw the council, composed of twelve men who had shark heads, emerge. After a while the king himself appeared. He had a whiting's head like many of the others, but he could speak. He had fins on his shoulders, and from his waist down he was a veritable whiting. He wore only an extremely radiant scarf made of the skin of goldfish and a helmet in the form of a crown, from which rose a codfish's tail as a plume. Four whiting carried him in a bowl of Japanese porcelain as large as a bathful of sea water. His greatest pride consisted in having it filled twice a day by the dukes and peers of his kingdom, and this position was extremely sought after.

Very large, the King of the Whiting had more the air of a monster than of anything else. After he had spoken to several petitioners, he noticed the prince. "Who are you, my friend?" he asked. "By what chance do I see a man here?"

"My lord," Zirphil said, "I'm the page the fairy Lumineuse promised you."

"I know what she's up to," the king laughed, showing teeth like those of a saw. "Lead him into my seraglio, and let him teach my crayfish to talk."

Immediately a squad of whiting surrounded him and led him away. As he passed through the apartments again, all the fish, even those in highest favor, professed a great deal of friendship for him by various signs. The whiting led him through a delightful garden at the end of which was a charming pavilion built entirely of mother-of-pearl and ornamented with great branches of coral. The favorite whiting brought him into a similarly decorated apartment that had windows overlooking a magnificent stretch of water. They indicated that this was to be his residence, and after showing him a little room at one corner of the salon, which he understood was to be his bedroom, they retired, and he remained alone, astonished to find himself something like a prisoner in the palace of his rival.

He was contemplating his situation when the doors of his room opened. Ten or twelve thousand crayfish, who were conducted by one larger than the rest, entered and placed themselves in straight lines that nearly filled the apartment. The one marching at their head mounted a table near him and said, "Prince, I know you, and you owe much to my care, but since it is rare to find gratitude in men, I won't tell you what I've done for you, for fear you'd destroy the sentiments you've aroused in me. Therefore, let me merely inform you that these are the crayfish of the King of the Whiting. They alone speak in this empire, and you've been chosen to teach them the language of refinement, the customs of the world, and the means of pleasing their sovereign. You'll find them intelligent, but you must choose ten every morning to pound in the king's mortar to make his broth."

Once this crayfish stopped speaking, the prince replied, "I had no idea, madam, that you had taken an interest in my affairs. The gratitude I already feel toward you should induce you to abandon the bad opinion you've developed toward men in general, for on the bare assurance you've given me of your friendship, I feel deeply obligated to you. But what I am anxious to learn is how I should go about reasoning with the beings whose education I am in charge of. If I could be sure that they had as much intelligence as you, I'd be honored to do this work. But if I find them difficult to teach, I'll have less courage to punish them for faults for which they are not responsible. And if I live with them, how can I have the heart to have them tortured?"

"You are obstinate and a great talker," the crayfish interrupted. "But we know exactly how to take care of you." Upon saying this, she rose from the table, and after jumping to the ground, she took her real form of Marmotte (for she was that wicked fairy).

"Oh heavens!" the prince cried. "So this is the person who boasts that she's interested in my affairs—she who's done nothing but make me miserable! Ah, Lumineuse, you've abandoned me!"

No sooner had he finished uttering those words than the marmot jumped through the window into the reservoir and disappeared, leaving him alone with twelve thousand crayfish. After reflecting somewhat on how he should proceed to educate them, during which time they waited in complete silence, it occurred to him that he might find his beautiful and unfortunate princess among them. "Hideous Marmotte has ordered me to pound ten of them every morning. And why should I be chosen to pound ten of them every morning if not to drive me mad? Never mind, let's look for her. Let's at least try to recognize her even if I die of grief before her eyes." Then he asked the crayfish if they would kindly permit him to search for one of his acquaintances among them.

"We know nothing about it, my lord," offered one of them. "But you can make whatever inquiry you please up to the time we must return to the reservoir, for we spend every night there."

Zirphil began his inspection, and the more he looked, the less he discovered, but he surmised from the few words that he drew from those he interrogated that they were all princesses transformed by Marmotte's wickedness. This caused him inconsolable grief because he had to choose ten for the king's broth.

When evening came, the crayfish repeated that they had to retire to the reservoir. Not without pain did he relinquish his search for the sweet princess. He had been able to interrogate only a hundred and fifty crayfish during the entire day, but since he was certain that at least she was not among them, he decided to take ten from that number. No sooner did he choose them than he proceeded to carry them to the king's offices. Suddenly he heard peals of laughter from the victims he was about to crush and stopped dead, so surprised that he could not speak. As he continued walking, he interrupted them to inquire what they found so amusing under their present circumstances. They renewed their loud laughter so heartily that he could not help participating in their mirth in spite of himself. They wanted to speak, but could not do so because they were laughing so hard. They could only utter, "Oh, I can't say any more!" "Oh, I'll die from it!" "No, there's nothing in the world so amusing!" And then they roared again.

At last he reached the palace with them all laughing together, and after he showed them to a pike-headed man who seemed to be the head cook, a mortar of green porphyry ornamented with gold was placed before him. Into this he put his ten crayfish, and prepared to pound them. Just then the bottom of the mortar opened and emitted a radiant flame that dazzled the prince. Then it closed again and appeared perfectly empty: the crayfish had vanished. This simultaneously astonished and gratified him because he had been loath to pound such merry creatures. On the other hand, the man-pike seemed sadly distressed by this incident and wept bitterly. The prince was just as much surprised by this as he was by the laughter of the crayfish. However, he could not determine the reason for this, since the pike-head could not talk.

He returned to his pretty rooms and was disturbed to find the crayfish had already gone back to the reservoir. The next morning they reentered without Marmotte, and he looked for his princess. Since he was still not able to discover her, he again chose ten of the youngest crayfish for pounding. Then the same thing occurred—they laughed, and the man-pike wept when they disappeared in the flame. For three months this extraordinary scene was repeated every day. He heard nothing from the King of the Whiting, and he was uneasy only because he had not discovered his beautiful princess.

One evening, after returning from the kitchen to his apartment, he crossed the king's gardens and passed near a palisade surrounding a charming grove. In the middle of it was a little sparkling fountain, where he heard someone chatting. Since he believed that all the inhabitants of that kingdom were incapable of speaking, this surprised him. He advanced quietly and heard a voice that said, "But, Princess, if you don't reveal yourself, your husband will never find you."

"What can I do?" said the other voice, which he recognized as the one he had so often heard. "Marmotte's cruelty compels me to remain silent, and I can't reveal myself without risking his life as well as my own. The wise Lumineuse, who's helping him, is hiding my features from him in order to protect both of us. It's absolutely necessary that he pound me. It's an irrevocable sentence."

"But why must he pound you?" the other inquired. "You've never told me your history. Your confidante, Citronette, would have told me if she hadn't been chosen for the king's broth last week."

"Alas!" the princess replied. "That unfortunate lady has already undergone the torture that still awaits me. If only I were in her place! I'm sure she's in her grotto by this time."

"But," the other voice replied, "since it's such a beautiful night, tell me now why you've been subjected to Marmotte's vengeance. I've already told you who I am, and I'm burning with impatience to know more about you."

"Although it will revive my grief," the princess remarked, "I can't refuse to satisfy you, especially since I must talk about Zirphil. I take pleasure in everything that pertains to him."

You can easily judge how delighted the prince felt at this fortunate moment. He glided quietly into the grove, but since it was very dark, he did not see anything. However, he listened with all his might, and this is what he heard word for word:

My father was king of a country near Mount Caucasus. He reigned to the best of his ability over a people of incredible wickedness. They were perpetually revolting, and often the windows of his palace were broken by stones they hurled. The queen, my mother, who was a very accomplished woman, composed speeches for him to make to the disaffected, but if he succeeded in appeasing them one day, the next produced new troubles. The judges became tired of condemning people to death, and the executioners of hanging them. At last things reached such a state that my father saw that all our provinces were united against us, and he decided to withdraw from the capital so that he would no longer have to witness so many unpleasant scenes. He took the queen with him and left the government of the kingdom to one of his ministers, who was very wise and less timid than my father. My mother was expecting to give birth to me and traveled with some difficulty to the foot of Mount Caucasus, which my father had chosen for his abode. Our wicked subjects joyfully fired guns at their departure and strangled our minister the next day, saying that he had wanted to carry matters with too high a hand and that they preferred their former sovereign. My father was not at all flattered by their preference and remained hiding in his little retreat, where I soon saw the light of day.

They named me Camion because I was so tiny. Moreover, since the king and queen were tired of the honors that had cost them so dearly, they concealed my high birth from me. I was brought up as a shepherdess. At the end of ten years (which appeared to them like ten minutes because they were so happy in their retreat), the fairies of the Caucasus, who had become infuriated by the wickedness of the people of our kingdom, decided to restore order there. One day, as I was tending my sheep in the meadow next to our garden, two old shepherdesses approached and begged me to give them shelter for the night. They had such a dejected air that my soul was moved with compassion. "Follow me," I said. "My father, who's a farmer, will gladly welcome you." I ran to the cottage to announce their arrival to him. He came to greet them and received them with a good deal of kindness, as did my mother. Then I brought in my sheep and set milk before our guests. Meanwhile, my father prepared them a nice little supper, and the queen—who, as I told you before, was a clever woman—entertained them in a wonderful manner.

I had a little lamb of which I was extremely fond, and my father called me to bring it to him so he might kill and roast it. I was not accustomed to oppose his will and therefore took it to him. But I was so distressed that I sat down to weep beside my mother, who was so occupied in talking to these good women that she did not pay any attention to me. "What's the matter with the little Camion?" one of them said, who saw me in tears.

"Alas, madam!" I said to her. "My father's roasting my pet lamb for your supper."

"What!" said the one who had not yet spoken. "Is it on our account that pretty Camion is thus distressed?" Standing up, she struck the ground with her stick, and a magnificently set table rose from it. The two old women became two beautiful ladies dressed in dazzling precious stones. I was so transfixed that I did not even pay attention when my little lamb bounded into the room and made a thousand capers that amused the entire company. After kissing the hands of the beautiful ladies, I ran to pet him. Imagine my shock when I found his wool made all of silver purl and covered with knots of rose-colored ribbon.

My father and mother fell at the feet of the fairies, for, I need not tell you, this is what they were. The more majestic of them raised them, saying, "King and queen, we've known you for a long time, and your misfortunes have aroused our pity. Don't imagine that greatness exempts anyone from the evils of human-kind. You must know through experience that the more ele-vated the rank, the more keenly these evils are felt. Your patience and virtue have raised you above your misfortunes, and it's time to give you your reward. I'm the fairy Lumineuse, and I've come to inquire what your majesties would find most pleasant. Come, speak! Don't worry about putting our power to the test. Con-sult each other, and your wishes will be fulfilled. But say noth-ing with regard to Camion: her destiny is separate from yours. The fairy Marmotte has been envious of the splendid fate prom-ised her and has obscured it for a time. But we do know Camion will learn the value of her happiness only by experiencing the evils of life. We can protect her only by softening them. That's all we're permitted to tell you. Now, speak. We can do anything you want with that one exception."

After this speech the fairies fell silent. The queen turned to the king so that he might reply, for she was crying because I was doomed to be unhappy. But my father was in no better condi-tion to speak than she was. He uttered pitiful cries, and on see-ing them in tears, I left my lamb to come weep with them. The fairies waited patiently and in perfect silence until our tears dried. At last my mother nudged the king gently: they were waiting for his reply. He took his handkerchief from his eyes and said that since it was fated that I should be miserable, they could offer him nothing that would please him. "I refuse the happiness you promise me because I'll always feel embittered by thinking about what dear Camion has to dread." Seeing that the poor man could say no more, the queen begged the fairies to take their lives on the day my sad destiny was to be fulfilled because her only wish was not to be compelled to witness my misery. The good fairies were touched by the extreme grief that reigned in the royal family and talked together in a whisper. At last Lumineuse said to the queen, "Be consoled, madam. The misfortunes threatening Camion are not so great and they'll end happily. Indeed, from the moment that the husband destined for her obeys the commands of fate, our sister's malevolence will have no more power over her. Believe me, she'll be happy with him, for the prince we've chosen is worthy of her.

"All we can tell you is that you must never forget to lower your daughter every morning into your well. She must bathe in it for half an hour, every morning. If you observe this rule strictly, she may escape the evil with which she is threatened. At the age of twelve, the critical period of her fate will commence. If she reaches the age of thirteen safely, there'll be nothing more to fear. This is all that concerns her. Now, make a wish for yourselves, and we'll satisfy your desires."

The king and queen looked at each other, and after a short silence the king asked to become a statue until I had completed my thirteenth year. The queen made a modest request, that the temperature of the well in which I was to be dipped always correspond to the season. The fairies were charmed by this excess of parental tenderness and added that the water would be orange-flowered water, and that the king could resume his natural form whenever the queen threw this water on him. "You can, of course, become a statue again whenever you please." After lauding the king and queen for their moderation, they eventually took their leave of us with the promise: "We'll aid you whenever you need help if you just burn a bit of the silver purl with which Camion's lamb is covered."

When they vanished, I felt anguish for the first time in my life as I watched my father become a great black marble statue. The queen burst into tears, and I did, too, but since everything must have an end, I stopped crying and occupied myself by consoling my mother because I felt a sudden increase of both sense and sensitivity.

The queen spent her days at the feet of the statue, and I milked my ewes after bathing each day as they had ordered.

We lived off the food produced by the milk because the queen would not take anything else, and only out of love for me could she be prevailed upon to go on with a life so filled with bitterness. "Alas, my daughter!" she sometimes said. "Our grandeur and high birth have been of no use to us! (By this time she had revealed my rank to me.) It would have been better to be born into the lower classes. A crown has brought such disaster to us! Only virtue and my affection for you, my dear Camion, enable me to withstand these catastrophes. There are moments when my soul seems eager to leave me, and I confess, I feel pleasure in thinking that I shall soon die. It's not for me you should weep, but for your father, whose grief is even greater than mine. It has brought him to the extremity of desiring a fate worse than death. Never forget, my dear, the gratitude you owe him."

"Alas, madam!" I said. "I'm incapable of ever forgetting it, and still less can I forget that you're keeping yourself alive only in order to help me."

I was bathed regularly every day, and every day my mother sadly viewed the king as an inanimate statue. However, she did not dare recall him to life for fear of inflicting him with the pain of witnessing my threatened misfortune. Since the fairies had not specified what we were to fear, we lived in mortal dread. My mother in particular imagined no end of frightful things because her imagination had an unlimited scope to cover. As for me, I did not trouble myself much about it, for youth is the only time that we enjoy the present.

My mother told me repeatedly that she felt a great desire to bring my father back to life again, an inclination I shared as well. At last, after six months had passed and she found that the fairies' bath had greatly enriched both my body and mind, she decided to satisfy this longing, if only to give the king the pleasure of seeing my progress. Therefore, she asked me to bring her some water from the well. Accordingly, after my bath I drew up a vase of this marvelous water, and no sooner did we sprinkle the statue than my father became a man again. The queen threw herself at his feet to ask pardon for having troubled his repose. He raised her and after embracing her tenderly, he readily forgave her and she introduced me to him.

"I'm ashamed to tell you that he was both delighted and surprised. For how can you believe me, beautiful princess, when I am the most hideous of crayfish?" the voice said hesitatingly.

"Alas! I don't have any trouble believing you," replied the one to whom she spoke. "I too might boast of having been beautiful, but how is it possible to appear so in these frightful shells? Please continue, for I'm eager to hear the rest of your story."

"Very well, then," said the other voice:

The king was enchanted with me and gave me numerous caresses. Then he asked the queen if she had any news to tell him. "Alas!" she said. "Who in this desolate spot could come and tell me any? Besides, since I've been solely occupied in lamenting your transformation, I've taken little interest in the world, which means nothing to me without you."

"Well," the king said, "I'll tell *you* some news then, for don't think that I've always been asleep. The fairies who are protecting us have disclosed to me the punishment of my subjects. They've made an immense lake out of my kingdom, and all the inhabitants are men-fish. A nephew of the fairy Marmotte whom they have set up as their king persecutes them with unparalleled cruelty: he devours them for the least fault. At the end of a certain time a prince will arrive who'll dethrone him and reign in his stead. It's in this kingdom that Camion will attain perfect happiness. This is all I know, and it wasn't a bad way of spending my time, given the fact that I was able to discover these things," he said laughing. "The fairies came every night to inform me of what was going on, and I would have perhaps learned much more if you had let me remain a statue a little longer. However, I'm so delighted to see you once more that I don't think I'll want to become a statue again very soon."

We spent some time in the happiest manner possible. Nevertheless the king and queen were rather anxious as I approached the age of thirteen. Whenever the queen bathed me, she took great care to ensure the prediction would not be fulfilled. But who can boast of escaping her destiny? One morning, when my mother had risen early and was gathering some flowers to decorate our cottage—my father was fond of them—she saw an ugly animal, a marmot, come out from beneath a tuberose. This beast threw itself on her and bit her nose. She fainted from the pain of the bite, and when my father did not see her return at the end of an hour, he went looking for her. You can imagine how upset he was at finding her covered with blood and nearly dead! He uttered fearful cries and I ran to his aid. Together we carried the queen into the house and put her to bed, where it took more than two hours for her to revive. At last she began to give some signs of life, and we had the pleasure of seeing her recover from all but the pain of the bite, which caused her a good deal of suffering.

Right away she asked, "Did Camion go bathing?" We had quite forgotten it, though, in our anxiety about her. She was very alarmed at hearing this. However, on seeing that nothing had happened to me as yet, she became reassured.

The day passed without any other trouble. The king had taken out his gun and went searching all over for the horrid beast without being able to find it. The next day at sunrise the queen awoke and came to fetch me to make up for the fault of the preceding morning. She lowered me into the well as usual, but alas, it was our unlucky day! Although the heavens were quite serene, all at once a dreadful clap of thunder pierced the air. Suddenly the sky was on fire, and a flaming dart soared from a burning cloud and flew into the well. In her fright my mother let go of the cord holding me, and I sank to the bottom. Although I was not hurt, you can imagine how horrified I was at discovering that I had been partially transformed into an enormous whale. I bobbed to the surface again and called the queen with all my might. She did not reply, and I wept bitterly as much for her loss as for my transformation. Then I felt an invisible power forcing me to descend to the bottom of the well. Upon reaching it I entered a crystal grotto where I found a kind of nymph. She was quite ugly, resembling an immensely fat frog. However, she smiled at my approach and said to me, "Camion, I'm the Nymph of the Bottomless

Well. I have orders to welcome you and to make you undergo the penance to which you've been sentenced for having failed to bathe. Follow me, and don't try to object."

"Alas, what could I do? I was so distressed and so faint at finding myself on dry ground that I didn't have the strength to speak. She dragged me, not painlessly, into a salon of green marble adjoining the grotto. There she put me into an immense golden tub filled with water, and I began to recover my senses. The good nymph appeared delighted at this. "I'm called Citronette," she said. "I've been appointed to wait on you, so you can order me to do anything you want. I know the past and the present perfectly, but I cannot determine the future. Command me, and at least I can make the time of your penance less annoying to you."

I embraced the good Citronette after she said these words and told her about my past. Then I inquired about the fate of the king and queen. She was about to reply when a hideous marmot as large as a human being entered the salon. I was petrified with horror. She walked on her hind legs and leaned on a gold wand, giving her a dignified air. She approached the tub—in which I would gladly have drowned myself because I was so frightened—and she raised her wand to touch me. "Camion," she said, "you're in my power, and nothing can release you except your obedience and that of the husband whom my sisters have destined for you. Listen to me, and set aside your fear. It doesn't befit a person of your rank.

"Ever since your childhood I have wanted to care for you and marry you to my nephew, the King of the Whiting. Lumineuse and two or three of my other sisters combined to deprive me of this right. I was provoked, and, not being able to revenge myself on them, I decided to punish you for their audacity. Therefore, I condemned you to become a whale for at least half the term of your existence. My sisters protested so strongly against what they called my injustice that I reduced my term by over three-quarters, but I reserved the right of marrying you to my nephew in return for my compliance. Lumineuse, who's imperious and unfortunately my superior, would not listen to this arrangement. She had predestined you to a prince whom she protected. I was then compelled to consent to her plan in spite of my resentment.

All that I could obtain was that the first person to rescue you from my claws would become your husband. Here are their portraits," she continued, showing me two gold miniature cases, "which will enable you to recognize them. But if one of them comes to rescue you, he must become your fiancé when you're in the tub, and he must tear off the whale skin before you can leave it. If he doesn't, you'll remain a fish forever. My nephew wouldn't hesitate a moment to carry out this order, but Lumineuse's favorite will consider it a horrible task because he has the air of a delicate gentleman. So you'd better put your mind to work and think up a way to make him skin you. After that you'll no longer be unhappy, if you can call it unhappiness to be a beautiful, fat, and well-fed whale up to your neck in water."

I did not reply, dejected as much by my present state as the thought of the flaying to which I had to submit myself. Marmotte disappeared and left me with the two miniature cases. I was weeping over my misfortunes without dreaming of looking at the portraits when sympathetic Citronette said, "Come, we musn't lament over catastrophes that can't be remedied. Let's see if I can't help console you. But first, try not to weep so much, for I have a tender heart and can't see your tears without feeling inclined to mix mine with them. Let's chase them away by looking at these portraits."

Upon saying this, she opened the first case and showed it to me. We both shrieked like Melusine at seeing a hideous whiting's head. True, it was painted to give all the advantages that could be given, yet in spite of that, nothing so ugly has ever been seen in the memory of humankind. "Take it away," I cried. "I can't bear the sight of it any longer. I'd rather be a whale all my life than marry that horrible whiting!"

She didn't give me time to finish heaping abuse on this monster, but exclaimed, "Look at this darling young man! Oh, as far as he's concerned, if he were to skin you, I'd be delighted."

I looked quickly to see if what she said was true, and I was soon quite convinced. A noble, charming expression, with fine eyes full of tenderness, adorned a face both mild and majestic. An air of intelligence permeated this fascinating and delightful portrait. A profusion of black hair with natural curls gave him a look that

Citronette mistook for indifference, but which I interpreted, and I think rightly so, as conveying precisely the opposite sentiment.

I gazed at this handsome face without being aware of how much pleasure I was having. Citronette noticed it first. "'Without a doubt," she cried, "that's the one we'll choose."

This banter roused me from my reverie, and blushing at my ecstasy, I said, "Why should I trouble myself? Ah, my dear Citronette, this appears to me very much like another one of cruel Marmotte's tricks. She's made full use of her art to compel me to long for some similar living being who's impossible to find."

"What?" Citronette commented. "You're already having such tender thoughts about this portrait? Ah, truly, I didn't expect that so soon." I blushed again at this jest and became quite embarrassed at finding that I had too innocently betrayed the effect this beautiful painting had produced on my heart. Citronette again read my thoughts. "No, no," she said, embracing me. "Don't repent of your feelings. Your frankness charms me, and to console you, I'll tell you that Marmotte is not deceiving you. There really is a prince who's the original of the portrait."

This assurance filled me with joy momentarily, but the next instant that feeling departed when I remembered that this prince would never see me. I was in the depths of the earth, and Marmotte would prefer to allow her monster of a nephew to penetrate my abode than give the least assistance to a prince she hated. Hadn't her sisters destined him for me without her consent? I no longer concealed what I thought from Citronette. Indeed, the attempt would have been useless because she read my deepest secrets with surprising ease. Therefore, I decided it would be better to be candid. Moreover, she deserved my trust since she was so attached to me. Naturally, I found it a great consolation because I've felt from that time on, one can have a lot of happiness in being able to talk to someone when one's heart is consumed by one object. In fact, this is when I began to fall in love, and Citronette helped clear up the confusion that the beginning of passion produces in the mind. Clever and clear-sighted, she soothed my grief by allowing me to talk about it, and when I had exhausted words, she gently changed the subject to something that almost always, however, touched on my troubles or my affection.

She informed me that the king, my father, had been transported to the abode of the King of the Whiting and that the
queen had become a crayfish the very moment she lost me. I
could not understand this and maintained, "One cannot just
become a crayfish."

"Well," she responded, "can you explain how you've become
a whale any better?"

She was right, of course. We are often surprised by things
that happen to others, even though we don't notice when we go
through even more astonishing things ourselves. I simply lacked
experience to grasp this. Citronette laughed frequently at my
innocence and was surprised to find me so eloquent in my affection, for truly I was spellbinding on that subject. And I found that
love makes the mind more active. I could not sleep and woke the
good-natured Citronette a hundred times during the night to talk
to her about my prince. She had told me his name, that he hunted
almost every day in the forest, and it was beneath this forest that
I was interred. She proposed that we try to attract him to our
dwelling, but I would not consent, although I was dying to do so.
I was afraid he would die for want of air. It was different for us
since we were accustomed to it. I was also afraid that I would be
taking too great a liberty. Besides, I was upset that I would have
to appear to him in the form of a whale, and I judged that his
aversion for me would equal that which the King of the Whiting's
portrait had aroused within me. Citronette reassured me, saying
that despite the whale's body, my face was charming. I believed it
sometimes, but more often I was uneasy, and after having looked
at myself, I could not imagine I was sufficiently beautiful to
inspire love in a man who had made me so well acquainted with
it. My self-love came to the aid of my prudence. Alas, how rarely
are our virtues traced to purer inspirations!

I spent my time by devising ways that I could catch sight of
him and make him see me. Each one that occurred to me I
rejected, one after the other. Citronette was a great help to me
at this time, for she had plenty of sense and even more gentleness and amiability. One day, when I was even sadder than
usual—for love has the peculiar property of infecting gentle
souls with melancholy—I saw the frightful Marmotte enter

with two persons whom I did not recognize at first. I imagined she had brought her wretched nephew with her, and I uttered frightful shrieks as they approached. "Why, she couldn't cry louder if they were skinning her!" the horrid Marmotte exclaimed. "Look what terrible harm's been done to her!"

"Good gracious, sister," said one of the persons accompanying her and whom I then remembered with joy as having seen previously in our village. "Let's set a truce to your stories of skinning, and let's tell Camion what we've come to tell her."

"Gladly," Marmotte said, "but on the conditions agreed upon."

"Camion," the good fairy said, without replying to Marmotte, "we've become too upset by your plight not to think of a remedy, particularly since you've not deserved your fate. My sisters and I have decided to ameliorate it as much as we can. Therefore, this is what we've decided to do. You're about to be presented at the court of the prince to whom I've destined you from birth. But, my dear child, you won't appear there as you are. You're to return three nights a week and to plunge back into your tub. Until you're married—"

"And skinned!" interrupted the odious Marmotte, laughing violently.

The good fairy merely turned toward her, shrugged her shoulders, and continued, "Until you're married, you'll be a whale in this place. We can tell you no more. You'll be informed of the rest by degrees, but above all keep your secret. If a word of this is revealed, neither I nor my sisters can do anything for you, and you'll be at the mercy of my sister Marmotte."

"That's what I hope," the wicked fairy said, "and I daresay I already see her in my power. A secret kept by a girl would be a miracle."

"That's her own affair," Lumineuse said, for it was she who had already spoken. "To proceed, my daughter," she said, "you'll become a little doll made of ivory, but you'll be capable of thinking and speaking, and we'll preserve all your features. I'll give you a week to consider whether my proposal suits you. Then we'll return, and you can tell me if you agree to it, or if you'd prefer one of the two husbands chosen for you."

I had no time to reply. The fairies departed after these words, leaving me astounded by what I had just seen and heard. I remained with Citronette, who believed that it was a great treat for me to become an ivory doll. I sighed when I thought that my prince would never take a fancy to such a bauble, but at last the desire to become acquainted with him overcame my anxiety to please him, and I decided to accept. In fact, I was quite eager because Zirphil (they had mentioned his name) might possibly be forestalled by the King of the Whiting, and this idea made me nearly die of grief.

Citronette told me that Prince Zirphil hunted daily in the forest above, and I made her take the form of a stag, hound, or wild boar every day so that she might bring me some news of him who occupied my heart. She described him to me as a hundred times more handsome than his picture, and my imagination embellished him to such a degree that I decided to see him or die.

One day before the expected arrival of the fairies, Citronette was roaming the forest in the form of a wild boar to find food for my curiosity when suddenly I saw her return, followed by the too charming Zirphil. I can't describe my joy and astonishment. What enchanted me most, though, was that this charming prince appeared equally delighted with me. Perhaps I desired this too much not to help deceiving myself. However, I thought I saw a look in his eyes that he knew the impression he had made. Citronette was more worried about my happiness than about our ecstasy. She aroused us by begging him either to skin or to marry me. Then I came to my senses and felt the danger of my situation. I joined in her entreaties and, thanks to our tears and pleas, we induced him to pledge himself to me. No sooner did I accept him than he vanished. I don't know how, but I found myself in my ordinary form, lying on a good bed. I was no longer a whale, but I was still in the depths of the earth in the green salon, and Citronette had lost the power of leaving it and of transforming herself.

I expected the fairies to be infuriated. My love had increased since I had become personally acquainted with the object of my desire, and I feared that my charming husband might be included in the vengeance of the fairies for not having waited until they could witness my marriage. Citronette had all she could do to reassure me, for I could not overcome my apprehension. At dawn

Marmotte appeared, but I saw neither Lumineuse nor her companion. Not seeming more irritable than usual, Marmotte touched me with her wand without a word, and I became a charming little doll, which she put in her toothpick case. Then she went to the queen-mother of my husband and gave me to her with orders to wed me to her son or to expect all the evil she could inflict. Moreover, she told her that I was her goddaughter and was called Princess Camion. In truth, I took a great fancy to my mother-in-law. I considered her charming since she was the mother of my adorable Zirphil, and my caresses were returned. Every night I was transported into the green salon and enjoyed the pleasure of meeting my husband, for the same power controlled him and transported him likewise into the subterraneous dwelling. I did not know why they forbade me to tell him my secret since I was married, but I kept it in spite of my great desire to tell him.

"You'll see," the speaker continued with a sigh, "how impossible it is to avoid one's fate. But it's beginning to get light, and I'm quite weary from being out of the water so long. Let's return to the reservoir, and tomorrow, if we're not selected for the soup of that worthless king, we'll resume the thread of our conversation at the same hour.—Come, let's go.'

Zirphil did not hear any more and returned to his apartment, quite concerned at not having given some indication to his princess that he was so near. Yet the fear of increasing her misfortunes by such an indiscretion consoled him. The misery of knowing she was likely to perish by his hand made him determined to continue his diligent search among the crayfish.

He went to bed but not to sleep, for he did not close his eyes all night. To have found his princess in the form of a crayfish, ready to be made into soup for the King of the Whiting, seemed a torture more frightful than even death itself. He believed that this had been her fate and was becoming terribly upset when he heard a great noise in the garden. At first he heard a jumbled sound, but after listening attentively, he distinguished flutes and conch shells. He rose and went to the window, from which he saw the King of the Whiting, accompanied by the dozen sharks who composed his council, advancing toward the pavilion. He rushed to open the door, and after the retinue entered, the king had his tub filled with sea water by the peers of the realm who had been carrying it. After a short repose he made the council take their places and addressed the young prince. "Whoever you may be," he said, "you've apparently decided to make me die of hunger because you've been sending me a broth everyday that I can't swallow. However, I must tell you, young man, that if you are in league with evil powers to poison me, you're on the wrong side. As nephew of the fairy Marmotte, nothing can harm me."

The prince was astonished at being suspected of such a base act and was about to make a proud reply. As he raised his hand, however, he happened to gaze at his ring and saw Lumineuse, who placed her finger to her lips to warn him to be silent. (He had not thought of consulting his ring before this because he had been so overwhelmed by his grief.) Accordingly, he held his tongue, but he betrayed his indignation by his expression, which the sharks noticed because they made signs that appeared to say that they agreed with him.

"Ho, ho!" the king said. "Since this myrmidon appears so angry, we must make him work in front of us. Let them go to my kitchen. Let them bring the mortar for the crayfish. I'll give my council a treat."

A pike-head began carrying out the king's commands at once. At the same time the twelve sharks took a large net, threw it from the window into the reservoir, and drew in three or four thousand crayfish. While the council fished and the pike-head fetched the king's mortar, Zirphil contemplated the situation. "The most crucial moment of my life is approaching. My happiness or misery will depend on what I do right now." He armed himself with resolve for whatever might happen, placing all his hopes in the fairy Lumineuse. He implored her, "Take my side," and at the same time he looked at his ring and saw the beautiful fairy, who made a sign to him to pound courageously. This signal revitalized him and relieved him of some of the pain he felt in consenting to such a cruel act.

At last the horrid mortar was produced. Zirphil approached it boldly, prepared to obey the king. The council ceremoniously put in the crayfish, and the prince tried to pound them.

Yet the same thing that had happened to the ones in the kitchen happened to them as well—the bottom of the mortar opened and flames devoured them. The king and his odious sharks amused themselves for a long time with this spectacle, never tiring of refilling the mortar. Finally, a single crayfish was left of the four thousand, one surprisingly large and fine. The king commanded it to be shelled so he could see if he would like to eat it raw. They gave it to Zirphil to shell, and he trembled all over at having to inflict this new torture. His trembling became even worse when this poor fish joined her two claws and said with eyes filled with tears, "Alas, Zirphil, what have I done to you to make you want to harm me so much?"

The prince was moved by these words, and his heart, pierced with grief. He looked at her sadly and at length took it upon himself to beg the king to allow her to be pounded. Ever covetous of his authority, the king was firm in his resolution. Indeed, he was enraged by this humble request and threatened to pound Zirphil himself if he did not shell it. The poor prince quivered as he touched the crayfish with a knife they supplied him. Again he looked at his ring and saw Lumineuse laughing and talking to a veiled person she held by the hand. He was baffled by this, and the king gave him no time to reflect. He cried out to him loudly to finish. The prince stuck the knife with such force under the shell of the crayfish that it cried piteously. He turned his eyes away from hers, unable to help shedding tears. Finally he resumed his task, but to his great astonishment, as he was about to finish the shelling, he found the wicked Marmotte in his hands. She jumped to the ground and uttered shrieks of mocking laughter. They were so loud and unpleasant that they prevented him from fainting; otherwise he would have slumped to the floor.

The king cried in surprise, "Why, it's my aunt!"

"Yes, it's no one but me," this annoying beast said. "But, my dear Whiting, I've come to tell you a terrible piece of news." Whiting grew pale at these words, and the council assumed an air of satisfaction that increased the bad mood of the king and his terrible aunt. "The fact is, my darling," Marmotte continued, "you must return to your watery dominions because this rash young man before you has chosen to display a constancy that nothing can shake. He's triumphed despite all the traps I set to prevent him from carrying off the princess I had destined for you."

Upon hearing these words, the King of the Whiting fell into such a rage that he could not contain himself. He flailed about and showed his violent temper. Despite Marmotte's attempts to calm him, he broke his bowl into a thousand pieces, and since he was on dry ground, he fainted. Mad with rage, Marmotte turned to Zirphil, who had remained a silent spectator during this tragic scene. "You've triumphed, Zirphil," she said, "thanks to the power of a fairy whom I must obey. But your troubles haven't ended yet. You won't be happy until you give me the case that contained the cursed Camion. Even Lumineuse has agreed to this, and I've obtained her consent to make you suffer until that time." After saying this she took the King of the Whiting on her shoulders and threw him into the reservoir along with the sharks, the palace, and all its inhabitants.

Zirphil found himself alone at the foot of a great mountain, in a country as arid as a desert. There was nothing to be seen— not a single house or even the large reservoir. Everything had vanished all at once. The prince was more upset than astonished by such an extraordinary event: he was accustomed to wonders but the continued persecution of the fairy Marmotte caused him to grieve.

"I'm sure that I've pounded my princess," he said. "Yes, I must have pounded her. Yet I'm none the happier for it. Ah, barbarous Marmotte! And you, Lumineuse, you've left me helpless even after I obeyed you at the expense of all that a heart as sensitive as mine could suffer!"

Grief and his scant rest of the night before threw him into such a state of weakness that he would have collapsed altogether if he had not summoned the courage to survive. "If I could only find some nourishment," he said. "However, I'm sure I can't find a single fruit in this horrible desert that can refresh me." No sooner had he uttered these words than his ring opened, and a tiny table covered with excellent viands emerged from it. Within seconds it grew large enough to accommodate him, and on it he found everything that could tempt his eyes and his appetite, for the repast was so beautifully arranged and the wine so delicious that nothing was lacking. He gave thanks to Lumineuse, for who else could have helped him so opportunely? He ate, drank, and felt his strength return.

After he had finished, the table shrank back into the ring. Since it was late, he did not make much progress in climbing the mountain, but stretched himself out under a wretched tree that had hardly enough leaves to protect him from the dew. "Alas!" he said as he lay down. "Such is the nature of man. He forgets the good that is past and concerns himself only with the evil in the present. Right now I'd gladly exchange that table for a couch a little less hard than this."

A moment later he felt himself lying in a comfortable bed, though he could see nothing because the darkness had seemingly increased. He ascertained that this was caused by large curtains surrounding his bed and protecting him from the cold and dew. After thanking the attentive Lumineuse again, he dropped off to sleep. At daybreak he awoke and found himself in a bed walled by curtains of yellow taffeta and silver. This bed had been placed in the middle of a satin tent of the same color, embroidered all over with bright silver letters forming Zirphil's name, and all of these supported by whales outlined by rubies. Everything that one could possibly need was to be found in this beautiful tent. If the prince had been in a more tranquil state of mind, he would have admired this elegant habitation, but he only glanced at the whales, dressed himself, and went out of the tent, which folded itself up and returned to the ring from which it had emerged.

He began to climb the mountain, no longer going to the trouble of looking for food or lodging because he was certain to have both as soon as he wished for them. His only worry was how to find Lumineuse, for his ring was mute on that subject, and he found himself in a country so unfamiliar and deserted that he was compelled to trust to chance.

After having spent several days in climbing without discovering anything, he arrived at the brink of a well that was cut into the rock. Seating himself beside it to rest, he began to exclaim as usual: "Lumineuse, why can't I find you?"

When he finished uttering these words, he heard a voice coming from the well: "Is it Zirphil who's speaking to me?"

His joy at hearing the voice was increased when he recognized whose it was. He rushed to the brink of the well and said, "Yes, it's Zirphil. And aren't you Citronette?"

"Yes," Citronette replied, emerging from the well and embracing the prince.

It is impossible to relate what pleasure Zirphil felt in seeing Citronette again. He overwhelmed the nymph with questions about the princess and herself. Finally, after the excitement of their initial encounter had subsided, they spoke more soberly with each other.

"I'm going to tell you everything you don't know," she said. "Ever since you pounded us, we've been enjoying a happiness lessened only by your absence. I've been awaiting your arrival here in behalf of the fairy Lumineuse to tell you what you still have to do in order to possess a princess who loves you as much as you love her. But since some time must elapse before you can attain this happiness, I'll tell you the rest of the marvelous story about your charming bride."

Zirphil kissed Citronette's hand a thousand times and followed her into her grotto, where he thought he would die of intermixed pleasure and woe, for in this spot had he seen his divine princess for the first time. After sharing a meal that sprang from the ring, he begged the good Citronette kindly to resume the narrative from the point that the princess had left off in the palace garden.

Since this is the spot where Lumineuse is to meet you, you'll learn all you want while waiting for her—you realize it's useless for you to run after her. She's entrusted you to my care, and a lover is less impatient when one talks to him about the lady he loves.

The fairy Marmotte knew about your marriage, and she had transformed our friend into an ivory doll, believing that you would be disgusted by her. Lumineuse conducted this affair herself, knowing that nothing could deprive you of the princess if you destroyed her enchantment by either marrying or skinning her. You chose the former alternative, and you know what followed. By night she resumed her natural form and lamented spending all her days in your royal mother's pocket, for Marmotte had been permitted by Lumineuse to torment the princess until you had fulfilled your destiny, which was to skin her. Marmotte was enraged at finding that you had married her before the King of the Whiting, her nephew.

Since the princess was no longer a whale, there was no fish to skin, but Marmotte, who kept creating new obstacles, was to make you pound her and had forbidden the princess to tell you anything about it at the cost of your life. Moreover, Marmotte promised her she would later enjoy the greatest happiness. "How will he ever make up his mind to pound me?" she asked while waiting for you. "Ah, my dear Citronette, if it were only my life that Marmotte threatened, I'd give it cheerfully to protect my husband from the tortures they've prepared for him. But they're also after his life—that life which is so dear to me. Ah, Marmotte! Babarous Marmotte! How can you find pleasure in making me so miserable when I've never given you any reason to harm me?" She knew the period prescribed for your separation from her, but she did not dare tell you. You know the last time that you saw her that you found her in tears, and you asked her why. She pretended to accuse you of inconstancy because of your attentions to little Camion. You appeased her supposed jealousy, and the fatal hour for Marmotte to fetch her arrived. You were transported to the palace of your father while the princess and I were changed into crayfish and placed into a little cane basket, which the fairy put under her arm. After getting into a chariot drawn by two adders, we arrived at the palace of the King of the Whiting. This palace had belonged to the princess's father, but the city had been changed into a lake and formed the reservoir that we inhabited. By the way, all the men-fish that you've seen had once been the wicked subjects of that good king.

I must tell you, my lord, that the unfortunate monarch and his wife were in despair the moment the princess sank to the bottom of the well. The fairies who had formerly come to their aid appeared and consoled them for their loss, but the unhappy couple knew that Camion was to be exiled to their kingdom and chose to be with her rather than far away in spite of what they had to fear from the cruelty and ferociousness of the King of the Whiting. The fairies did not conceal the princess's future fate from them, and her father asked to be cook of the kitchen and keeper of the King of the Whiting's mortar. The fairy immediately tapped her wand, and he became the pike-headed man you saw in that position. So you need no longer be surprised at his having wept bitterly whenever you brought the crayfish to pound. Since he knew that his daughter had to undergo this torture, he always thought she might be among them. The wretched monarch did not have a moment's rest because his daughter had no means of making herself known to him. What's more, the queen had requested to be changed into a crayfish in order to be with the princess.

As soon as we arrived at the palace, the fairy presented us to him and ordered him to have crayfish soup made for his dinner every day. We were then thrown into the reservoir. My first concern was to search for the queen in order to soothe the grief of the princess a little. But either by decree of fate or stupidity on my part, I found it impossible to discover her. We spent our days in this mournful search, and our most pleasant moments were those in which we recalled our past. Finally you arrived and they presented us to you, but the fairy had forbidden us to make ourselves known until you interrogated us, and we didn't dare to break this rule because we were severely punished for the most trivial offenses.

The princess told me she thought she was going to die of fright when she observed you talking with the cruel Marmotte. We saw you impatiently searching among our companions, and it was obvious you had little chance of reaching us by the direction you took. We knew we had to be pounded, but we also learned that we would be restored to our former condition immediately after and that the wicked Marmotte would have no further power over us. On the same day you were to begin inflicting this torture on us, we were all gathered in the reservoir weeping over our destiny when Lumineuse appeared. "Don't weep, my children," that remarkable fairy said. "I've come to inform you that you'll escape the punishment with which they've threatened you, provided you go cheerfully to the mortar and don't answer any questions addressed to you. I can say no more at present—I'm in a hurry, but do as I've told you and you won't regret it. The young princess whose fate appears to be the cruelest is not to lose hope—she'll soon find relief."

We all thanked the fairy and appeared before you fully determined to keep our secret. You spoke to some, who gave you only vague replies, and after you had chosen ten, we returned to the reservoir, where the assurance of our imminent rescue invigorated us with a natural gaiety.

Lumineuse's last words relieved the beautiful Camion's heart, and that made her charming in her mother's eyes and mine, and we three were inseparable. Eventually your choice fell on me and the queen, and we had no time to say adieu to the princess. An unknown power acted on us at the moment and caused us to become so cheerful that we thought we'd die of laughter at the absurd things we said to each other. You carried us to the kitchen, and no sooner did we touch the bottom of the fatal mortar than Lumineuse herself came to our aid and restored me to my natural form and transported me to my usual abode. I also had the consolation of seeing the queen and our companions resume their forms, but I don't know what happened to them. The fairy embraced me and told me to wait for you and reveal everything when you came searching for the princess.

"I've awaited this moment with impatience, as you can well believe, my lord," Citronette said to the prince, who had been listening most eagerly to her. "Yesterday I was just about to sit at the mouth of the well when Lumineuse appeared and said, 'Our children are about to be made happy, my dear Citronette. Zirphil has only to retrieve Marmotte's toothpick case to fulfill his tasks since he's finally skinned the princess.' 'Ah, great queen!' I cried. 'Are you sure of this? Have we really been so fortunate?' 'Yes,' she replied. 'It's quite true. He thought he had only skinned Marmotte, but in reality it was the princess. Marmotte was concealed in the handle of the knife that he used, and the instant he had finished his task, she caused the princess to vanish and appeared in her place in order to intimidate him again!'"

"What!" cried the prince. "I actually harmed my charming

bride? Was I so cruel? Did I torture her? Ah, heavens! She'll never pardon me. I don't deserve her pardon!" The unhappy Zirphil spoke so impetuously and upset himself so much that poor Citronette was sorry she had told him this news.

"What's that?" she said, seeing that he was quite overcome. "You didn't know it?"

"No, I didn't know that," he said. "What made me take the shell off that unfortunate and charming crayfish was the sight of Lumineuse in my ring speaking to a veiled person. She even laughed with her, and I imagined it was my princess. I thought that she had passed through the mortar like the rest. Ah, I'll never forgive myself for this mistake!"

"But, my lord," Citronette said, "the charm depended on your skinning or pounding her, and you hadn't done either. The person to whom Lumineuse spoke was the princess's mother. They were waiting for the end of your adventure in order to seize your bride and protect her for you. It was quite necessary for it to happen that way."

"Nevertheless," the prince said, "if I had known it, I'd rather have pierced my own heart with that horrid knife!"

"But consider," Citronette said, "that in piercing your heart, you'd have left the princess eternally in the power of your frightful rival. It is far better to have shelled her than to have died and left her in misery."

This argument obviously placated the prince, and he consented to some nourishment to maintain his strength. They had just finished when the roof of the salon opened and Lumineuse appeared, seated on a carbuncle drawn by a hundred butterflies. She descended from the carbuncle, assisted by the prince, who drenched the hem of her garment with a flood of tears. The fairy raised him, saying, "Prince Zirphil, today you're to reap the fruit of your heroic endeavors. Console yourself, for you shall finally enjoy happiness. I've vanquished Marmotte's fury by my pleas, and your courage has disarmed her. Come with me to receive your princess from her hands and mine."

"Ah, madam," the prince cried, throwing himself at her feet, "am I dreaming? Can it be that happiness is at last mine?"

"You can rest assured," the fairy said. "Come to your

kingdom and console the queen, your mother, for your absence and the death of the king, your father. Your subjects are waiting to crown you."

In the midst of his joy the prince felt a bitter pang on hearing about his father's death, but the fairy distracted him from his distress by seating himself beside her. Citronette she permitted to seat herself at their feet. Then the butterflies spread their radiant wings and set out for King Zirphil's empire.

On the way the fairy told him to open his ring, and he found the toothpick case he had to return to Marmotte. The king thanked the generous fairy a thousand times over, and they arrived at the capital of his dominions, where they were awaited with the utmost impatience. Zirphil's mother advanced to greet the fairy as she got out of her chariot, and all the people, who knew about Zirphil's return, shouted and acclaimed him. Such a reception relieved him somewhat of his grief, and he tenderly embraced his mother. Then they all went up to a magnificent apartment that the queen had prepared for the fairy.

No sooner did they enter than Marmotte arrived in a chariot lined with Spanish leather and drawn by eight winged rats. She brought with her the beautiful Camion as well as her father and mother. Lumineuse and the queen hastened to embrace Marmotte while Zirphil respectfully kissed her paw, which she laughingly extended to him. Thereupon he returned the toothpick case to her, and she permitted him to claim his bride and present her to the queen, who embraced her with a thousand expressions of joy.

The large, illustrious group of people began speaking all at once, and joy reigned supreme. Camion and her charming husband were the only ones unable to say a word, for they had too much on their minds. There was, however, an eloquence in their silence that affected everyone present. The good Citronette wept with happiness while kissing the hands of the divine princess.

At last Lumineuse took them both by the hand and advanced with them toward Zirphil's mother. "Behold, madam," she said. "Two young lovers who only await your consent to become happy. Do complete their happiness. My sister Marmotte, the king and queen here present, and I myself, all request that you do so."

The queen tenderly embraced the happy couple. "Yes, my children," she replied courteously, "live happily together, and permit me to participate in that happiness as I relinquish my crown to you."

Zirphil and the princess threw themselves at her feet, and she raised them and embraced them again. They implored her not to abandon them, but to help them by giving them her advice.

Then Marmotte touched the beautiful Camion with her wand: her clothes, already magnificent, became silver brocade embroidered with carat diamonds, and her beautiful locks fell down and rearranged themselves so exquisitely that the kings and queens declared that her appearance was perfectly dazzling. The toothpick case the fairy held was changed into a crown formed entirely from beautiful diamonds so well set that the whole palace became illuminated by it. Marmotte placed it on the head of the princess, and Zirphil in turn appeared in a suit similar to that of Camion's. Lastly, the ring that she had given him produced a crown exactly like hers.

They were married on the spot and proclaimed king and queen of that fine country. The fairies gave the royal wedding breakfast, and nothing was lacking. After spending a week overwhelming them with good things, they departed and conducted the king and queen, Camion's father and mother, back to their kingdom, where they had punished the old inhabitants and repopulated it with new people faithful to their master. As for Citronette, the fairies permitted her to come and spend some time with her beautiful queen, and they allowed Camion to see her whenever she pleased just by wishing for her.

At last the fairies departed, and never has the world seen two people so happy as King Zirphil and Queen Camion. Their greatest happiness they found in each other, and days seemed to them like moments. Having children completed their bliss, and they lived to an extreme old age loving and continually striving to please each other with the same ardor. When they died, their kingdom was divided, and after various changes it has come under the rule of one of their descendants and become the flourishing empire of the Great Mogul.

MARIE-CATHERINE D'AULNOY

BEAUTY WITH THE
GOLDEN HAIR

ONCE upon a time there was a princess who was more beautiful than anyone in the world, and she was called Beauty with the Golden Hair because her locks were radiant like the finest gold and fell in ringlets to her feet. She always appeared with her hair flowing, in curls and crowned with flowers, and her dresses were embroidered with diamonds and pearls. It was impossible to look upon her without adoring her.

Now, among her neighbors was a young king who was rich, handsome, and unmarried. When he heard about Beauty with the Golden Hair—though he had never seen her—he fell so deeply in love with her that he could neither eat nor drink. Therefore, he decided to send an ambassador to ask her hand in marriage. He had a magnificent coach made for this envoy, gave him upward of a hundred horses and as many servants, and charged him specifically not to return without the princess. From the moment the ambassador took his leave, the entire court talked of nothing else, and the king, who never doubted that Beauty with the Golden Hair would consent to his proposal, immediately ordered fine dresses and splendid furniture to be prepared for her.

While the craftsmen were hard at work, the ambassador arrived at Beauty's court and delivered his brief message. However, she was either out of temper that day or found the proposal displeasing, for she told the ambassador that she was grateful to the king, but she had no inclination to marry. The ambassador left the princess's court, despondent at not being able to bring her with him. He carried back all the king's presents he had brought, for the prudent beauty was perfectly aware that young ladies should never accept gifts from bachelors. So she had refused beautiful diamonds and other valuable articles, retaining only a quarter pound of English pins so as not to affront the king.

When the ambassador reached the king's capital, where he was so impatiently awaited, everybody was disturbed that he had not brought back Beauty with the Golden Hair. The king began to cry like a babe. They endeavored to console him, but without the least success.

At the king's court resided a young man who cut the finest figure in the kingdom. Indeed, he was as radiant as the sun. Due to his graceful manners and intelligence, he was called Avenant. Everybody loved him except envious colleagues, who were irritated that the king conferred favors upon him and confided to him daily about his affairs. Happening to be in the company of some people who were talking about the return of the ambassador, he told them the man had not done his best. "Why, if the king had sent me to Beauty with the Golden Hair," he said to them carelessly, "I'm certain she would have returned with me."

These mischief makers went directly to the king and said, "Sire, do you know what Avenant's been saying? He claims that if you had sent him to Beauty with the Golden Hair, he would have brought her back with him. See how malicious he is! He asserts he's handsomer than you, and that she would have become so fond of him that she would have followed him anywhere."

Upon hearing this, the king flew into a rage so terrible that he was quite beside himself. "Ha, ha!" he cried, "this petty minion laughs at my misfortune. He thinks he's superior to me. Go! Fling him into the great tower, and let him starve to death!"

The royal guards quickly searched out Avenant, who had quite forgotten what he had said. They dragged him to prison and beat him terribly. The poor youth had only a pittance of straw to lie upon and would have soon perished but for a tiny spring that trickled through the foundations of the tower. Since his mouth was continually parched with thirst, he kept refreshing himself by drinking drops of water from the spring.

One day when he was quite exhausted, he exclaimed with a

heavy sigh, "Why is the king complaining? There's not a subject more loyal than I am. I've never done anything to offend him."

Just then the king happened to pass near the tower, and upon hearing the voice of one he had loved so dearly, he stopped to listen, even though the people who were with him hated Avenant and said, "That doesn't concern you, sire. Don't you know he's a rogue?"

The king replied, "Leave me alone. I want to hear what he has to say."

After listening to Avenant's complaints, tears welled in his eyes. He opened the door of the tower and called to the prisoner. Avenant came, knelt before him with deep humility, and kissed his feet. "What have I done, sire, to have earned such severe treatment?"

"You've boasted that if I had sent you to Beauty with the Golden Hair, you would certainly have brought her back with you."

"It's true, sire," Avenant remarked. "I believe I would have impressed her with your majesty's high qualities in such a persuasive manner she could not have refused you. By saying that, sire, I uttered nothing that was intended to offend you."

The king saw clearly that Avenant was innocent. He cast an angry look at the maligners of his favorite and took him away, sincerely repenting the wrong he had done to him.

After giving Avenant an excellent supper, he called him into his cabinet and said to him, "Avenant, I still love Beauty with the Golden Hair. Her refusal has not discouraged me, but I don't know what step to make to induce her to marry me. I'm tempted to send you to her to see if you might succeed."

Avenant replied that he was ready to obey him completely, and that he could set out the next day.

"Wait," said the king, "I want to give you a splendid equipage."

"It's unnecessary," Avenant answered. "I only need a good horse and letters of recommendation from your majesty."

The king embraced him, for he was delighted to find Avenant prepared to start so quickly.

On that Monday morning Avenant took his leave of the

king and his friends, and proceeded on his mission, quite alone
and without pomp or fanfare. His mind was occupied solely
with schemes to induce the Beauty with the Golden Hair to
marry the king. He had a writing case in his pocket, and when
a good idea occurred to him for his introductory speech, he
dismounted from his steed and seated himself under a tree to
write it down so that he would not forget anything.

One morning he set out at the first peep of day, and while passing through a large meadow, a charming idea came into his head.
He dismounted and seated himself beside some willows and pop-
lars planted along the bank of a little river that bordered the
meadow. After he had noted down his thought, he looked about
him, delighted to find himself in such a beautiful spot. It was then
that he spotted not far from him on the grass a large, gilded carp
gasping and nearly exhausted: in trying to catch some flies, it had
leapt right out of the water. Although it was a fish-day and
Avenant might have carried it off for his dinner, he took pity on
it. Picking it up, he put it gently back into the river. As soon as
this lovely carp felt the freshness of the water, she began to
recover. Down to the very bottom she glided and then rose again
joyously to the bank of the stream. "Avenant," she said, "I thank
you for your kindness. If it weren't for you, I would have died.
You've saved me, and I shall do the same for you."

After this brief salute, she darted down again into the water,
leaving Avenant astonished by her clarity of mind and civility.

As he continued his journey, the next day he saw a crow in
great distress. The poor bird was being pursued by a large
eagle, a great predator of crows. The eagle had nearly caught it
and would have swallowed it like a lentil if Avenant had not
felt compassion for its misfortune. "Just look," he cried, "how
the strong oppress the weak. What right does the eagle have to
eat the crow?" He seized his bow and arrow, which he always
carried with him, and, taking good aim at the eagle, whizz!
sent the shaft right through its body, and it fell dead.

The crow was delighted. Fluttering over to a tree and land-
ing on a branch, it cried to him, "Avenant, you were very kind
to rescue me, I who am only a poor crow. Believe me, I shall
not be ungrateful and shall do as much for you."

Astonished by the crow's intelligence, Avenant resumed his journey. After entering a great wood early in the next morning, when there was scarcely light enough for him to see his way, he heard an owl screeching as though in desperate straits. "Eh, now," he said, "there's an owl in great trouble. It must be caught in some net." He searched all about and at last discovered some large nets that had been spread by fowlers during the night to catch small birds. "What a pity," he said, "that men are only made to torment each other, or to persecute poor animals that do them no mischief." He drew his knife and cut the cords. The owl took flight, but swiftly returned on the wing and cried, "Avenant, it's needless for me to make a long speech. You realize now that I'm beholden to you. Everything's quite clear. The hunters would soon have been here. They would have captured me, and I would now be dead but for your assistance. I have a grateful heart, and I shall do as much for you."

These were the three most important adventures that Avenant experienced during his journey. So eager was he to reach its end that he lost no time in proceeding to the palace of Beauty with the Golden Hair. Everything about it was remarkable. As he looked about, he saw heaps of diamonds, strewn about like pebbles. In addition, there were elegant clothes, candied preserves, and coins—it was the most wonderful sight in the world. Avenant thought in his heart, if he could persuade the princess to leave all this for the king his master, he would be lucky indeed. Dressing in a suit of brocade with a plume of carnations and white feathers, he combed and powdered himself, washed his face, and wrapped a richly embroidered scarf around his neck. Finally he took a little basket containing a beautiful little dog that he had bought as he had passed through Bologna. Avenant was so handsome, so charming, and did everything with so much grace that when he presented himself at the palace gate the guards saluted him most respectfully and ran to inform Beauty with the Golden Hair that Avenant, ambassador from the king, her nearest neighbor, requested an audience with her.

Upon hearing the name of Avenant, the princess said, "That's a good omen. I'll wager he's a handsome fellow and pleases everybody."

"Yes, indeed, madam!" all her maids of honor exclaimed. "We saw him from the loft in which we were trimming your flax, and as long as he remained beneath our windows, we couldn't work."

"Very nice," Beauty with the Golden Hair replied, "amusing yourselves by looking at young men! Here, give me my grand gown of blue embroidered satin and arrange my blonde hair with the utmost of taste. Get me some garlands of fresh flowers, my high-heeled shoes, and my fan. Have the servants sweep my chamber and dust my throne, for I want him to declare everywhere he goes that I'm truly Beauty with the Golden Hair."

All her women rushed about to dress her regally. Such was their hurry that they bumped into one another and scarcely made any progress. At length, however, the princess strolled through her great gallery of mirrors to see if anything was missing. Then she ascended her throne of gold, ivory, and ebony, which emitted a perfume-like balsam, and she commanded her maids of honor to take their instruments and sing very softly so as not to disturb the audience.

Ushered into the hall where all the audiences were held, Avenant was so carried away with astonishment that ever since that time he has frequently commented on how he was scarcely able to speak. Nevertheless, he took courage and delivered his speech to perfection. He begged the princess not to humiliate him by refusing to return with him.

"Gentle Avenant," she replied, "the arguments you have produced are all extremely good, and I assure you I would be very happy to favor you more than anyone, but you must know that about a month ago I was walking by the riverside with my ladies-in-waiting, and when I pulled off my glove to take some refreshment, my ring slipped from my finger and unfortunately fell into the stream. I valued it more than my kingdom, so you can imagine my grief over its loss. I have made a vow never to listen to any offers of marriage if the ambassador representing the prospective husband does not restore to me my ring. Now you see what you have to do in this matter, for even if you were to talk to me for two weeks, night and day, you could never persuade me to change my mind."

Avenant was very much surprised by this answer. He made the princess a low bow and begged her to accept the little dog, the basket, and the scarf. But she replied that she would not accept any presents, and asked him to go and reflect on what she had said. When he returned to his lodgings, he went to bed without eating any supper, and his little dog, whose name was Cabriolle, would take none himself and lay down beside his master. All night long Avenant kept sighing. "How can I hope to find a ring that fell into a great river a month ago?" he said. "It would be folly to attempt looking for it. The princess set this condition only because she knew I could not possibly fulfill it." And then the despondent fellow sighed again.

Cabriolle, who had heard him, said, "My dear master, I beseech you not to despair of your misfortune. You're too likable not to be happy. Let's go to the riverside as soon as it is daylight."

Avenant gave him two little pats without saying a word, and since he was worn out with fretting, he fell asleep. As soon as Cabriolle saw the day break, he frisked about so that he woke Avenant. "Dress yourself, master, and let's go out."

Avenant was quite willing. He arose, dressed, and descended into the garden. From there he strayed automatically toward the river, where he strolled along the banks with his hat pulled over his eyes and his arms folded. He was thinking only of taking his departure when suddenly he heard his name being called: "Avenant! Avenant!" He looked all around and saw no one. He thought he was dreaming and had resumed his walk when again the voice called: "Avenant! Avenant!"

"Who's calling me?" he cried.

Tiny Cabriolle, who was gazing down into the water, replied, "I can't believe my eyes, but I see a golden carp there."

Immediately the carp appeared on the surface and said to Avenant, "You saved my life in the meadow of nettle trees, where I would have perished if it hadn't been for your aid. I promised to do as much for you. Here, dear Avenant, is the ring that belongs to Beauty with the Golden Hair."

Avenant stooped, took the ring out of the carp's mouth, and thanked his friend a thousand times. Instead of returning to his lodgings, he went directly to the palace, followed by little Cabriolle, who was very glad he had induced his master to take a walk by the riverside. The princess was informed that Avenant requested to see her.

"Alas," she said, "the poor boy is coming to take his leave of me. He's convinced that it's impossible to provide me with what I want and is about to return with these tidings to his master."

After Avenant was introduced, he presented her with the ring. "Madam, I've obeyed your commands. Are you willing now to accept the king my master for your husband?"

When she saw her ring in perfect condition, she was so astonished that she thought she was dreaming. "My gracious Avenant, you must be truly favored by some good fairy. Naturally, there's no other way you could have done it."

"Madam" he answered, "I'm not acquainted with any fairy, but I was most desirous of obeying you."

"Since you are so obliging," she continued, "you must do me another service, if I am to marry. Not far from here lives a prince named Galifron, who has gotten it into his head he will make me his wife. He declared his intention to me accompanied by the most terrible threats. For instance, if I refuse him, he will ravage my kingdom. But you be the judge if I should accept him. He's a giant who's taller than a tower, and he eats men like a monkey eats chestnuts. When he ambles about his country, he carries in his pockets small cannons, which he uses for pistols, and when he shouts, those near him become deaf. I sent word to him that I didn't want to marry and that he must excuse me, but he's not stopped persecuting me. He kills all my subjects, and before anything can be done, you must fight him and bring me his head."

Avenant was astounded at this proposition. He pondered it for a few minutes and answered, "Well, madam, I'll fight Galifron. Even though I believe I'll lose, I'll die like a brave man."

The princess was in turn surprised by his determination. She said a thousand things to prevent his undertaking such an adventure, but they were all for naught. He withdrew to seek out weapons and anything else he might require. After he had made his preparations, he placed little Cabriolle in his basket again, mounted a fine horse, and rode toward Galifron's country. Along the way he asked people where Galifron was to be found, and everyone told him he was a demon whom nobody dared approach. The more he heard about him, the more his alarm increased. Cabriolle encouraged him by saying, "My dear master, when you fight him I'll bite his legs. Then as he stoops to get rid of me, you can kill him easily."

Avenant admired the wit of the little dog, but he knew well enough that his help would be of little avail. Finally he arrived in the vicinity of Galifron's castle. All the roads to it were strewn with the bones and bodies of men whom he had eaten or torn to pieces. Avenant did not wait long before he saw the monster coming through a wood. His head was visible above the highest trees, and he sang in a terrible voice:

> "Ho! bring me some babies, fat or lean,
> So I can crush them between my teeth!
> I could eat oh so many, many, many,
> That the world would not be left with any, any!"

Avenant immediately began to sing in the same spirit:

> "Ho! Here comes Avenant on the spot
> To take out your teeth and make them rot.
> I'm not the greatest man you'll ever view,
> But I'm big enough to conquer you!"

The rhymes were not quite adapted to the music, but he made them up in a great hurry, and it is really a miracle they were not much worse because he was terribly frightened. When Galifron heard these words, he looked all around him and caught sight of Avenant, who, sword in hand, uttered several taunts to provoke him. However, they were not necessary, for Galifron was in a dreadful rage. He snatched an iron club and would have crushed the gentle Avenant with one blow if a crow had not landed on his head at that instant and adroitly pecked out both his eyes with its beak. As blood poured down his face, he swung the club all about him like a madman. Avenant avoided his blows and kept thrusting with his sword until the giant fell down bleeding from a thousand wounds. Then Avenant ran his sword up to the hilt into Galifron's heart. Rejoicing in his good fortune, Avenant quickly cut off his head, and the crow, who had perched itself on the nearest tree, said to him, "I didn't forget the service you rendered me in killing the eagle that pursued me. I promised you I would return the favor. I trust I have done so today."

"I owe everything to you, Monsieur Crow," Avenant replied, "and I shall remain your servant."

Immediately Avenant mounted his horse, laden with the horrible head of Galifron. When he reached the city, the people followed him, crying, "Behold the brave Avenant, who has slain the monster!"

When the princess heard the uproar, she so trembled for fear they were coming to announce Avenant's death that she did not dare inquire what had happened. But within minutes she saw Avenant enter carrying the giant's head. The very sight of this filled her with terror, though there was no longer any reason to be alarmed.

"Madam," Avenant said to the princess, "your enemy is dead. I trust you'll no longer refuse the king my master."

"Ah, pardon me," Beauty with the Golden Hair said, "but I still must refuse him, unless you bring me some water from the Gloomy Grotto before my departure. Nearby is a deep cavern that is six miles long. At its mouth are two dragons who prevent anyone from entering: flames spew from their jaws and eyes. Inside the cavern is a deep pit into which you must descend: it is full of toads, adders, and serpents. At the bottom of this pit is a small hole, and the fountain of health and beauty flows through it. It is absolutely crucial that I obtain some of this water. Whatever it washes becomes something marvelous. If people are handsome, they remain so forever; if ugly, they become beautiful; if young, they remain young; if old, they become young again. You may well imagine, Avenant, that I would not leave my kingdom without some of this wonderful water."

"Madam," he replied, "you are so beautiful already that this water will be quite useless to you. But I'm an unfortunate ambassador, whose death you desire. So I shall go now to search for what you desire with the certainty that I'll never return."

Beauty with the Golden Hair remained immovable, and Avenant set out with little Cabriolle to seek the water of beauty in the Gloomy Grotto. Everyone he met on the road exclaimed, "It's a pity to see such a charming young man wantonly court destruction. He's going alone to the grotto, but even if he had a hundred men to back him, he'd not be able to accomplish his mission. Why does the princess demand the impossible?" Avenant kept going without saying a word, but he was in very low spirits.

When he was almost at the top of a mountain, he sat down to rest a little, allowing his horse to graze and Cabriolle to run after flies. He knew that the Gloomy Grotto was not far away and looked around to see if he could spot it. He caught sight of a tremendous chasm, as black as ink, from which thick smoke was rising. The next moment he saw one of the dragons, spitting out fire from his mouth and eyes. It had a green and yellow body, great claws, and a long tail wrapped in more than a hundred coils. Cabriolle saw all this as well and was so frightened he did not know where to hide himself.

Perfectly convinced he was going to his death, Avenant drew his sword and descended toward the cavern with a phial that Beauty with the Golden Hair had given him to fill with the water of beauty. He said to his little dog, Cabriolle, "It's all over for me. I'll never be able to obtain the water guarded by those dragons. When I'm dead, fill the phial with my blood and carry it to the princess so that she may see what her whim has cost. Then go to the king my master and tell him my sad story." As he uttered these words, he heard a voice calling: "Avenant! Avenant!"

"Who's calling me?" he cried. In the hollow of an old tree he spied an owl who said to him, "You let me out of the fowler's net, in which I was ensnared, and saved my life. I promised I would do the same for you, and now's the time. Give me your phial. I'm familiar with all the windings in the Gloomy Grotto. I'll fetch you some of the water of beauty."

You can imagine how delighted Avenant was to hear this. He quickly handed the phial to the owl, who entered the grotto without the least difficulty. In less than a quarter of an hour the bird returned with the phial full of water and tightly capped. Avenant was in ecstasy. He thanked the owl heartily, and after climbing back up the mountain, he returned to the city filled with joy. Once there he went straight to the palace and presented the phial to Beauty with the Golden Hair, who no longer had any excuses to make. Thanking him, she gave orders for everything to be prepared for her departure, and at last set out with him on their journey. She found him an exceedingly pleasant companion and said to him more than once, "If you had wished it, I would have made you king, and there would have been no occasion for us to leave my realm."

But his answer was always: "I'd never betray my master, not for all the kingdoms on the face of the earth, even though I find you more beautiful than the sun."

Finally they arrived at the king's capital city. Upon hearing that Beauty with the Golden Hair was approaching, his majesty went to meet her and gave her the most superb presents in the world. The marriage was celebrated with such great rejoicing that people could talk of nothing else. But Beauty with the Golden Hair, who secretly loved Avenant, was never happy when he was out of her sight. "I'd never have come here, except that he did impossible things for my sake. You should feel deeply indebted to him. He obtained the water of beauty for me so that I'll never grow old and always remain beautiful."

The envious courtiers, who heard the queen express herself in this way, said to the king, "You're not jealous and yet you have good cause to be so. The queen is so deeply in love with Avenant that she can neither eat nor drink. She can talk about nothing but him and about your obligation to him. Yet anyone you had sent to her would have done as much."

"Now that I think upon it, that's quite true," said the king. Let him be put in the tower with irons on his hands and feet."

Avenant was seized, and in return for his faithful service was fettered hand and foot in a dungeon. He was allowed to see no one but the jail keeper, who threw him a morsel of black bread through a hole and gave him some water in a clay pan. His little dog, Cabriolle, however, did not desert him. He came daily to console him and tell him all the news. When Beauty with the Golden Hair heard of Avenant's disgrace, she flung herself at the king's feet. With tears running down her cheeks, she implored him to release Avenant from prison. But the more she pleaded, the more angry the king became, for he thought to himself, "It's because she loves him." So he refused to budge in the matter, and the queen gave up urging him and fell into a deep melancholy.

Because of this, the king took it into his head that perhaps she did not think him handsome enough. He longed to wash his face with the water of beauty in the hope that the queen would then feel more affection for him. The phial full of this water stood on the chimneypiece in the queen's chamber, where she had placed it for the pleasure of looking at it more frequently. Unfortunately, one of her chambermaids, trying to kill a spider with a broom, knocked the phial off, and it broke in the fall. All the water was lost. Quickly, she swept the fragments of glass away, and not knowing what to do, it suddenly occurred to her that she had seen a phial full of water in the king's cabinet. It was as clear as the water of beauty and looked exactly the same. So, without saying a word to anyone, she adroitly managed to get it and placed it on the queen's chimneypiece.

The water in the king's cabinet, however, was used to execute princes and great noblemen who committed criminal offenses. Instead of beheading or hanging them, their faces were rubbed with this water, which had the fatal property of throwing them into a deep sleep from which they never awakened. So one evening the king happened to take the phial that he thought contained the water of beauty and, rubbing the contents well over his face, he fell into a profound slumber and died.

Little Cabriolle was the first to hear the news of the king's death and ran to tell Avenant, who begged him to find Beauty with the Golden Hair and remind her of the poor prisoner. Cabriolle slipped quietly through the crowd, for there was great confusion at court due to the king's death, and he said to the queen, "Madam, do not forget poor Avenant."

She immediately recalled all that he had endured for her and his utter fidelity. Leaving the palace without speaking to a soul, she went directly to the tower, where she took the irons off his hands and feet with her own hands. Putting a crown of gold upon his head and a royal mantle over his shoulders, she said, "Come, charming Avenant, I want to make you king and take you for my husband."

He threw himself at her feet in joy and gratitude. Everybody was delighted to have him for their master. Their wedding was the most splendid the world has ever seen, and Beauty with the Golden Hair reigned long and happily with the handsome Avenant.

> A kindly action never fail to do.
> The smallest returns a blessing to you.
> When Avenant saved the carp and crow,
> And even showed compassion for the woes
> Of a poor and unfortunate owl,
> Who would have dreamed a mere fish or fowl
> Would place him on the pinnacle of fame?
> Yet his bravery ignited the princess's flame,
> And he induced her to give her accord.
> Unshaken in his loyalty he stood on the ford.
> Innocent victim of a rival's hate.
> When all seemed lost—when faced by his dark fate—
> Just Providence reversed the ruthless doom
> And gave virtue the throne, tyranny a tomb.

THE RAM

IN those happy times when fairies still existed, there reigned a king who had three daughters. Young and beautiful, all three possessed considerable qualities, but the youngest was the most charming and the favorite by far. Indeed, they called her Merveilleuse. Her father gave her more gowns and ribbons in a month than he gave the others in a year, and she was so good-natured that she shared everything with them so that there might be no misunderstandings.

Now, the king had some evil neighbors who grew tired of keeping peace with him. Therefore, they formed a powerful alliance and compelled him to arm his country in self-defense. Once he had raised a large army, he assumed command and rode off to battle. The three princesses remained with their tutors in a castle, and every day they received good news about the king's exploits. One time he took a city, another he won a battle. Finally he succeeded in routing his enemies and driving them out of his dominions. Then he returned to the castle as fast as he could to see his little Merveilleuse, whom he adored so much.

The three princesses had ordered three satin gowns to be made for themselves—one green, one blue, one white. Jewels were selected to match their dresses—the green enriched with emeralds, the blue with turquoises, and the white with diamonds. Thus attired, they went to meet the king, singing the following verses, which they had written to celebrate his victories:

> "With conquest crowned on many a glorious plain,
> What joy to greet our king and sire again!
> Welcome him back, victorious, to these halls,

With new delights and countless festivals.
Let shouts of joy and songs of triumph prove
His people's loyalty, his daughters' love!"

When the king saw his lovely daughters in such splendid attire, he embraced them all tenderly, but caressed Merveilleuse more than the others. A magnificent banquet was set up, and the king and his three daughters sat down to eat. Since it was his habit to draw inferences from everything, he said to the eldest, "Tell me, please, why have you put on a green gown?"

"Sire," she answered, "having heard of your achievements, I imagined that green would express the joy and hope with which your return inspired me."

"That is very prettily said," the king exclaimed. "And you, my child," he continued, "why are you wearing a blue gown?"

"My liege," the princess said, "I want to indicate that we should constantly implore the gods to protect you. Moreover, your sight is to me like that of Heaven and all the Heavenly Host."

"You speak like an oracle," the king said. "And you, Merveilleuse, why have you dressed yourself in white?"

"Because, sire," she answered, "it becomes me better than any other color."

"What?" the king cried, very much offended. "Was that your only motive, you little coquette?"

"My motive was to please you," said the princess. "It seems to me that I ought to have no other."

The king, who loved her dearly, was so perfectly satisfied with this explanation that he declared himself quite pleased by the little turn she had given to her meaning and the art with which she had at first concealed the compliment.

"Now, then," he said, "I've had an excellent supper, but I won't yet go to bed. Tell me what you all dreamed of the night before my return."

The eldest said she had dreamed that he had brought her a gown with gold and jewels that glistened brighter than the sun. The second said she had dreamed he had brought her a golden distaff to spin herself some shifts. The youngest said she had dreamed that he had married off her second sister and on the wedding day he had offered her a golden vase and said, "Merveilleuse, come here. Come here so you can wash."

Infuriated by this dream, the king knit his brow and made such an exceedingly wry face that everybody saw he was enraged. He retired to his room and flung himself onto the bed, but he could not forget his daughter's dream. "This insolent creature," he said, "she wants to turn me into her servant. I wouldn't be at all surprised if she put on that white satin dress without thinking of me at all. She doesn't take me seriously. But I'll frustrate her wicked designs while there's still time." He rose in a fury, and though it was still dark outside, he sent for the captain of his guards and said, "You heard Merveilleuse's dream. It forecasts strange things against me. I command you to seize her immediately, take her into the forest, and kill her. Afterward, you're to bring me her heart and tongue so I'll be sure you haven't deceived me. If you fail, I'll have you put to death in the most cruel manner imaginable."

The captain of the guards was astounded by this barbarous order. He did not dare argue with the king, however, for fear of increasing his rage and causing him to give the horrifying order to another. He assured him he would take the princess and kill her and bring him her heart and tongue.

The captain strode directly to the princess's apartment, where he had some difficulty in obtaining permission to enter, for it was still quite early. He informed Merveilleuse that the king desired to see her. She arose immediately, and a tiny Moorish girl named Patypata carried her train. A young ape and a little dog who always accompanied her also ran after her. The ape was called Grabugeon and the little dog, Tintin. The captain of the guards made Merveilleuse descend into the garden, where he told her the king was taking in the fresh morning air. She entered it, and the captain pretended to look for the king. When he did not find him, he said, "No doubt his majesty has walked farther on into the wood." He opened a small gate and led the princess into the forest. It was just getting light, and the princess saw that her escort had tears in his eyes and was so dejected that he could not speak.

"What's the matter?" she inquired kindly. "You seem very much distressed."

"Ah, madam," he exclaimed, "how could I be otherwise, for I've been given the most dreadful order that has even been given! The king has commanded me to kill you in this forest and to take your heart and tongue to him. If I fail to do so, he will put me to death."

Turning pale with terror, the poor princess began to weep softly, like a lamb about to be sacrificed. Then she turned her beautiful eyes to the captain of the guards and looked at him without anger. "Do you really have the heart to kill me?" she asked. "I've never done you any harm, and I've always spoken well of you to the king. If I really deserved my father's hate, I'd suffer the consequences without a murmur. But alas, I've always shown him so much respect and affection that he has no just reason to complain."

"Fear not, beautiful princess," said the captain, "I'm incapable of such a barbarous deed. I'd rather have him carry out his threat and kill me. But if I were to kill myself, you would be no better off. We must find some way that will enable me to return to the king and convince him you're dead."

"What way is there?" asked Merveilleuse. "He's ordered you to bring him my heart and tongue, and if you don't, he won't believe you."

Patypata had witnessed everything, though neither the captain nor the princess was aware of her presence because they were so overcome by sadness. Advancing courageously, she threw herself at Merveilleuse's feet. "Madam," she said, "I want to offer you my life. You must kill me. I'd be most happy to die for such a good mistress."

"Oh, I could never permit it, my dear Patypata!" the princess said, kissing her. "After such an affectionate proof of your friendship, your life is as dear to me as my own."

Then Grabugeon stepped forward and said, "You have good reason, Princess, to love such a faithful slave as Patypata. She can be of much more use to you than I. Now it's my turn to offer you my heart and tongue with joy, for I wish to immortalize myself in the annals of the empire of monkeys."

"Ah, my darling Grabugeon," Merveilleuse replied, "I can't bear the idea of taking your life."

"I'd find it intolerable," exclaimed Tintin, "good little dog as I am, if anyone but myself were to sacrifice his life for my mistress. Either I die or nobody dies."

Upon saying this, a geat dispute arose between Patypata, Grabugeon, and Tintin, and they exchanged a great many harsh words. At last Grabugeon, who was quicker than the others, scampered up to the top of a tree and flung herself down headfirst, killing herself on the spot. As much as the princess grieved over her loss, she agreed to let the captain of the guards cut out her tongue since the poor thing was dead. To their dismay, however, it was so small (for the creature was not much bigger than one's fist) that they felt certain the king would not be deceived by it.

"Alas, my dear little ape," cried the princess, "there you lie, and your sacrifice hasn't saved my life!"

"That honor has been reserved for me," interrupted the Moor, and as she spoke, she snatched the knife that had been used on Grabugeon and plunged it into her bosom. The captain of the guards would have taken her tongue, but it was so black that he knew he would not be able to deceive the king with it.

"Look at my misfortune!" the princess said tearfully. "I lose all those I love, and yet my fate remains unchanged."

"Had you accepted my offer," Tintin said, "you would have only had to mourn my loss, and I would have had the satisfaction of being the only one mourned."

Merveilleuse kissed her little dog and wept such bitter tears over him that she became quite exhausted. She turned hastily away, and when she ventured to look around again, her escort was gone, and she found herself alone with the dead bodies of her Moor, her ape, and her little dog. She could not leave the spot until she had buried them in a hole that she found by chance at the foot of a tree. Afterward she scratched these words into the tree:

> Three faithful friends lie buried in this grave.
> They saved my life with deeds most brave.

Then she began to think about her own safety. It was certainly dangerous for her to remain in that forest, especially since it was so close to her father's castle. The first person who saw her would recognize her. Then again, she might be attacked and devoured like a chicken by the lions and wolves that infested it. So she set off walking as fast as she could.

The forest was so enormous, however, and the sun so strong that she was soon nearly ready to collapse from heat, fear, and exhaustion. She looked around in every direction, but was unable to see an end to the woods. Every movement frightened her. She continually imagined that the king was in hot pursuit, seeking to kill her. Indeed, she uttered so many cries of woe that it is impossible to repeat them all here.

As she walked on, not following any particular path, the thickets tore her beautiful dress and scratched her ivory skin. At last she heard some sheep bleating. "It is probably some shepherds with their flocks," she said. "Perhaps they'll be able to direct me to a village where I can disguise myself in peasant garb. Alas, kings and queens are not always the happiest people in the world! Who in all this kingdom would have ever believed that I'd become a fugitive, that my father would want to take my life without reason, and that I'd have to disguise myself to save my neck?"

Even as she made these remarks, she was approaching the spot where she had heard the bleating. Upon reaching an open glade encircled by trees, she was astonished to see a large ram with gilded horns and fleece whiter than snow. He had a garland of flowers around his neck, his legs were entwined with ropes of enormous pearls, and chains of diamonds hung all about him. As he lay on a couch of orange blossoms, a pavilion of gold cloth suspended in the air sheltered him from the rays of the sun. There were a hundred brightly decked sheep all around him, and instead of browsing on grass, some were having coffee, sherbet, ices, and lemonade; others, strawberries and cream, and preserves. Some were playing at *basset*, others at *lansquenet*. Several wore collars of gold ornamented with numerous fine emblems, earrings, ribbons, and flowers. Merveilleuse was so astounded that she remained stock still. Her eyes were roving in search of the shepherd in charge of this extraordinary flock when the beautiful ram ran over to her in a sprightly manner. "Approach, divine princess," he said. "You have nothing to fear from such gentle and peaceful animals of our kind."

"What a miracle! A talking ram!" the princess exclaimed.

"What's that, madam?" the ram replied. "Your ape and your little dog spoke very prettily. Why weren't you surprised by that?"

"A fairy endowed them with the gift of speech, which made everything less miraculous," Merveilleuse stated.

"Perhaps we had a similar experience," the ram answered, smiling sheepishly. "But what caused you to come our way, my princess?"

"A thousand misfortunes, my lord ram," she said to him. "I'm the most unhappy person in the world. I'm seeking a place of refuge from my father's fury."

"Come, madam," the ram replied, "come with me. I can offer you one that will be known only by you, and you will be completely in charge of everything there."

"I can't follow you," Merveilleuse said. "I'm about to die from exhaustion."

The ram with golden horns called for his chariot, and immediately six goats were led forward, harnessed to a pumpkin of such tremendous size that two persons could sit in it with the greatest ease. The hollowed-out pumpkin was dry inside and fitted with splendid down cushions and lined all over with velvet. Getting into the pumpkin, the princess was astounded by such a unique equipage. The master ram seated himself in the pumpkin beside her, and the goats took them at full gallop to a cave. The entrance was blocked by a large stone, but the golden-horned ram touched the stone with his foot and it fell away at once. He told the princess, "Enter without fear."

She imagined that the cave would be a horrible place, and if she had not been so afraid of being captured, nothing would have induced her to go into it, but her fear was so great that she would have thrown herself into even a well to avoid capture. So she followed the ram without hesitation. He walked in front of her to show her the way down, which ran so very deep that she thought she was going at least to the other end of the earth. At moments she feared he was conducting her to the region of the dead.

Suddenly she came upon a vast meadow bursting with a thousand different flowers whose sweet aroma surpassed that of any she had ever smelled. A broad river of orange-flower water flowed around it; fountains of Spanish wine, rossolis, hippocras, and a thousand other liqueurs formed charming cascades and rivulets. The meadow was home to entire avenues of unusual trees, and partridges greased and dressed better than those eaten at the restaurant La Guerbois hung from the branches. In other avenues the branches were festooned with quails, young rabbits, turkeys, chickens, pheasants, and orto-lans. In certain parts, where from afar the atmosphere appeared hazy, it rained bisques d'écrevisse and other soups, foies gras, ragouts of sweetbreads, white puddings, sausages, tarts, pat-ties, jam, and marmalade. There were also louis d'ors, crowns, pearls, and diamonds. Showers so rare—and so useful—would no doubt have attracted excellent company if the great ram had been more inclined to mix in general society, but all the chron-icles in which he is mentioned concur in assuring us that he was as reserved as a Roman senator.

Merveilleuse had arrived in this beautiful region during the finest time of the year. Thus, she was fortunate to see that there was also a palace, surrounded by long rows of orange trees, jasmines, honeysuckles, and tiny musk roses, whose interlaced branches formed cabinets, halls, and chambers, all hung with gold and silver gauze and furnished with large mir-rors, chandeliers, and remarkable paintings. The master ram told the princess to consider herself the sovereign of this realm. "I have been suffering from grief for many years, and it is now up to you to make me forget all my misfortunes."

"Your behavior is so generous, charming ram," she said, "and everything I see appears so extraordinary that I don't know what to make of it."

No sooner had she uttered these words than a group of the most remarkable and beautiful nymphs appeared before her. They gave her fruit in baskets of amber, but when she stepped toward them, they shrank back slightly. When she extended her hands to touch them, she felt nothing—they were only phantoms. "What does this mean?" she exclaimed. "Who are these things around me?" She began to weep, and King Ram (for so they called him), who had left her momentarily, returned and found her in tears, causing him such despair that he felt he would die at her feet.

"What's the matter, lovely princess?" he inquired. "Has anyone here been disrespectful to you?"

"No," she answered, "I can't complain. It's only that I'm not accustomed to living among the dead and with sheep that talk. Everything here frightens me, and though I'm greatly obliged to you for bringing me here, I'd be even more obliged if you'd bring me back into the world."

"Don't be alarmed," the ram replied. "Please deign to listen to me calmly, and you shall hear my sad story:

I was born to inherit a throne. A long line of kings, my ancestors, had ensured that the kingdom I'd be taking over was the finest in the universe. My subjects loved me. Feared and envied by my neighbors, I was thus justly respected. It was said that no king had ever been more worthy of such homage, and my physical appearance was not without its attractions as well.

I was extremely fond of hunting, and once, when I was zealously pursuing a stag, I became separated from my attendants. Suddenly seeing the stag plunge into a pond, I spurred my horse in after him. This was as unwise as it was bold. But instead of the coldness of water, I felt an extraordinary heat. The pond dried up, and through an opening gushing with terrible flames I fell to the bottom of a precipice, where nothing was to be seen but fire.

I thought I was lost when I suddenly heard a voice saying, "No less fire could warm your heart, ungrateful one!"

"Hah! Who is it that complains of my coldness?" I said.

"An unfortunate who adores you without hope," the voice replied.

Just then the flames were extinguished, and I perceived a fairy whose age and ugliness had horrified me ever since I had known her in my early childhood. She was leaning on a young slave of incomparable beauty, and the golden chains she wore sufficiently indicated who she was. "What miracle is this, Ragotte?" I asked her (since that was the fairy's name). "Have you really ordered this?"

"Who else should have ordered it?" the fairy replied. "Has it taken you this long to learn the way I feel? Must I undergo the shame of explaining myself? Have my eyes, once so certain of their power, lost all their influence? Just look how low I'm stooping! I'm the one who's confessing my weakness to you, who, great king though you may be, are less than an ant compared to a fairy like me."

"I am whatever you please," I said impatiently, "but what is it you demand of me? Is it my crown, my cities, my treasures?"

"Ah, wretch," she replied disdainfully, "if I so desired it, my scullions would be more powerful than you. No, I demand your heart! My eyes have asked you for it thousands and thousands of times. You haven't understood them, or rather, you don't want to understand them. If you had been desperately in love with someone else," she continued, "I wouldn't have interrupted the progress of your ardor, but I had too great an interest in you not to discover the indifference that reigned in your heart. Well, then, love me!" she added, rolling her eyes and pursing her mouth to make it look more pleasant. "I'll be your little Ragotte, and I'll add twenty kingdoms to what you possess already, a hundred towers filled with gold, five hundred filled with silver—in a word, all you can wish for."

"Madame Ragotte," I said to her, "I would never think of declaring myself to a person of your merit at the bottom of a pit in which I expect to be roasted. I implore you, by all the charms that you possess, to set me free, and then we'll consider together what we can do to satisfy you."

"Ha, traitor!" she exclaimed, "if you loved me, you wouldn't seek the road back to your kingdom. You'd be happy in a grotto, in a foxhole, in the woods or the desert. Don't think that I'm such an ingenue. You hope to escape, but I warn you that you'll remain here. Your first task will be to tend my sheep. They are intelligent animals and speak just as well as you do."

Upon saying this, she took me to the plain where we now stand and showed me her flock. I paid scant attention to them, for I was struck by the marvelous beauty of the slave beside her. My eyes betrayed me. The cruel Ragotte noticed my admiration and attacked her. She plunged a bodkin into one of her eyes with such violence that the adorable girl fell dead on the spot. At this horrible sight I threw myself on Ragotte, and with my sword in hand, I would have made her into a sacrificial victim for the spirits of the underworld if she hadn't used her power to freeze me as I stood. All my efforts were in vain. I fell to the ground and sought some way to kill myself and end my agony. But the fairy said to me with an ironical smile, "I want you to become acquainted with my power. You're a lion right now, but soon you'll become a sheep."

As she pronounced this sentence, she touched me with her wand, and I found myself transformed as you now behold me. I haven't lost the faculty of speech, nor the sense of torment caused by my condition. "You are to be a sheep for five years," she said, "and absolute master of this beautiful realm. Meanwhile I'll move far from here so I won't have to see your handsome face. But I'll brood over the hate I owe you."

Then she disappeared and, in truth, if anything could have relieved my misfortune, it would have been her absence. The talking sheep you see here acknowledged me as their king, and they informed me that they were unfortunate mortals who had in various ways offended the vindictive fairy. They had been changed into a flock, and some had to serve longer penances than others. In fact, every now and then they become what they were before and leave the flock. As for the shadows you've seen, they are Ragotte's rivals and enemies whom she has deprived of life for a century or so and who will return to the world later on. The young slave I mentioned is among them. I've seen her several times with great pleasure, although she didn't speak to me. When first I approached her, I was disturbed to discover it was nothing but her shadow. However, I noticed that one of my sheep was giving this phantom a lot of attention and learned that he was her lover. Ragotte had separated them out of jealousy, and this is the reason why I've avoided the shadow of the slave since then. During the past three years I've longed only for my freedom.

"In the hope of regaining it, I frequently wander into the forest," he continued. "It was there that I saw you, beautiful princess. Sometimes you were in a chariot that you drove yourself with more skill than Apollo does his own. Sometimes you followed the chase on a steed that seemed would obey no other rider, or you were in a race with the ladies of your court, flying lightly over the plain, and you won the prize like another Atalanta. Ah, Princess, if I had dared to speak to you during this time in which my heart paid you secret homage, what wouldn't I have said? But how would you have received the declaration of an unhappy sheep like me?"

Merveilleuse was so stirred by all she had heard that she scarcely knew how to answer him. She said something civil, however, which gave him some hope, and also told him that she was less alarmed by the ghosts now that she knew their owners would revive again. "Alas," she continued, "if my poor Patypata, my dear Grabugeon, and the pretty Tintin, who died to save me, could have met with a similar fate, I wouldn't be so melancholy here."

Despite the disgrace of the royal ram, he still possessed some remarkable prerogatives. "Go," he said to his grand equerry (a splendid-looking sheep), "go fetch the Moor, the ape, and the little dog. Their shadows will amuse our princess."

A moment later they appeared, and although they did not approach near enough for Merveilleuse to touch them, their presence was a great consolation to her.

The royal ram possessed all the intelligence and refinement required for pleasant conversation, and he adored Merveilleuse so much that she began to have some regard for him and soon after came to love him. A pretty sheep, so gentle and affectionate, is not a displeasing companion, particularly when one knows that he is a king and that his transformation will eventually end. Thus the princess spent her days peacefully, awaiting a happier future. The gallant ram devoted himself entirely to her. He gave fetes, concerts, and hunts in which his flock aided him and even the shadows played their part.

One day when his couriers arrived—for he regularly sent out couriers for news and always obtained the best—he learned that the eldest sister of Princess Merveilleuse was about to marry a great prince, and the most magnificent preparations were being made for the wedding.

"Ah," the young princess said, "how unfortunate I am to be deprived of witnessing so many fine things! Here I am underground, among ghosts and sheep, while my sister is about to be made a queen. Everybody will pay their respects to her, and I'm the only one who won't be able to share in her joy."

"What reason do you have to complain, madam?" asked the king of the sheep. "Have I refused you permission to attend the wedding? Depart as soon as you please. Only give me your word that you'll return. If you don't agree to that, I'll perish at your feet, for my love for you is too passionate and I'd never be able to live if I lost you."

Touched, Merveilleuse promised the ram that nothing in the world could prevent her return. So he provided her with an equipage befitting her birth. She was superbly attired, and nothing was omitted to embellish her beauty. She got into a chariot of mother-of-pearl drawn by six Isabella-colored hypogriffins that had just arrived from the other end of the earth. She was accompanied by a great number of exceedingly handsome, richly attired officers. These the royal ram had ordered to come from a distant land to form the princess's train.

She arrived at her father's court at the moment the marriage was being celebrated. As soon as she appeared, she dazzled everyone by her glittering beauty and the jewels that adorned her. She heard nothing but acclamation and praise. The king gazed at her with such zeal and pleasure that she was afraid he would recognize her, but he was so convinced that his daughter was dead that he did not have the least inkling who she was.

Nevertheless, she was so afraid that she might be detained that she did not stay to the end of the ceremony. She departed abruptly, leaving a small coral box garnished with emeralds, on which was written in diamonds: "JEWELS FOR THE BRIDE." They opened it immediately, and what extraordinary things they found! The king, who was burning to know who she was,

was despondent about her departure. He gave strict orders that if she ever returned, they were to shut the gates and detain her.

Brief though the absence of Merveilleuse had been, it had seemed like ages to the ram. Waiting for her by the side of a fountain in the thickest part of the forest, he had immense treasures displayed there with the intention of giving them to her in gratitude for her return. As soon as he saw her, he ran toward her, romping and frisking like a real sheep. He lay down at her feet, kissed her hands, and told her all about his anxiety and impatience. His love for her so inspired him that he managed to speak with an eloquence that completely captivated the princess.

A short time afterward, the king was to marry off his second daughter, and Merveilleuse heard about it. Once again she asked the ram for permission to attend a fete in which she took the closest interest. Of course, he felt a pang he could not suppress when he heard her request, for a secret presentiment warned him of a catastrophe. But since we cannot always avoid evil, and since his consideration for the princess overruled any other feeling, he did not have the heart to refuse her. "You desire to leave me, madam," he said, "and I must blame my sad fate for this unfortunate situation more than you. In consenting to your wish, I'll never make you a greater sacrifice."

She assured him that she would return as quickly as she had the first time. "I would be deeply grieved if anything were to keep me from you. I beg you, don't worry about me."

She went in the same pomp as before and arrived just as they were beginning the marriage ceremony. Although everyone was following the nuptials, her presence caused exclamations of joy and admiration that drew the eyes of all the princes to her. They could not stop gazing at her: her beauty, they felt, was so extraordinary that they could easily have been convinced that she was more than mortal.

The king was charmed to see her once more, and he never took his eyes off her, except to order all the doors to be closed to prevent her departure. When the ceremony was nearly concluded, the princess rose hastily in order to disappear in the throng but was shocked and distressed to find that all the gates had been locked against her.

The king approached with a respectful, submissive air that reassured her. He begged her not to deprive them so soon of the pleasure of admiring her and requested that she remain and grace the banquet he was about to give the princes and princesses who had honored him with their presence on this occasion. He led her into a magnificent salon, in which the entire court was assembled, and offered her a golden basin and a vase filled with water so that she might wash her beautiful hands. No longer could she restrain her feelings. She flung herself at his feet, embraced his knees, and exclaimed, "Look, my dream has come true! You've offered me water to wash with on my sister's wedding day without anything evil happening to you."

The king had no difficulty recognizing her, for he had been struck by her strong resemblance to Merveilleuse more than once. "Ah, my dear daughter!" he cried, embracing her with tears in his eyes. "Can you ever forgive my cruelty? I wanted to take your life because I thought your dream predicted I would lose my crown. Indeed, it did just that, for now that your two sisters are married, each has a crown of her own. Therefore, mine shall be yours." Upon saying this, he rose and placed his crown on the princess's head, crying, "Long live Queen Merveilleuse!"

The entire court took up the shout. The two sisters threw their arms around her neck and kissed her a thousand times. Merveilleuse was so happy she could not express her joy. She cried and laughed at the same time. She embraced one, talked to another, thanked the king, and in the midst of all this, she recalled the captain of the guard, to whom she was so much indebted. When she asked eagerly to see him, though, they informed her he was dead, and she felt a pang of sorrow.

After they sat down to dinner, the king asked her to relate all that had happened to her ever since the day he had given his fatal orders. She immediately began telling the story with the most remarkable grace, and everybody listened to her attentively.

While she was engrossed in telling her story to the king and her sisters, though, the enamored ram watched for the princess as the hour set for her return passed. Indeed, his anxiety became so extreme that he could not control it. "She'll never come back!" he cried. "My miserable sheep's face disgusts her. Oh, unfortunate lover that I am, what will become of me if I have lost Merveilleuse? Ragotte! Cruel fairy! How you have avenged yourself for my indifference to you!" He indulged in such lamentations for hours, and then, as night approached without any signs of the princess, he ran to the city. When he reached the king's palace, he asked to see Merveilleuse, but since everybody was now aware of her adventures and did not want her to return to the ram's realm, they harshly refused to let him see her. He uttered cries and lamentations capable of moving anyone except the Swiss guard who stood sentry at the palace gates. At length, broken-hearted, he flung himself to the ground and breathed his last sigh.

The king and Merveilleuse were completely unaware of the sad tragedy that had taken place. The king suggested to his daughter that she ride in a triumphal coach and show herself to everyone in the city by the lights of thousands and thousands of torches illuminating the windows and all the great squares. But what a horrible spectacle she encountered as she left the palace gates—her dear ram stretched out breathless on the pavement! Jumping out of the coach and running to him, she wept and sobbed, for she knew that her delay in returning had caused the royal ram's death. In her despair she felt she would die herself.

Now we know that people of the highest rank are subject, like all others, to the blows of fortune, and that they frequently experience the greatest misery at the very moment they believe themselves to have attained their heart's goal.

> The choicest blessings sent by Heaven
> Often tend to cause our ruin.
> The charms, the talents, that we're given,
> May often end on a sad tune.
> The royal ram would have surely seen
> Happier days without the charms that led

The cruel Ragotte to love, then hurl her mean
But fatal vengeance on his head.
In truth he should have had a better fate,
For spurning a sordid Hymen's chains;
Honest his love—unmasked his hate—
How different from our modern swains!
Even his death may well surprise
The lovers of the present day:
Only a silly sheep now dies,
Because his ewe has gone astray.

THE GREEN SERPENT

ONCE upon a time there was a great queen who, having given birth to twin daughters, invited twelve fairies who lived nearby to come and bestow gifts upon them, as was the custom in those days. Indeed, it was a very useful custom, for the power of the fairies generally compensated for the deficiencies of nature. Sometimes, however, they also spoiled what nature had done its best to make perfect, as we shall soon see.

When the fairies had all gathered in the banquet hall, they were about to sit at the table and enjoy a magnificent meal. Suddenly the fairy Magotine entered. She was the sister of Carabossa and no less malicious. Shuddering when she saw her, the queen feared some disaster since she had not invited her to the celebration. However, she carefully concealed her anxiety, personally went looking for an armchair for the fairy, and found one covered with green velvet and embroidered with sapphires. Since Magotine was the eldest of the fairies, all the rest made way for her to pass and whispered to one another, "Let us quickly endow the infant princesses, sister, so that we may get the start on Magotine."

When the armchair was set up for her, she rudely declined it, saying that she was big enough to eat standing. She was mistaken in this, though, because the table was rather high and she was not tall enough to see over it. This annoyance increased her foul mood even more.

"Madam," the queen said, "I beg you to take your seat at the table."

"If you had wished me to do so," the fairy replied, "you would have sent an invitation to me as you did to the others, but you only want beauties with fine figures and fine dresses like my sisters here. As for me, I'm too ugly and old. Yet despite it all, I have just as much power as they. In fact, without boasting about it, I may even have more."

All the fairies urged her strongly to sit at the table, and at length she consented. A golden basket was placed before them, containing twelve bouquets composed of jewels. The fairies who had arrived first each took a bouquet, leaving none for Magotine. As she began to mutter between her teeth, the queen ran to her room and brought her a casket of perfumed Spanish morocco covered with rubies and filled with diamonds, and asked her to accept it. But Magotine shook her head and said, "Keep your jewels, madam. I have more than enough to spare. I came only to see if you had thought of me, and it's clear you've neglected me shamefully."

Thereupon she struck the table with her wand, and all the delicacies heaped on it were turned into fricasseed serpents. This sight horrified the fairies so much that they flung down their napkins and fled the table. While they talked with one another about the nasty trick Magotine had played on them, that cruel fairy approached the cradle in which the princesses, the loveliest children in the world, were lying wrapped in golden swaddling. "I endow you with perfect ugliness," she quickly said to one, of them, and she was about to utter a malediction on the other when the fairies, greatly disturbed, ran and stopped her. Then the mischievous Magotine broke one of the window panes, dashed through it like a flash of lightning, and vanished from sight.

All the good gifts that the benevolent fairies proceeded to bestow on the princess did not alleviate the misery of the queen, who found herself the mother of the ugliest being in the universe. Taking the infant in her arms, she had the misfortune of watching it grow more hideous by the moment. She struggled in vain to suppress her tears in the presence of their fairy ladyships, whose compassion is impossible to imagine. "What shall we do, sisters?" they said to one another. "How can we ever console the queen?" They held a grand council about the matter, and at the end they told the queen not to give in to her grief since a time would come when her daughter would be very happy.

"But," the queen interrupted, "will she become beautiful again?"

"We can't give you any further information," the fairies replied. "Be satisfied, madam, with the assurance that your daughter will be happy."

She thanked them very much and did not forget to give them many presents. Although the fairies were very rich, they always liked people to give them something. Throughout the world this custom has been passed down from that day to our own, and time has not altered it in the least.

The queen named her elder daughter Laidronette and the younger Bellotte. These names suited them perfectly, for Laidronette, despite her boundless intelligence, became too frightful to behold, whereas her sister's beauty increased hourly until she looked thoroughly charming.

After Laidronette had turned twelve, she went to the king and queen, and threw herself at their feet. "Please, I implore you, allow me to shut myself up in a lonely castle so that I will no longer torment you with my ugliness." Despite her hideous appearance, they could not help being fond of her, and not without some pain did they consent to let her depart. However, since Bellotte remained with them, they had ample consolation.

Laidronette begged the queen not to send anyone except her nurse and a few officers to wait on her. "You needn't worry, madam, about my being abducted. I can assure you that, looking as I do, I shall avoid even the light of day."

After the king and queen had granted her wishes, she was conducted to the castle she had chosen. It had been built many centuries before, and the sea crashed beneath its windows and served it as a moat. In the vicinity was a large forest in which one could stroll, and in several fields leading to the forest, the princess played various instruments and sang divinely.

Two years she spent in this pleasant solitude, even writing several volumes recording her thoughts, but the desire to see her father and mother again induced her to take a coach and revisit the court. She arrived just as they were to celebrate the marriage of Bellotte. Everyone had been rejoicing, but the moment they saw Laidronette, their joy turned to distress. She was neither kissed nor hugged by any of her relatives. Indeed, the only thing they said to her was that she had grown a good deal uglier, and they advised her not to appear at the ball. "However, if you wish to see it, we shall find some hole for you to peep through."

She replied that she had come there neither to dance nor to hear the music, that she had been in the desolate castle so long that she had felt a longing to pay her respects to the king and the queen. Painfully aware that they could not endure the sight of her, she told them that she would therefore return to her wilderness, where the trees, flowers, and springs she wandered among did not reproach her for her ugliness. When the king and queen saw how hurt she was, they told her reluctantly that she could stay with them two or three days. Good-natured as always, though, she replied, "It would be harder for me to leave you if I were to spend so much time in your good company." Since they were all too eager for her to depart, they did not press her to stay, but coldly remarked that she was quite right.

For coming to her wedding the Princess Bellotte gave her a gift of an old ribbon that she had worn all winter in a bow on her muff, and Bellotte's fiancé gave her some zinzolin taffeta to make a petticoat. If she had expressed what she thought, she would have surely thrown the ribbon and rag of zinzolin in her generous donors' faces, but she had such good sense, prudence, and judgment that she revealed none of her bitterness. With her faithful nurse she left the court to return to her castle, her heart so filled with grief that she did not say a word during the entire journey.

One day as she was walking on one of the gloomiest paths in the forest, she saw a large green serpent at the foot of a tree. As it reared its head, it said to her, "Laidronette, you aren't the only unhappy creature. Look at my horrible form. And yet at birth I was even handsomer than you."

Terrified, the princess heard not one half of this. She fled from the spot, and for many days thereafter did not dare to leave the castle, so afraid was she of another such encounter.

Eventually she tired of sitting alone in her room, however, and one evening she went for a walk along the beach. She was strolling slowly, pondering her sad fate, when she noticed a small gilt barque painted with a thousand different emblems gliding toward her. With a sail made of gold brocade, a mast of cedar, and oars of eagle wood, it appeared to be drifting at random. When it landed on the shore, the curious princess stepped on board to inspect all of its beautiful decorations. She found its deck laid with crimson velvet and gold trimmings, and all the nails were diamonds.

Suddenly the barque drifted out to sea again, and the princess, alarmed at her impending danger, grabbed the oars and endeavored in vain to row back to the beach. The wind rose and the waves became high. She lost sight of land and, seeing nothing around her but sea and sky, resigned herself to her fate, fully convinced not only that it was unlikely to be a happy one, but also that this was another one of the fairy Magotine's mean tricks. "If I must die, why do I have such a secret dread of death?" she asked. "Alas, have I ever enjoyed any of life's pleasures so much that I should now feel regret at dying? My ugliness disgusts even my family. My sister is a great queen, and I'm consigned to exile in the depths of a wilderness where the only companion I've found is a talking serpent. Wouldn't it be better for me to perish than to drag out such a miserable existence?" Having thus reflected, she dried her tears and courageously peered out to discover whence death would come, inviting its speedy approach. Just then she saw a serpent riding the billows toward the vessel, and as it approached her, it said: "If you're willing to be helped by a poor green serpent like me, I have the power to save your life."

"Death is less frightful to me than you are," the princess exclaimed, "and if you want to do me a kind favor, never let me set eyes on you again."

The green serpent gave a long hiss (the manner in which serpents sigh), and without saying a word it immediately dove under the waves.

"What a horrible monster!" the princess said to herself. "He has green wings, a body of a thousand colors, ivory claws, fiery eyes, and a bristling mane of long hair on his head. Oh, I'd much rather die than owe my life to him! But what motive does he have in following me? How did he obtain the power of speech that enables him to talk like a rational creature?"

As she was entertaining these thoughts, a voice answered her: "You had better learn, Laidronette, that the green serpent is not to be despised. I don't mean to be harsh, but I assure you that he's less hideous in the eyes of his species than you are in the eyes of yours. However, I do not desire to anger you but to lighten your sorrows, provided you consent."

The princess was dumbfounded by this voice, and the words it uttered seemed so unjust to her that she could not suppress her tears. Suddenly, though, a thought occurred to her. "What am I doing? I don't want to cry about my death just because I'm reproached for my ugliness!" she exclaimed. "Alas, shouldn't I perish as though I were the grandest beauty in the world? My demise would be more of a consolation to me."

Completely at the mercy of the winds, the vessel drifted on until it struck a rock and immediately shattered into pieces. The poor princess realized that mere philosophizing would not save her in such a catastrophe, and grabbed on to some pieces of the wreck, so she thought, for she felt herself buoyed in the water and fortunately reached the shore, coming to rest at the foot of a towering boulder. Alas, she was horrified to discover that her arms were wrapped tightly around the neck of the green serpent! When he realized how appalled she was, he retreated from her and said, "You'd fear me less if you knew me better, but it is my hard fate to terrify all those who see me."

With that he plunged into the surf, and Laidronette was left alone by the enormous rock. No matter where she glanced, she could see nothing that might alleviate her despair. Night was approaching. She was without food and knew not where to go. "I thought I was destined to perish in the ocean," she said sadly, "but now I'm sure that I'm to end my days here. Some sea monster will come and devour me, or I'll die of hunger." Rising, she climbed to the top of the crag and sat down. As long as it was light, she gazed at the ocean, and when it became dark, she took off her taffeta petticoat, covered her head with it, and waited anxiously for whatever was to happen next. Eventually she was overcome by sleep, and she seemed to hear the music of some instruments. She was convinced that she was dreaming, but a moment later she heard someone sing the following verse, which seemed to have been composed expressly for her:

> "Let Cupid make you now his own.
> Here he rules with gentle tone.
> Love with pleasure will be sown.
> On this isle no grief is known."

The attention she paid to these words caused her to wake up. "What good or bad luck shall I have now?" she exclaimed. "Might happiness still be in store for someone so wretched?" She opened her eyes timidly, fearing that she would be surrounded by monsters, but she was astonished to find that in place of the rugged, looming rock was a room with walls and ceiling made entirely of gold. She was lying in a magnificent bed that matched perfectly the rest of this palace, which was the most splendid in the universe. She began asking herself a hundred questions about all of this, unable to believe she was wide awake. Finally she got up and ran to open a glass door that led onto a spacious balcony, from which she could see all the beautiful things that nature, with some help from art, had managed to create on earth: gardens filled with flowers, fountains, statues, and the rarest trees; distant woods, palaces with walls ornamented with jewels, and roofs composed of pearls so wonderfully constructed that each was an architectural masterpiece. A calm, smiling sea strewn with thousands of vessels, whose sails, pennants, and streamers fluttered in the breeze, completed the charming view.

"Gods! You just gods!" the princess exclaimed. "What am I seeing? Where am I? What an astounding change! What has become of the terrible rock that seemed to threaten the skies with its lofty pinnacles? Am I the same person who was shipwrecked last night and saved by a serpent?" Bewildered, she continued talking to herself, first pacing, then stopping. Finally she heard a noise in her room. Reentering it, she saw a hundred pagods advancing toward her. They were dressed and made up in a hundred different ways. The tallest were a foot high, and the shortest no more than four inches—some were beautiful, graceful, pleasant, others hideous, dreadfully ugly. Their bodies were made of diamonds, emeralds, rubies, pearls, crystal, amber, coral, porcelain, gold, silver, brass, bronze, iron, wood, and clay. Some were without arms, others without feet, others had mouths extending to their ears, eyes askew, noses broken. In short, nowhere in the world could a greater variety of people be found than among these pagods.

Those pagods who presented themselves to the princess were the deputies of the kingdom. After a speech containing some very judicious ideas, they informed her that they had traveled about the world for some time past, but in order to obtain their sovereign's permission to do so, they had to take an oath not to speak during their absence. Indeed, some were so scrupulous that they would not even shake their heads or move their hands or feet, but the majority of them could not help it. This was how they had traveled about the universe, and when they returned, they amused the king by telling him everything that had occurred, even the most secret transactions and adventures in all the courts they had visited. "This is a pleasure, madam," one of the deputies added, "which we shall have the honor of occasionally affording you, for we have been commanded to do all we can to entertain you. Instead of bringing you presents, we now come to amuse you with our songs and dances."

They began immediately to sing the following verses while simultaneously dancing to the music of tambourines and castanets:

> "Sweet are pleasures after pains,
> Lovers, do not break your chains;
> Trials though you may endure,
> Happiness they will insure.
> Sweet are pleasures after pains,
> Joy from sorrow luster gains."

When they stopped dancing and singing, their spokesman said to the princess, "Here, madam, are a hundred pagodines, who have the honor of being selected to wait on you. Any wish you may have in the world will be fulfilled, provided you consent to remain among us."

The pagodines appeared in their turn. They carried baskets cut to their own size and filled with a hundred different articles so pretty, so useful, so well made, and so costly that Laidronette never tired of admiring and praising them, uttering exclamations of wonder and delight at all the marvels they showed her. The most prominent pagodine, a tiny figure made of diamonds, advised her to enter the grotto of the baths, since the heat of the day was increasing. The princess proceeded in the direction indicated between two ranks of bodyguards, whose appearance was enough to make one die with laughter.

She found two baths of crystal in the grotto ornamented with gold and filled with scented water so delicious and uncommon that she marveled at it. Shading the baths was a pavilion of green and gold brocade. When the princess inquired why there were two, they answered that one was for her, and the other for the king of the pagods.

"But where is he, then?" the princess asked.

"Madam," they replied, "he is presently with the army waging war against his enemies. You'll see him as soon as he returns."

The princess then inquired if he were married. They answered no. "Why, he is so charming that no one has yet been found who would be worthy of him." She indulged her curiosity no further, but disrobed and entered the bath. All the pagods and pagodines began to sing and play on various instruments. Some had theorbos made out of nut shells; others, bass viols made out of almond shells, for it was, of course, necessary that the instruments fit the size of the performers. But all the parts were arranged in such perfect accord that nothing could surpass the delight their concert gave her.

When the princess emerged from her bath, they gave her a magnificent dressing gown. A pair of pagods playing a flute and oboe marched before her, and a train of pagodines singing songs in her praise trailed behind. In this state she entered a room where her toilet was laid out. Immediately the pagodines in waiting, and those of the bedchamber, bustled about, dressed her hair, put on her robes, and praised her. There was no longer talk of her ugliness, of zinzolin petticoats, or greasy ribbons.

The princess was truly taken aback. "To whom am I indebted for such extraordinary happiness?" she asked herself. "I was on the brink of destruction. I was waiting for death to come and had lost hope, and yet I suddenly find myself in the most magnificent place in the world, where I've been welcomed with the greatest joy!"

Since the princess was endowed with a great deal of good sense and breeding, she conducted herself so well that all the wee creatures who approached her were enchanted by her behavior. Every morning when she arose, she was given new dresses, new lace, new jewels. Though it was a great pity she was so ugly, she who could not abide her looks began to think they were more appealing because of the great pains they took in dressing her. She rarely spent an hour without some pagods coming to visit and recounting to her the most curious and private events of the world: peace treaties, offensive and defensive alliances, lovers' quarrels and betrayals, unfaithful mistresses, distractions, reconciliations, disappointed heirs, matches broken off, old widows remarrying foolishly, treasures discovered, bankruptcies declared, fortunes made in a minute, favorites disgraced, office seekers, jealous husbands, coquettish wives, naughty children, ruined cities. In short, they told the princess everything under the sun to entertain her. She occasionally saw some pagods who were so corpulent and had such puffed-out cheeks that they were wonderful to behold. When she asked them why they were so fat, they answered, "Since we're not permitted to laugh or speak during our travels and are constantly witnessing all sorts of absurdities and the most intolerable follies, our inclination to laugh is so great that we swell up when we suppress it and cause what may properly be called risible dropsy. Then we cure ourselves as soon as we get home." The princess admired the good sense of the pagodine people, for we too might burst with laughter if we laughed at all the silly things we see every day.

Scarcely an evening passed without a performance of one of

the best plays by Corneille or Molière. Balls were held frequently, and the smallest pagods danced on a tightrope in
order to be better seen. What's more, the banquets in honor of
the princess might have served for feasts on the most solemn
occasions. They also brought her books of every description—
serious, amusing, historical. In short, the days passed like
minutes, although, to tell the truth, all these sprightly pagods
seemed insufferably little to the princess. For instance, whenever she went out walking, she had to put some thirty or so
into her pockets in order for them to keep up. It was the most
amusing thing in the world to hear the chattering of their little
voices, shriller than those of puppets in a show at the fair.

One night when the princess was unable to fall asleep, she
said to herself, "What's to become of me? Am I to remain here
forever? My days are more pleasant than I could have dared to
hope, yet my heart tells me something's missing. I don't know
what it is, but I'm beginning to feel that this unvarying routine
of amusements is rather insipid."

"Ah, Princess," a voice said, as if answering her thoughts,
"isn't it your own fault? If you'd consent to love, you'd soon
discover that you can abide with a lover for an eternity without wishing to leave. I speak not only of a palace, but even the
most desolate spot."

"What pagodine addresses me?" the princess inquired. "What
pernicious advice are you giving me? Why are you trying to disturb my peace of mind?"

"It is not a pagodine who forewarns you of what will sooner
or later come to pass," the voice replied. "It's the unhappy
ruler of this realm, who adores you, madam, and who can't
tell you this without trembling."

"A king who adores me?" the princess replied. "Does this
king have eyes or is he blind? Doesn't he know that I'm the
ugliest person in the world?"

"I've seen you, madam," the invisible being answered, "and
have found you're not what you represent yourself to be.
Whether it's for your person, merit, or misfortunes, I repeat: I
adore you. But my feeling of respect and timidity oblige me to
conceal myself."

"I'm indebted to you for that," the princess responded. "Alas, what would befall me if I were to love anyone?"

"You'd make a man who can't live without you into the happiest of beings," the voice said. "But he won't venture to appear before you without your permission."

"No, no," the princess said. "I wish to avoid seeing anything that might arouse my interest too strongly."

The voice fell silent, and the princess continued to ponder this incident for the rest of the night. No matter how strongly she vowed not to say the least word to anyone about it, she could not resist asking the pagods if their king had returned. They answered in the negative. Since this reply did not correspond in the least with what she had heard, she was quite disturbed. She continued making inquiries: was their king young and handsome? They told her he was young, handsome, and very charming. She asked if they frequently received news about him.

They replied, "Every day."

"But," she added, "does he know that I reside in his palace?"

"Yes, madam," her attendants answered, "he knows everything that occurs here concerning you. He takes great interest in it, and every hour a courier is sent off to him with an account about you."

Lapsing into silence, she became far more thoughtful than she had ever been before.

Whenever she was alone, the voice spoke to her. Sometimes she was alarmed by it, but at others she was pleased, for nothing could be more polite than its manner of address. "Although I've decided never to love," the princess said, "and have every reason to protect my heart against an attachment that could only be fatal to it, I nevertheless confess to you that I yearn to see a king who has such strange tastes. If it's true that you love me, you're perhaps the only being in the world guilty of such weakness for a person so ugly."

"Think whatever you please, adorable princess," the voice replied. "I find that you have sufficient qualities to merit my affection. Nor do I conceal myself because I have strange tastes. Indeed, I have such sad reasons that if you knew them, you wouldn't be able to refrain from pitying me."

The princess urged him to explain himself, but the voice stopped speaking, and she heard only long, heavy sighs.

All these conversations made her very uneasy. Although her lover was unknown and invisible to her, he paid her a thousand attentions. Moreover, the beautiful place she inhabited led her to desire companions more suitable than the pagods. That had been the reason why she had begun feeling bored, and only the voice of her invisible admirer had the power to please her.

One very dark night she awoke to find somebody seated beside her. She thought it was the pagodine of pearls, who had more wit than the others and sometimes came to keep her company. The princess extended her arm to her, but the person seized her hand and pressed it to a pair of lips. Shedding a few tears on it, the unseen person was evidently too moved to speak. She was convinced it was the invisible monarch.

"What do you want of me?" she sighed. "How can I love you without knowing or seeing you?"

"Ah, madam," he replied, "why do you make conditions that thwart my desire to please you? I simply cannot reveal myself. The same wicked Magotine who's treated you so badly has condemned me to suffer for seven years. Five have already elapsed. There are two remaining, and you could relieve the bitterness of my punishment by allowing me to become your husband. You may think that I'm a rash fool, that I'm asking an absolute impossibility. But if you knew, madam, the depth of my feelings and the extent of my misfortunes, you wouldn't refuse this favor I ask of you."

As I have already mentioned, Laidronette had begun feeling bored, and she found that the invisible king certainly had all the intelligence she could wish for. So she was swayed by love, which she disguised to herself as pity, and replied that she needed a few days to consider his proposal.

The celebrations and concerts recommenced with increased splendor, and not a song was heard but those about marriage. Presents were continually brought to her that surpassed all that had ever been seen. The enamored voice assiduously wooed her as soon as it turned dark, and the princess retired at an earlier hour in order to have more time to listen to it. Finally she consented to marry the invisible king and promised him that she would not attempt to look upon him until the full term of his penance had expired. "It's extremely important," the king said, "both for you and me. Should you be imprudent and succumb to your curiosity, I'll have to begin serving my sentence all over again, and you'll have to share in my suffering. But if you can resist the evil advice that you will soon receive, you'll have the satisfaction of finding in me all that your heart desires. At the same time you'll regain the marvelous beauty that the malicious Magotine took from you."

Delighted by this new prospect, the princess vowed a thousand times that she would never indulge her curiosity without his permission. So the wedding took place without any pomp and fanfare, but the modesty of the ceremony affected their hearts not a whit.

Since all the pagods were eager to entertain their new queen, one of them brought her the history of Psyche, written in a charming style by one of the most popular authors of the day. She found many passages in it that paralleled her own adventures, and they aroused in her a strong desire to see her father, mother, sister, and brother-in-law. Nothing the king could say to her sufficed to quell this whim.

"The book you're reading reveals the terrible ordeals Psyche experienced. For mercy's sake, try to learn from her experiences and avoid them."

After she promised to be more than cautious, a ship manned by pagods and loaded with presents was sent with letters from Queen Laidronette to her mother, imploring her to come and pay a visit to her daughter in her own realm. (The pagods assigned this mission were permitted, on this one occasion, to speak in a foreign land.)

And in fact, the princess's disappearance had affected her relatives. They believed she had perished, and consequently her letters filled them with gladness. The queen, who was dying to see Laidronette again, did not lose a moment in departing with her other daughter and son-in-law. The pagods, the only ones who knew the way to their kingdom, safely conducted the entire royal family, and when Laidronette saw them, she thought she would die from joy. Over and over she read the story of Psyche to be completely on her guard regarding any questions that they might put to her and to make sure she would have the right answers. But the pains she took were all in vain—she made a hundred mistakes. Sometimes the king was with the army; sometimes he was ill and in no mood to see anyone; sometimes he was on a pilgrimage and at others hunting or fishing. In the end it seemed that the barbarous Magotine had unsettled her wits and doomed her to say nothing but nonsense.

Discussing the matter together, her mother and sister concluded that she was deceiving them and perhaps herself as well. With misguided zeal they told her what they thought and in the process skillfully plagued her mind with a thousand doubts and fears. After refusing for a long time to acknowledge the justice of their suspicions, she confessed at last that she had never seen her husband, but his conversation was so charming that just listening to him was enough to make her happy. "What's more," she told them, "he has only two more years to spend in this state of penance, and at the end of that time, I shall not only be able to see him, but I myself shall become as beautiful as the orb of day."

"Oh, unfortunate creature!" the queen exclaimed. "What a devious trap they've set for you! How could you have been so naive as to listen to such tales? Your husband is a monster, and that's all there is to it, for all the pagods he rules are downright monkeys."

"I believe differently," Laidronette replied. "I think he's the god of love himself."

"What a delusion!" Queen Bellotte cried. "They told Psyche that she had married a monster, and she discovered that it was Cupid. You're positive that Cupid is your husband, and yet it's certain he's a monster. At the very least, put your mind to rest. Clear up the matter. It's easy enough to do."

This was what the queen had to say, and her husband was even more emphatic. The poor princess was so confused and disturbed that, after having sent her family home loaded with presents that sufficiently repaid the zinzolin taffeta and muff ribbon, she decided to catch a glimpse of her husband, come what may. Oh, fatal curiosity, which never improves in us despite a thousand dreadful examples, how dearly you are about to make this unfortunate princess pay! Thinking it a great pity not to imitate her predecessor, Psyche, she shone a lamp on their bed and gazed upon the invisible king so dear to her heart. When she saw, however, the horrid green serpent with his long, bristling mane instead of a tender Cupid young, white, and fair, she let out the most frightful shrieks. He awoke in a fit of rage and despair.

"Cruel woman," he cried, "is this the reward for all the love I've given you?"

The princess did not hear a word. She had fainted from fright. Within seconds the serpent was faraway. Upon hearing the uproar caused by this tragic scene, some pagods ran to their post, carried the princess to her couch, and did all they could to revive her. No one can possibly fathom Laidronette's depths of despair upon regaining consciousness. How she reproached herself for the misfortune she had brought upon her husband! She loved him tenderly, but she abhorred his form and would have given half her life if she could have taken back what she had done.

These sad reflections were interrupted by several pagods who entered her room with fear written on their faces. They came to warn her that several ships of puppets with Magotine at their head had entered the harbor without encountering any resistance. Puppets and pagods had been enemies for ages and had competed with each other in a thousand ways, for the puppets had always enjoyed the privilege of talking wherever they went—a privilege denied the pagods. Magotine was the queen of the puppets, and her hatred for the poor green serpent and the unfortunate Laidronette had prompted her to assemble her forces in order to torment them just when their suffering was most acute.

This goal she easily accomplished because the queen was in such despair that although the pagods urged her to give the necessary orders, she refused, insisting that she knew nothing of the art of war. Nevertheless, she ordered them to convene all those pagods who had been in besieged cities or on the councils of the greatest commanders and told them to take the proper steps. Then she shut herself up in her room and regarded everything happening around her with utter indifference.

Magotine's general was that celebrated puppet Punch, and he knew his business well. He had a large body of wasps, mayflies, and butterflies in reserve, and they performed wonders against some lightly armed frogs and lizards. The latter had been in the pay of the pagods for many years and were, if truth be told, much more frightening in name than in action.

Magotine amused herself for some time by watching the combat. The pagods and pagodines outdid themselves in their efforts, but the fairy dissolved all their superb edifices with a stroke of her wand. The charming gardens, woods, meadows, fountains, were soon in ruins, and Queen Laidronette could not escape the sad fate of becoming the slave of the most malignant fairy that ever was or will be. Four or five hundred puppets forced her to go before Magotine.

"Madam," Punch said to the fairy, "here is the queen of the pagods, whom I have taken the liberty of bringing to you."

"I've known her a long time," Magotine said. "She was the cause of my being insulted on the day she was born, and I'll never forget it."

"Alas, madam," the queen said, "I believed you were sufficiently avenged. The gift of ugliness that you bestowed on me to such a supreme degree would have satisfied anyone less vindictive than you."

"Look how she argues," the fairy said. "Here is a learned doctor of a new sort. Your first job will be teaching philosophy to my ants. I want you to get ready to give them a lesson every day."

"How can I do it, madam?" the distressed queen replied. "I know nothing about philosophy, and even if I were well versed in it, your ants are probably not capable of understanding it."

"Well now, listen to this logician," exclaimed Magotine. "Very well, Queen. You won't teach them philosophy, but despite yourself you'll set an example of patience for the entire world that will be difficult to imitate."

Immediately thereafter, Laidronette was given a pair of iron shoes so small that she could fit only half her foot into each one. Compelled nevertheless to put them on, the poor queen could only weep in agony.

"Here's a spindle of spider webs," Magotine said. "I expect you to spin it as fine as your hair, and you have but two hours to do it."

"I've never spun, madam," the queen said. "But I'll try to obey you even though what you desire strikes me to be impossible."

She was immediately led deep into a dark grotto, and after they gave her some brown bread and a pitcher of water, they closed the entrance with a large rock. In trying to spin the filthy spider webs, she dropped her spindle a hundred times because it was much too heavy. Even though she patiently picked it up each time and began her work over again, it was always in vain. "Now I know exactly how bad my predicament is. I'm wholly at the mercy of the implacable Magotine, who's not just satisfied with having deprived me of all my beauty, but wants some pretext for killing me." She began to weep as she recalled the happiness she had enjoyed in the kingdom of Pagodia. Then she threw down her spindle and exclaimed, "Let Magotine come when she will! I can't do the impossible."

"Ah, Queen," a voice answered her. "Your indiscreet curiosity has caused you these tears, but it's difficult to watch those we love suffer. I have a friend whom I've never mentioned to you before. She's called the Fairy Protectrice, and I trust she'll be of great service to you."

All at once she heard three taps, and without seeing anyone, she found her web spun and wound into a skein. At the end of the two hours Magotine, who wanted to taunt her, had the rock rolled from the grotto mouth and entered it, followed by a large escort of puppets.

"Come, come, let us see the work of this idle hussy who doesn't know how to sew or spin."

"Madam," the queen said, "it's quite true I didn't know how, but I was obliged to learn."

When Magotine saw the extraordinary result, she took the skein of spider web and said: "Truly, you're too skillful. It would be a great pity not to keep you employed. Here, Queen, make me some nets with this thread strong enough to catch salmon."

"For mercy's sake!" the queen replied. "You see that it's barely strong enough to hold flies."

"You're a great casuist, my pretty friend," Magotine said, "but it won't help you a bit." She left the grotto, had the stone replaced at the entrance, and assured Laidronette that if the nets were not finished in two hours, she was a lost creature.

"Oh, Fairy Protectrice!" the queen exclaimed, "if it's true that my sorrows can move you to pity, please don't deny me your assistance."

No sooner had she spoken than, to Laidronette's astonishment, the nets were made. With all her heart she thanked the friendly fairy who had granted her this favor, and it gave her pleasure to think that it must have been her husband who had provided her with such a friend. "Alas, green serpent," she said, "you're much too generous to continue loving me after the harm I've done you."

No reply was forthcoming, for at that moment, Magotine entered. She was nonplussed to find the nets finished. Indeed, they were so well made that the work could not have been done by common hands. "What?" she cried. "Do you have the audacity to maintain that it was you who wove these nets?"

"I have no friend in your court, madam," the queen said. "And even if I did, I'm so carefully guarded that it would be difficult for anyone to speak to me without your permission."

"Since you're so clever and skillful, you'll be of great use to me in my kingdom."

She immediately ordered her fleet to make ready the sails and all the puppets to prepare themselves to board. The queen she had heavily chained down, fearing that in some fit of despair she might fling herself overboard.

One night when the unhappy princess was deploring her sad fate, she perceived by the light of the stars that the green serpent was silently approaching the ship.

"I'm always afraid of alarming you," he said, "and despite the reasons I have for not sparing you, you're extremely dear to me."

"Can you pardon my indiscreet curiosity?" she replied. "Would you be offended if I said:

> "Is it you? Is it you? Are you again near?
> My own royal serpent, so faithful and dear!
> May I hope to see my fond husband again?
> Oh, how I've suffered since we were parted then!"

The serpent replied as follows:

> "To hearts that love truly, to part causes pain,
> With hope even to whisper of meeting again.
> In Pluto's dark regions what torture above
> Our absence forever from those whom we love?"

Magotine was not one of those fairies who fall asleep, for the desire to do mischief kept her continually awake. Thus, she did not fail to overhear the conversation between the serpent king and his wife. Flying like a Fury to interrupt it, she said, "Aha, you amuse yourselves with rhymes, do you? And you complain about your fate in bombastic tones? Truly, I'm delighted to hear it. Proserpine, who is my best friend, has promised to pay me if I lend her a poet. Not that there is a dearth of poets below, but she simply wants more. Green serpent, I command you to go finish your penance in the dark manor of the underworld. Give my regards to the gentle Proserpine!"

Uttering long hisses, the unfortunate serpent departed, leaving the queen in the depths of sorrow. "What crime have we committed against you, Magotine?" she exclaimed heatedly. "No sooner was I born than your infernal curse robbed me of my beauty and made me horrible. How can you accuse me of any crime when I wasn't even capable of using my mind at that time? I'm convinced that the unhappy king whom you've just sent to the infernal regions is as innocent as I was. But finish your work. Let me die this instant. It's the only favor I ask of you."

"You'd be too happy if I granted your request." Magotine said. "You must first draw water for me from the bottomless spring."

As soon as the ships had reached the kingdom of puppets, the cruel Magotine took a millstone and tied it around the queen's neck, ordering her to climb to the top of a mountain that soared high above the clouds. Upon arriving there, she was to gather enough four-leaf clovers to fill a basket, descend into the depths of the next valley to draw the water of discretion in a pitcher with a hole in the bottom, and bring her enough to fill her large glass. The queen responded that it was impossible to obey her: the millstone was more than ten times her weight and the pitcher with a hole in it could never hold the water she wished to drink. "Nay, I cannot be induced to attempt anything so impossible."

"If you don't," Magotine said, "rest assured that your green serpent will suffer for it."

This threat so frightened the queen that she tried to walk despite her handicap. But, alas, the effort would have been for naught if the Fairy Protectrice, whom she invoked, had not come to her aid.

"Now you can see the just punishment for your fatal curiosity," the fairy said. "Blame no one but yourself for the condition to which Magotine has reduced you."

After saying this, she transported the queen to the top of the mountain. Terrible monsters that guarded the spot made supernatural efforts to defend it, but one tap of the Fairy Protectrice's wand made them gentler than lambs. Then she proceeded to fill the basket for her with four-leaf clovers.

Protectrice did not wait for the grateful queen to thank her, for to complete the mission, everything depended on her. She gave the queen a chariot drawn by two white canaries who spoke and whistled in a marvelous way. She told her to descend the mountain and fling her iron shoes at two giants armed with clubs who guarded the fountain. Once they were knocked unconscious, she had only to give her pitcher to the canaries, who would easily find the means to fill it with the water of discretion. "As soon as you have the water, wash your face with it, and you will become the most beautiful person in the world." She also advised her not to remain at the fountain, or to climb back up the hill, but to stop at a pleasant small grove she would find on her way. She could remain there for three years, since Magotine would merely suppose that she was either still trying to fill her pitcher with water or had fallen victim to one of the dangers during her journey.

Embracing the knees of the Fairy Protectrice, the queen thanked her a hundred times for the special favors she had granted her. "But, madam," the queen added, "neither the success I may achieve nor the beauty you promise me will give me the least pleasure until my serpent is transformed."

"That won't occur until you've spent three years in the mountain grove," the fairy said, "and until you've returned to Magotine with the four-leaf clovers and the water in the leaky pitcher."

The queen promised the Fairy Protectrice that she would scrupulously follow her instructions. "But, madam," she added, "must I spend three years without hearing any news of the serpent king?"

"You deserve never to hear any more about him for as long as you live," the fairy responded. "Indeed, can anything be more terrible than having made him begin his penance all over again?"

The queen made no reply, but her silence and the tears flowing down her cheeks amply showed how much she was suffering. She got into her little chariot, and the canaries did as commanded. They conducted her to the bottom of the valley, where the giants guarded the fountain of discretion. She quickly took off her iron shoes and threw them at their heads. The moment the shoes hit them, they fell down lifelessly like colossal statues. The canaries took the leaky pitcher and mended it with such marvelous skill that there was no sign of its having ever been broken.

The name given to the water made her eager to drink some. "It will make me more prudent than I've been," she said. "Alas, if I had possessed those qualities, I'd still be in the kingdom of Pagodia." After she had drunk a long draught of the water, she washed her face with some of it and became so very beautiful that she might have been mistaken for a goddess rather than a mortal.

The Fairy Protectrice immediately appeared and said, "You've just done something that pleases me very much. You knew that this water could embellish your mind as well as your person. I wanted to see to which of the two you would prefer the most, and it was your mind. I praise you for it, and this act will shorten the term of your punishment by four years."

"Please don't reduce my sufferings," the queen replied. "I deserve them all. But comfort the green serpent, who doesn't deserve to suffer at all."

"I'll do everything in my power," the fairy said, embracing her. "But since you're now so beautiful, I want you to drop the name of Laidronette, which no longer suits you. You must be called Queen Discrète."

As she vanished, the queen found she had left a pair of dainty shoes that were so pretty and finely embroidered that she thought it almost a pity to wear them. Soon thereafter she got back into her little chariot with her pitcherful of water, and the canaries flew directly to the grove of the mountain.

Never was a spot as pleasant as this. Myrtle and orange trees intertwined their branches to form long arbors and bowers that the sun could not penetrate. A thousand brooks running from gently flowing springs brought a refreshing coolness to this beautiful abode. But most curious of all were the animals there, which gave the canaries the warmest welcome in the world.

"We thought you had deserted us," they said.

"The term of our penance is not over yet," the canaries replied. "But here is a queen whom the Fairy Protectrice has ordered us to bring you. Try to do all you can to amuse her."

She was immediately surrounded by all sorts of animals, who paid her their best compliments. "You shall be our queen," they said to her. "You shall have all our attention and respect."

"Where am I?" she exclaimed. "What supernatural power has enabled you to speak to me?"

One of the canaries whispered in her ear, "You should know, madam, that several fairies were distressed to see various persons fall into bad habits on their travels. At first they imagined that they needed merely to advise them to correct themselves, but their warnings were paid no heed. Eventually the fairies became quite upset and imposed punishments on them. Those who talked too much were changed into parrots, magpies, and hens. Lovers and their mistresses were transformed into pigeons, canaries, and lapdogs. Those who ridiculed their friends became monkeys. Gourmands were made into pigs and hotheads into lions. In short, the number of persons they punished was so great that this grove has become filled with them. Thus, you'll find people with all sorts of qualities and dispositions here."

"From what you've just told me, my dear canary," the queen said, "I've reason to believe that you're here only because you loved too well."

"It's quite true, madam," the canary replied. "I'm the son of a Spanish grandee. Love in our country has such absolute power over our hearts that one cannot resist it without being charged with the crime of rebellion. An English ambassador arrived at the court. He had a daughter who was extremely beautiful, but insufferably haughty and sardonic. In spite of all this, I was attracted to her. My love, though, was greeted with so much disdain that I lost all patience. One day when she had exasperated me, a venerable old woman approached and reproached me for my weakness. Yet everything she said only made me more obstinate. When she perceived this, she became angry. 'I condemn you,' she said, 'to be a canary for three years, and your mistress to be a wasp.' Instantly I felt an indescribable change come over me. Despite my affliction I could not restrain myself from flying into the ambassador's garden to determine the fate of his daughter. No sooner had I arrived than I saw her approach in the form of a large wasp buzzing four times louder than all the others. I hovered around her with the devotion of a lover that nothing can destroy, but she tried several times to sting me. 'If you want to kill me, beautiful wasp,' I said, 'it's unnecessary to use your sting. You only have to command me to die, and I'll obey you.' The wasp did not reply, but landed on some flowers that had to endure her bad temper.

"Overwhelmed by her contempt and the condition to which I was reduced, I flew away without caring where my wings would take me. I eventually arrived at one of the most beautiful cities in the universe, which they call Paris. Wearily, I flung myself on a tuft of large trees enclosed within some garden walls, and before I knew who had caught me, I found myself behind the door of a cage painted green and ornamented with gold. The apartment and its furniture were so magnificent that I was astounded. Soon a young lady arrived. She caressed me and spoke to me so sweetly that I was charmed by her. I did not live there long before learning whom her sweetheart was. I witnessed this braggart's visits to her, and he was always in a rage because nothing could satisfy him. He was always accusing her unjustly, and one time he beat her until he left her for dead in the arms of her women. I was quite upset at seeing her suffer this unworthy treatment, and what distressed me even more was that the blows he dealt the lovely lady served only to increase her affection.

"Night and day I wished that the fairies who had transformed me into a canary would come and set to rights such ill-suited lovers. My wish was eventually fulfilled. The fairies suddenly appeared in the apartment just as the furious gentleman was beginning to make his usual commotion. They reprimanded him severely and condemned him to become a wolf. The patient lady who had allowed him to beat her, they turned into a sheep and sent her to the grove of the mountain. As for myself, I easily found a way to escape. Since I wanted to see the various courts of Europe, I flew to Italy and fell into the hands of a man who had frequent business in the city. Since he was very jealous of his wife and did not want her to see anyone during his absence, he took care to lock her up from morning until night, and I was given the honor of amusing this lovely captive. However, she had other things to do than to attend to me. A certain neighbor who had loved her for a long time came to the top of the chimney in the evening and slid down it into the room, looking blacker than a devil. The keys that the jealous husband kept with him served only to keep his mind at ease. I constantly feared that some terrible catastrophe would happen when one day the fairies entered through the keyhole and surprised the two lovers. 'Go and do penance!' the fairies said, touching them with their wands. 'Let the chimney sweeper become a squirrel and the lady an ape, for she is a cunning one. And your husband, who is so fond of keeping the keys of his house, shall become a mastiff for ten years.'

"It would take me too long to tell you all the various adventures I had," the canary said. "Occasionally I was obliged to visit the grove of the mountain, and I rarely returned there without finding new animals, for the fairies were always traveling and were continually upset by the countless faults of the people they encountered. But during your residence here you'll have plenty of time to entertain yourself by listening to the accounts of all the inhabitants' adventures."

Several of them immediately offered to relate their stories whenever she desired. She thanked them politely, but since she felt more inclined to meditate than to talk, she looked for a spot where she could be alone. As soon as she found one, a little palace arose on it, and the most sumptuous banquet in the world was prepared for her. It consisted only of fruits, but they were of the rarest kind. They were brought to her by birds, and during her stay in the grove there was nothing she lacked.

Occasionally she was pleased by the most unique entertainments: lions danced with lambs; bears whispered tender things to doves; serpents relaxed with linnets; a butterfly courted a panther. In short, no amour was categorized according to species, for it did not matter that one was a tiger or another a sheep, but simply that they were people whom the fairies had chosen to punish for their faults.

They all loved Queen Discrète to the point of adoration, and everyone asked her to arbitrate their disputes. Her power was absolute in this tiny republic, and if she had not continually reproached herself for causing the green serpent's misfortunes, she might have accepted her own misfortune with some degree of patience. However, when she thought of the condition to which he was reduced, she could not forgive herself for her indiscreet curiosity.

Finally the time came for her to leave the grove of the mountain, and she notified her escorts, the faithful canaries, who wished her a happy return. She left secretly during the night to avoid the farewells and lamentations, which would have cost her some tears, for she was touched by the friendship and respect that all these rational animals had shown her.

She did not forget the pitcher of discretion, the basket of four-leaf clovers, or the iron shoes. Just when Magotine believed her to be dead, she suddenly appeared before her, the millstone around her neck, the iron shoes on her feet, and the pitcher in her hand. Upon seeing her, the fairy uttered a loud cry. "Where have you come from?"

"Madam," the queen said, "I've spent three years drawing water into the broken pitcher, and I finally found the way to make it hold water."

Magotine burst into laughter, thinking of the exhaustion the poor queen must have experienced. But when she examined her more closely, she exclaimed, "What's this I see? Laidronette has become quite lovely! How did you get so beautiful?"

The queen informed her that she had washed herself with the water of discretion and that this miracle had been the result. At this news Magotine dashed the pitcher to the ground. "Oh, you powers that defy me," she exclaimed, "I'll be revenged. Get your iron shoes ready," she said to the queen. "You must go to the underworld for me and demand the essence of long life from Proserpine. I'm always afraid of falling ill and perhaps dying. Once I have that antidote in my possession, I won't have any more cause for alarm. Take care, therefore, that you don't uncork the bottle or taste the liquor she gives you, or you'll reduce my portion."

The poor queen had never been so taken aback as she was by this order. "Which way is it to the underworld?" she asked. "Can those who go there return? Alas, madam, won't you ever tire of persecuting me? Under what unfortunate star was I born? My sister is so much happier than I. Ah, the stars above are certainly unfair."

As she began to weep, Magotine exulted at her tears. She

laughed loudly and cried, "Go! Go! Don't put off your departure a moment, for your journey promises to benefit me a great
deal." Magotine gave her some old nuts and black bread in a
bag, and with this handsome provision the poor queen started
on her journey. She was determined, however, to dash her brains
out against the first rock she saw to put an end to her sorrows.

She wandered at random for some time, turning this way
and that, thinking it most extraordinary to be sent like this to
the underworld. When she became tired, she lay down at the
foot of a tree and began to think of the poor serpent, forgetting all about her journey. Just then appeared the Fairy Protectrice, who said to her, "Don't you know, beautiful queen, that
if you want to rescue your husband from the dark domain
where he is being kept under Magotine's orders, you must seek
the home of Proserpine?"

"I'd go much farther, if it were possible, madam," she replied,
"but I don't know how to descend into that dark abode."

"Wait," said the Fairy Protectrice. "Here's a green branch.
Strike the earth with it and repeat these lines clearly." The
queen embraced the knees of her generous friend and then said
after her:

> "You who can wrest from mighty Jove the thunder!
>   Love, listen to my prayer!
>   Come, save me from despair,
> And calm the pangs that rend my heart asunder!
> As I enter the realm of Tartarus, be my guide.
> Even in those dreary regions you hold sway.
> It was for Proserpine, your subject, that Pluto sighed;
> So open the path to their throne and point the way.
> A faithful husband from my arms they tear!
> My fate is harder than my heart can bear;
>   More than mortal is its pain;
>   Yet for death it sighs in vain!"

No sooner had she finished this prayer than a young child
more beautiful than anything we shall ever see appeared in the

midst of a gold and azure cloud. He flew down to her feet with
a crown of flowers encircling his brow. The queen knew by his
bow and arrows that it was Love. He addressed her in the following way:

> "I have heard your tender sighs,
> And for you have left the skies.
> Love will chase your tears away,
> And try his best in every way.
> Shortly shall your eyes be blest
> With his sight you love the best.
> Then the penance will be done,
> And your foe will be overcome."

The queen was dazzled by the splendor that surrounded
Love and delighted by his promises. Therefore, she exclaimed:

> "Earth, my voice obey!
> Cupid's power is like my own.
> Open for him and point the way
> To Pluto's dark and gloomy throne!"

The earth obeyed and opened her bosom. The queen went
through a dark passage, in which she needed a guide as radiant as her protector, and finally reached the underworld. She
dreaded meeting her husband there in the form of a serpent,
but Love, who sometimes employs himself by doing good
deeds for the unfortunate, had foreseen all that was to be foreseen: he had already arranged that the green serpent become
what he was before his punishment. Powerful as Magotine
was, there was nothing she could do against Love.

The first object the queen's eyes encountered was her charming husband. She had never seen him in such a handsome form,
and he had never seen her as beautiful as she had become. Nevertheless, a presentiment, and perhaps Love, who made up the
third in the party, caused each of them to guess who the other
was. With extreme tenderness the queen said to him:

"I come to share your prison and your pain.
Though doomed no more the light of heaven to see,
Here let but love unite our hearts again,
No terrors these sad shades will have for me!"

Carried away by his passion, the king replied to his wife in a
way that demonstrated his ardor and pleasure. But Love, who
is not fond of losing time, urged them to approach Proserpine.
The queen offered Magotine's regards and asked her for the
essence of long life. Proserpine immediately gave the queen a
phial very badly corked in order to induce her to open it. Love,
who is no novice, warned the queen against indulging a curiosity that would again be fatal to her. Quickly the king and
queen left those dreary regions and returned to the light of day
with Love accompanying them. He led them back to Magotine
and hid himself in their hearts so that she would not see him.
His presence, however, inspired the fairy with such humane
sentiments that she received these illustrious unfortunates graciously, although she knew not why. With a supernatural effort
of generosity she restored the kingdom of Pagodia to them, and
they returned there immediately and spent the rest of their days
in as much happiness as they had previously endured trouble
and sorrow.

Too oft is curiosity
    The cause of fatal woe.
A secret that may harmful be,
    Why should we seek to know?

It is a weakness of womankind,
    For witness the first created,
From whom Pandora was designed,
    And Psyche imitated.

Each one, despite a warning, on the same
    Forbidden quest intent,
Did bring about her misery and become
    Its fatal instrument.

Psyche's example failed to save
     Poor Laidronette from erring.
Like warning she was led to brave.
     Like punishment incurring.

Alas, for human common sense,
     No tale, no caution, schools!
The proverb says, Experience
     Can make men wise, and change dumb fools.

But when we're told, yet fail to listen
     To the lessons of the past,
I fear the proverb lies quite often,
     Despite the shadows forward cast.